The Dance of Rotten Sticks

a novel

by

Jeff Vande Zande

MONTAG

First Montag Press E-Book and Paperback Original Edition August 2024

Copyright © 2024 by Jeff Vande Zande

Montag Press ISBN: 978-1-957010-46-5
Design © 2024 Amit Dey
Author Photo: Matt Brown

Montag Press Team:
Cover: Rick Febre
Editor: John Rak
Co-Editor: Lindsay Krumbein
Managing Director: Charlie Franco

A Montag Press Book
www.montagpress.com
Montag Press
777 Morton Street, Unit B
San Francisco CA 94129 USA

Printed & Digitally Originated in the United States of America
10 9 8 7 6 5 4 3 2 1

This novel initially depicts tragedy and quotidian life in a way drawing from realism and naturalism, but a troubling undercurrent gradually and then starkly emerges. From the title, drawn from one of Theodore Roethke's more uncanny and enigmatic poems, to its unexpected last act, Vande Zande presents us with an intriguing and nuanced Midwestern gothic.

—William Barillas,
author of The Midwestern Pastoral:
Place and Landscape in Literature
of the American Heartland

DEDICATION

For Allecia and the beauty of third acts.

"Mother me out of here. What more will the bones allow?
Will the sea give the wind suck? A toad folds into a stone.
These flowers are all fangs. Comfort me, fury.
Wake me, witch, we'll do the dance of rotten sticks."

—from "The Shape of the Fire"
Theodore Roethke

ACKNOWLEDGMENT

I owe much of the authenticity of this novel's details to my brother-in-law, Kelley Stanley, who is retired from the U.S. Fish and Wildlife Service.

CHAPTER 1

Suspended over the stubbled cornfield behind O'Rourke's restaurant, a full moon haunted the winter landscape with a chilling bluish light. Holding the door open, Isaac shivered. The outside temperature had dropped ten degrees during the course of their meal. He offered his arm to Gwen when she came through the door. She was wearing one of his favorite dresses, and he wasn't pleased to see it zipped away inside her winter coat.

He smiled. "Supposed to be slippery tonight," he said. The weatherman had talked about how the nighttime hours would fall below freezing, which didn't combine well with the light drizzle they'd had all day. The coldest temperatures weren't expected until after midnight.

She gripped her fingers into the crook of his elbow. Guiding her cautiously over the snow-dusted parking lot to the passenger side of the car, he opened the door for her.

Gwen climbed in. "Such a gentleman tonight," she said.

"Well, I should be. How many date nights do we get?" He waited for Gwen to gather her coat hem and purse in with her.

"More now that Ashley can watch the little ones."

"True," he said. He looked her over. "All set?"

She nodded and he closed the door. Going around to his side, he pushed off with his foot and slid across the icy parking lot in front of the car. He spread his arms when he came to a stop in a gesture that said, "Ta da!" She shook her head at him through the windshield.

They had six miles of county roads before they'd get to the highway. He was pretty certain that the road commission would have salted the main roads. In six miles they'd be much safer.

"I told Ashley we'd be home by eleven," Gwen said. She glanced at the speedometer.

"Text her and tell her we're going to be late. I'm not taking any chances with black ice." Conditions were perfect for intermittent patches of the invisible hazard.

Tapping her phone, Gwen muttered something under her breath about "Ol' Grandpa Isaac." For a moment, only the lit rectangle of her screen was visible in the darkness of the passenger side before his eyes adjusted to the ghostly glow. She thumbed in a text, hit send, and then her side went black in the absence of light. His pupils adjusted again, and her silhouette blossomed into his side vision.

"You know what next week is, right?" she asked in a playful voice.

The car shimmied as the tires rolled from swatches of wet pavement to iced pavement, and Isaac tightened both hands on the wheel. He glanced just beyond the shoulder where the ground dipped into a five-foot deep drainage ditch running along the side of the road like an open wound. A nightmare to slide down into that. He regripped the wheel. "You got me," he said. "What?"

She snickered. "I knew you'd forget. You're supposed to come with me to Madame Zara's."

He shook his head. "Like I've said before, I guarantee you that's not her real name."

"Yes it is, and you're changing the subject."

The snowy cornfields on either side of the car transitioned into a stretch of trees just beyond the shoulders of the road. No more ditches.

"Look," he said, more pouty than argumentative, "I didn't mind buying you those readings for Christmas, but I don't understand why I'm getting dragged into it."

"Oh, come on. It's my last one." She set her hand on his thigh. "Last week she told me that I'm about to go through a metamorphosis. She thought she might be able to get a clearer picture if you came ... you know, if you're somehow connected to the change."

He shook his head, smirking. "A metamorphosis? Seriously, you know those people say stuff that's just vague enough that almost anything they predict could come true. You could get a new haircut, and she'd say, 'See, a metamorphosis!'"

"It could be something with work," she said, ignoring him. "But Madame Zara felt pretty sure that you had something to do with—"

"I don't want to talk about that, hon." Isaac looked at her and then back to the road. "You know I don't believe in that crap."

She took her hand from his leg and set it in her lap. "You're no fun."

"That's because I haven't gotten you home to the bedroom, yet."

"Oh, sorry," she said, "that's what I was referring to."

"Hey," he said. His smile faded quickly when the car lurched over the centerline. He backed his foot off the gas.

Gwen's hand reached over and grabbed his thigh reflexively. "Wow, it is slick," she said.

"I told you."

Though the speed limit was 50 miles an hour, he kept the gauge hovering right around 35. The dashboard vents finally started to blow warm air.

"You know what I am looking forward to?" he asked. "In about four months we can all go to the cabin." He remembered the whirlwind of those days during the past autumn. In the space of 72 hours, they'd found the cabin, driven to see it, and finally purchased it.

Gwen was quiet a moment. "I still don't think the kids should go this first time," she said. She glanced out her window at the outlines of trees flickering by. "We don't even have a boat yet. If something bad happens with one of the kids, we're stuck on an island waiting for Caleb to come get us."

He sniffed in a long breath. "You really think something will happen to Carson?"

"Something could happen to any of them. I just think it's safer. For one, that lake is deep, and Carson isn't doing much more than a dog paddle. I'd be so worried about him falling in."

He backed off the gas more as headlights turned toward them out of a curve in the road ahead. Momentarily blinded, he shielded his eyes and waited for the wash of halogen to pass. "Turn off your brights, asshole!" he shouted.

"I'm sure he heard you. Did your tantrum make you feel better?" Gwen asked. She smiled.

"Yes. It did." He reached to turn down the heat. Then, he gripped both hands on the wheel again. "You know, I just think that if we don't get Ashley up there this summer, we never will. Once she hits sixteen, it's car and job and nothing with family." He stared ahead into the darkness beyond the headlights. "She's growing up fast."

She turned towards him in his peripheral vision. "Well, then maybe we can take her up with us, but not Carson ... not the first trip. I just want to get a sense that it's safe up there for him. He can stay with my mom."

Ah yes, Helen, patron saint of Flawless Motherhood. Poor kid would spend his mornings eating high fiber cereal, and the afternoons using his recommended thirty-seven minutes of screen time watching PBS. "Or he could stay with my brother."

Gwen laughed. "Adam? He's trying to get tenure. I highly doubt he wants to spend days at a time with a five-year-old."

"True."

"Why are you always so resistant when it comes to my mom?"

Isaac glanced at her and then back to the road. "You gotta admit, she can be a little much."

"Sure," Gwen said, "But she's also been there for us when we've needed her. She's lonely. Don't make an issue of it, please."

Isaac turned his gaze from the windshield to her face. "Okay," he said. "Sorry."

Gwen cleared her throat. "And with her anxiety, I'd say Emily holds off for a trip or two."

Why am I even arguing? he wondered. Just the two of us at the cabin doing whatever we want? It'd be heaven. "Sounds good. I agree," he said. He turned his attention back to the road.

A chill crawled up Isaac's spine. He shivered violently, and his vision clouded with memories of sledding as a child ... plummeting downhill with no real way to control the sled.

"You okay?"

He looked at her blurred face absently, and the steering wheel bucked out of his grip. As the car veered again over the centerline, something swooped out of the darkness and burst into a smear of crimson and black against the driver's side windshield, blinding him.

"Isaac!"

The car fishtailed to the left, and he jerked the wheel, sending them into a full spin in the other direction. The brake lights swept arcs of red over the snow-covered ground.

"Isaac! Isaac!"

His mind surfaced from its fugue, and his hands fumbled on the jerking steering wheel. The vehicle spun twice and then careened over the shoulder into the trees where it crashed to a violent stop.

CHAPTER 2

A creature rustled under the lilac bushes out beyond the edges of the screened-in porch's halo of light. Vaguely sweet with ozone, the humid air foreshadowed a rain shower or coming storm. Isaac took a sip from his tumbler of whiskey. The liquor burned soothingly sliding down his throat. The animal out in the darkness stirred again in the leaf litter. It was the only sound in the still night aside from the hum of some distant air conditioning units in his neighbors' windows. Whatever the animal—a possum or raccoon or even a skunk—it bothered Isaac that their nocturnal foraging went on undisturbed even as they moved in the shadows of what he considered a house of mourning. Things just go on, he lamented, even though it didn't feel like they should. He took a longer drink.

The sound of wings flapped through the darkness. Something landed in the branches of the maple tree above the lilacs. It sounded too big to be a nighthawk. Murmurous among the leaves, it steadied itself on its perch. He guessed that by the sounds it was probably an owl waiting for the chance to kill whatever animal was foraging on the ground. Isaac shivered with a sudden chill.

An insect—large, iridescent, and green—ricocheted off of the screen in front of him and back out into the darkness. Many of Isaac's nights were spent watching bugs trying to get to the light coming from the kitchen behind him. Two years before, it had been Gwen's idea to screen in the back porch. She'd barely had the chance to enjoy it. Just one full summer, really.

His phone's screen glowed with an incoming call. With a local area code, the number looked vaguely familiar ... something about the three sevens in a row at the end. He answered.

"Is this Isaac Fletcher?" a woman's shaky voice asked.

"Yeah," he said. Calls that started that way were never good in his experience. "Who is this?"

"Who I am isn't important, but what I know is—"

"I'm hanging up."

"No, don't. Please." She cleared her throat. "My name is Madame Zara, and I need to tell you something. It's urgent."

The medium? He rolled his eyes. That's why the number was familiar. He'd hung up on her when she'd called three weeks after Gwen's funeral to ask about her health.

She sounded like she might be drunk. Probably had to drink to muster the courage to cold call widows and widowers. She'd likely spin some yarn about how she could help him contact Gwen from beyond the grave ... for the right price. There was enough of that going on in his house already. "Seriously, it's after eleven o'clock."

"You must protect your mind," she said. "Do you have iron nails on your property? You'd need only three."

"Jesus Christ. What the hell are—"

"You're going to lose her."

There it is, Isaac thought. He squeezed the phone. "What, you're seeing my wife dying in your crystal ball all of a sudden ... six months after the fact?" He took a drink. "Calling me like this is pretty twisted shit, bitch."

"I only want to help."

He snickered. "Yeah ... yourself. To my money."

"No, I've seen ... I mean, if he takes an animal's life, your thoughts will not be your own—"

"Do you even hear yourself, lady?"

"Please. You need to listen to—"

"Piss off and don't call here again," he said. He blocked her number and then set the phone back on the armrest.

Isaac stared out into the darkness and took sips from his drink. His heart rate slowed with the passing minutes. How many calls had he already taken from life insurance people trying to get him to purchase a supplemental policy. The children only had one remaining parent, they argued. Being a widower had put a target on his back for all kinds of salespeople, including phony fortune tellers. Even a few churches had reached out, expressing how he could find family within their congregation.

Leeches ... all of them leeches.

Hearing small footfalls shuffling across the kitchen linoleum, he reached to set his drink on the floor. He hoped it wasn't Carson. Ever since the accident, his son had started sleepwalking, though a doctor said the two weren't related. Isaac knew that as a sudden single father, he hadn't been doing very well with keeping up on the kids' checkups. In Carson's case, a visit to the doctor was unavoidable. He had started getting out of bed a couple hours after Isaac made sure he was asleep. Most nights, Isaac would be on the screened-in porch, and he'd hear his little boy opening and closing drawers in the kitchen. The first time he tried to tell him it was too late for a snack, but Carson didn't seem to hear him. He kept up with his routine of drawer and cupboard opening, and sometimes calling out heartbreakingly for his mother.

On other nights, he just mumbled gibberish as he wandered around the kitchen. The doctor had called it "sleepwalk babble" when Isaac asked about it. Gwen had been a sleepwalker herself as a child. For a few weeks, Carson came into the kitchen almost every other night, and Isaac would sit with an amused smile, sipping his drink, and listening until he'd hear his little guy wander back up the stairs. Then, one night, a tinkling sound sent Isaac bolting to the sliding glass door to witness Carson with his pajama bottoms and underwear around his ankles. He was urinating into the vertical space between the refrigerator and pan drawer.

Isaac made an appointment with the doctor the next day, only to be told that Carson would eventually grow out of it. "You don't see a lot of sleepwalking in kids after they turn eight."

Isaac rubbed his palm over his stubbled cheek. "He's five. We're talking three more years of this?"

The doctor had told him to childproof the house. "Just move anything breakable or sharp away from table edges." He recommended too that maybe Carson should try naps again.

"Naps? Are you sure this isn't in any way related to ... I mean, with his mother?"

"I really don't think so."

Holding his son's hand, Isaac had left the doctor's office with few answers and the new fear that Carson could possibly hurt himself some night. But then, as though out of pity for his weary father, the boy suddenly stopped his "somnambulistic excursions," as the doctor had called them. It had been nearly two months since Carson had left his bed to haunt the house with his sleepwalking.

Isaac sat in the porch's stillness listening for drawers or cupboards being opened.

"Daddy?"

He jumped and turned. Emily, his ten-year-old, stood framed in the sliding glass doorway, a silhouette sandwiched between the light of the kitchen and the half-dark of the porch. Isaac's hand lay splayed over his heart.

"What's wrong, Daddy?"

He exhaled breathily. "Nothing, honey. You just startled me."

The bird out in the darkness lurched. Its wings sounded like sheets of paper caught in the branches.

Emily stepped back into the light of the kitchen. Her blonde hair was disheveled, and she wore a fairy Halloween costume from years ago. Only one of the glittery wings was still attached, and it was creased with folds from being stored away for so long. "What was that?" she asked. She stared out into the blackness of the backyard.

"I think it's an owl, but I'm not sure." He forced a smile. "You can come out here. What are you wearing?"

She stepped onto the porch and peered tentatively into the dark yard in the direction of the bird. "Mommy made it for me a few years ago. Remember? She wanted to see me in it again."

Isaac took his glasses off and rubbed his fingertips into his eyelids. Still with the ghostly visits crap, he thought. It can't be healthy. Sighing, he slipped his glasses back on and patted his good leg. "Come here and sit on my lap. Don't worry about that owl. He's not going to do anything to us."

Emily leaned her upward gaze out toward the darkness one more time, and then turned and walked toward him. She climbed onto his right leg and rested her upper half against him. Her head laid against his sternum. The fragrance of some fruity lotion wicked up from her skin.

Isaac stroked his fingers softly over her long hair. "So, what makes you think Mom wanted you to wear this? It's awfully small on you."

"She told me."

His hand stopped stroking. "Honey ..."

"Daddy, she did. In a dream she told me."

He started stroking her hair again. "Baby, those are just dreams, though."

Her arm came up, and her little hand clutched his left shoulder. "They seem real. It's like she's with me for a while."

He shifted all of his weight onto the leg pinned under Emily. Lifting with his hand from the underside of his knee, he stretched out his bad leg on the glass tabletop. He closed his eyes, waiting for the throbbing to subside. "Dreams can feel like that," he said between clenched teeth. "Is that why you're up? Did the dream wake you?"

Her head shook back and forth on his chest. "No, the dream was last night. I just woke up tonight. I don't know why."

"Yeah," he said. He leaned down to kiss the top of her head. Her hair smelled like her mother's, and it left him speechless for a moment. "You're usually my sound sleeper," he finally managed. He cleared his throat. "And you hardly ever pee on the kitchen floor."

She giggled. "Daddy! I never do."

"I know you don't," he said, smiling.

On the other side of the fence, a yard light came on casting a jaundiced glow. It was soon followed by the sound of Isaac's neighbor wheeling a garbage can down to the road.

Shit, he thought, garbage night. The idea of going around the house gathering up from the various receptacles and replacing bags instantly drained him. His hand groped along the floor for his drink until he remembered Emily sprawled over him. He brought his hand back up again and rested it on the top of her head. Something about the solidness of it – her soft hair, the scalp, the bone underneath – rooted him for a moment. There was something there worth the effort of being a better man. This little girl, his daughter—Carson and Ashley too—they were why he needed to keep going and get out of his rut of self-pity. Maybe even knock off the booze.

Then, too, the skull under his hand terrified him. It was as fragile as it was solid, as though his fingers might involuntarily seize up, squeezing in and shattering the bone. Unable to shake the image, he lifted his hand from her head and dangled it over the arm of his chair. They needed him to be a man that he wasn't really sure he could be.

The neighbor's yard light winked out again.

"What are we going to do for my birthday?" Emily asked. Her voice was half muffled from talking into his shirt. "It's next week."

The news sent something churning up from his guts and into his throat like heartburn. His forehead flushed with a sickly heat. "What?" he asked, though he knew what she'd said. Gwen had always taken care of the birthday party details and remembered specific dates. Three months ago, Ashley's birthday had been easy. Believing that most men were either predators or parasites, he'd bought and wrapped for her a dispenser of mace. "Always carry it in your front pocket," he'd said, "just to be safe." She'd taken it with an ironic smile, humoring him, and he guessed it would probably just end up in a drawer in her room. He also sprung for her and her friends to go to the mall, eat in the food court, and then go to a movie afterwards. Finally, he'd upgraded her phone, which had been a big hit.

Carson had told her happy birthday. Emily drew her a picture. Nothing to it.

But that wasn't an option with a soon-to-be eleven-year-old. Not a kid like Emily. She'd want a party of some kind ... something special with the family. She might even want to go out to the cemetery to visit her mother's grave.

It was August already. Why hadn't his brain put two and two together? Get it together, man. Forgetting your kid's birthday is next level checked out.

Emily pulled her head from his chest and sat up. She pointed. "Daddy, look," she said, her voice a whispered excitement.

He looked in the direction that she was pointing. The wing span of a large moth lay silhouetted against the porch screen. It would have easily filled the palm of his hand.

Emily slipped off his lap and started tiptoeing towards it.

"Careful. It will fly away." He watched it intermittently close its wings and then open the spread of them again against the mesh of screen. Its body was off-white, but the wings were chartreuse like the color of the green snakes he and his brother used to find under boards as kids. He absently touched his fingertips down the side of his cheek until the word surfaced from memory. He snapped his fingers. "That's a Luna moth," he said. He pointed at it. "It's pretty rare to—"

"It's Mom," Emily said. She reached to touch a single finger against the screen.

He sighed. "Honey..."

She turned and looked at him, her eyes bright with what, to her, was the absolute truth. "Daddy, it is. It's her," she said. She turned her attention back to the insect.

The moth didn't fly away. It spun a circle around Emily's fingertip like a pinwheel in slow motion. She had read somewhere that butterflies and moths were the returned spirits of the recently departed. Damn internet, Isaac thought. What was the harm, though, in letting her believe it? It was probably a comfort. He studied her standing at the screen. She was getting bigger, and would likely soon withdraw from him as her body started to go through its own metamorphosis. She needed her mother now more than ever, maybe even just the idea of her. Emily could be anxious, and sometimes fixated on the smallest thing, like a hypochondriac. Unlike Ashley and Carson, who would take nasty falls as children and get right back up again, Emily was sensitive and had no tolerance for discomfort or pain. She'd always cry and want to be held.

He couldn't get his own life together. How could he possibly help her cross the bridge ahead on her path? Even with the question lingering in his mind, he had trouble imagining her coming into puberty while wearing an ill-fitting fairy costume with its one deformed wing.

After a moment, the moth launched away from the screen and disappeared into the darkness.

"That probably *was* Mom," he said.

She turned towards him quickly, her face alert. "You think so too?"

Isaac nodded. "I do." Then he smiled. "And since that *was* her, she got to see you in your costume just like she wanted. Now, when you go up to bed, you can change into something that fits. You wouldn't be comfortable sleeping in that anyway." She probably had been trying to sleep in it. He guessed that the constriction had woken her.

Emily reached and rubbed her sides up into her armpits. "It is tight under my arms."

"Well, there you go. Change out of it when you get up to your room."

She walked to him and spread her arms. He did the same, and she fell into him for a hug.

"We'll do something special for your birthday, too. Don't you worry about it," he said into the hair above her ear. He kissed the top of her head.

"Okay," she said. "Night and love you."

"I love you too. But get up to bed now and get to sleep. Chop-chop."

Emily left the hug, crossed through the sliding glass doorway, and disappeared into the kitchen.

Isaac listened to her soft footsteps that soon faded out altogether. He dropped his arm over the side of his chair and groped until his fingertips found the cool rim of his drink. Raising it into the half-light, he studied the ice cubes melted down to slivers. He set a few more cubes afloat. The result was too watery for his taste, and so he added some whiskey for balance, nodding his approval at the next burning sip. He'd have to put something together soon ... some kind of birthday gift and some kind of party. I'll figure it out, Isaac thought. He took another, longer drink.

A sharp twinge jolted the muscles of his left thigh. He grimaced through the act of setting his foot on the porch floor and massaged the heel of his palm into the sore spot. The pain ebbed slowly. After a minute, he straightened the limb out onto the table top again. Every night was a routine of constant adjustments. He couldn't remember how long it'd been since he'd quit going to physical therapy. He'd only gone to two or three appointments. That was a mistake, he thought, shaking his head. But then, what wasn't?

The animal rustled again on the ground. "Go to hell," Isaac muttered. Gwen had always made sure to throw overripe apples or stale bread into the backyard for "the critters." How did they thank her? By carrying on as though she weren't gone ... as though she hadn't died. He remembered a poem about some painting. *Icarus' Fall* or something like that. Was the painter Auden? No, maybe that was the poet. Some bit of a line stuck in his thoughts: "...how everything turns away quite leisurely from the disaster." He shook his head and took another sip of his drink.

He'd been introduced to the poem in some literature class he had to take back in college. The professor projected the painting in the front of the room and then read the poem aloud, his voice coming disembodied from the darkness at the edges of the lit screen. Isaac could still picture the farmer in the foreground, bent to his task of plowing, unaffected by Icarus drowning in the dark stain of water nearby. Closer to the tragedy, the fisherman on the shore didn't look up from his angling. He had to have heard the boy's screams. The men climbing the rigging of a nearby sailing ship paid no attention to the flailing legs sinking through the surface. Even the daydreaming shepherd's skittish sheep took no notice.

If the themes of how we are so often alone in our misfortunes hadn't meant much to Isaac in his early twenties, they certainly made palpable sense given the last six months. At the time, the only thing about that literature class that had made much sense was sitting next to Gwen.

He took another drink, and his mind drifted. Stopped at a red light just days before, he had watched a couple strolling up to the crosswalk. They were smiling, and from his first glance, he loathed them for their happiness. The man had leaned down and said something to the blonde woman, and they'd both laughed as though nothing bad would ever happen to them. Worse, Isaac thought, more like nothing bad ever happened to anyone. He was drowning in his own misery just ten feet away, unacknowledged. So close, how could they not feel his pain? They had to have felt it. They just didn't care.

Soon, the light turned green, and he lifted his leaden foot from the brake to the gas. Ten minutes later, parked outside of a grocery store, knowing that his kids needed his inert body to bring food home, he'd sat motionless, his blood a stagnant syrup. His fingers gripped the door handle, but did nothing else. He had waited for the deadening lethargy to pass. He knew that he should have felt bad for flipping the middle finger to the couple at the crosswalk as he'd pulled away, but there'd been something satisfying about shocking something sour into their goddamned perfect day. Waiting another five minutes in the Meijer parking lot, he'd shifted his car into reverse and picked up fast food to bring home. Again.

He gulped another mouthful of whiskey.

A sliver of light shone from under his upside-down phone on the armrest of his Adirondack chair, like light coming from under a door into a dark room. He picked it up to find a text from his younger brother, Adam. He squinted into the brightness of the screen, trying to adjust to the sudden light. Only two words: "You up?" Probably just checking to see how I'm doing, he thought.

"Shitty," he said aloud. He set the phone down again.

Against his will, as it often did, his mind went to the idea of a raven. He could still hear the deputy that had spoken as Isaac had drifted in and out of consciousness on the gurney. "A seat belt and airbag failure is bizarre enough. What the hell was that raven doing out there?" the deputy had asked a fellow officer on the scene. The cop wasn't wrong. Something had been off about that bird. It had careened out of the darkness into Isaac's windshield like a missile. If he closed his eyes, he could still see the blinding Rorschach of blood and feathers. He purposely didn't close his eyes, didn't want to see it. Even with them open, he could hear it. He spent many of his waking hours trying not to hear it, trying not to remember the sound of it, but it was lodged in his head like some kind of colossal tinnitus ringing his ears. The metal collapsing in on itself. The thunder of the splintering oak. The shattering windshield.

The final gasp from the passenger seat.

He tilted his drink to his lips, but felt only the ice and a trickle of watery whiskey. He fumbled his arm over the side of his seat and groped his fingers along the floor until he found the pint bottle. Holding it in the pale light, he assessed the contents through the green glass. He'd already finished more than half of it. Setting the tumbler on his armrest, he reached down again, found the ice bucket, and retrieved several cubes. He dropped them into his glass and opened the bottle. He listened to the liquid settling over the ice – a miniature, discordant concert of tiny chimes.

Isaac had started buying pints rather than fifths. If he had access to a fifth, he was damn near useless in the morning. He'd tell Ashley that he was having a migraine. Then, through the pounding of his hangover headache, he'd listen to her getting Carson and Emily up and ready for school. "Come on guys, the bus will be here soon," he'd hear her announce. His guilt would never let him go back to sleep until long after they'd left the house.

The pint kept him honest, or at least kept him from blacking out. One Saturday in June, his son had found him sprawled out on the floor of the screened-in porch. Fortunately, the youngest had discovered him, and not one of the other kids. Isaac had explained that he wasn't sleeping but listening closely for the sound of termites. "I can hear them better if I close my eyes." Isaac's remorse coiled in his chest when Carson lay on the porch floor next to him and pressed his ear to the wood. "What do they sound like, Daddy?" he'd asked. He closed his eyes to listen. That night Isaac had devised the plan to only purchase a pint each day. He knew the liquor wouldn't hit him so hard if he could ever drum up enough of an appetite to really eat.

His leg stiffened painfully again. He pulled it from the table and set it flat-footed against the floor. Kneading, he twisted his knuckles as deep as he could into the tissue. The pain though, as it did some nights, felt more like it was in the bone than the muscle. Isaac picked up his phone to check the weather app. Sure enough, the forecast called for an all-day rain starting at about four o'clock in the morning. Ever since the accident, his body had become like a human barometer. His leg throbbed its own prediction of precipitation.

He thought of the metal in his body. Open reduction internal fixation - that's what the surgeon had called his procedure. He had a rod through the bone, and screws holding a plate that helped everything heal in place. "The rest falls on you," his doctor had said. "You'll have to be diligent with everything the physical therapist wants you to do. It's not a quick recovery." Isaac took a sip of his drink and pressed the heel of his palm into the muscle. I'm just sitting too much, he decided.

Shivering again, he guessed that the coming rain was dropping the evening temperature. He took a warming sip of his freshened drink. The owl, or whatever it was, flapped its wings a moment, adjusting itself for better purchase. Isaac set his head back and closed his eyes.

CHAPTER 3

A sudden light woke Isaac from his half slumber on the porch. He blinked open his eyes. Phone glowing, he guessed it was his brother again, calling rather than texting. It'd be good to talk to him. He picked it up and looked at the screen only to see his mother-in-law's name. His instinct was to decline the call, but this would be the third or fourth time in a week that she'd tried to reach him. He took a quick sip of his drink and then pressed the green icon. The bird rustled again in the branches of the maple. The nighttime yard was always full with the muted sounds of animals moving about. Easy prey for an owl. What was taking the bird so long to make its move?

Isaac set the phone to his ear. "Hey, Helen, how are you?"

"Isaac? Where have you been?" she asked, her voice an octave above its normal pitch. "I've called you several times this week."

He switched the phone to his other hand and then grabbed his thigh, flexing and releasing his fingers in the flesh. "Just busy. The kids. You know." He cleared his throat. "Work has me at a desk, but there's still work to do. How are you doing?"

"I've been calling in the evenings, too. Ashley says you stay up almost all night."

"That's a bit of an exaggeration," he said. He rolled his eyes. "But I'm awake right now and talking to you. What's up?"

"I'd just appreciate if you'd call me back when you see that I've called. It's tough being left in the dark."

He shook his head bitterly. In the dark? She probably texted Ashley 20 times a day. He'd held off on getting a phone for Emily so far, but he knew Helen was at least emailing with her too. The idea hit him suddenly. A phone! That could be a great birthday gift. He made a mental note. "I'm sorry," he said into his own phone. "I promise to be better about that."

"You've made that promise before."

He sighed. "I double promise. I'm sorry. Okay?" With his pain in check, he released his thigh from his grip. "Was there anything else you wanted to talk about?" He switched hands and ears. Using his finger, he slid his glasses back into place on the bridge of his nose.

Helen cleared her throat. "It's Emily's birthday next week."

"I'm aware." His hand found and tightened around his whiskey glass. She liked to act as though he was incapable of remembering anything.

"Have you made plans? I'd like to be invited."

He looked up into the darkness of the ceiling, shaking his head. What a martyr. "Of course you're going to be invited. I just haven't had much of a chance to ask her what she wants to do. When the plans are firm, I'll give you a call."

"There's a butterfly house near you guys in Midland. She'd probably—"

"Helen. I've got this."

She took in a long breath and then exhaled. "Do you?"

He stared out into the darkness of the backyard. The animal began foraging again. You're a goner, he thought. "Look, I'm perfectly capable of planning—"

"I'm not just talking about the birthday. It's everything. It's ... well, Ashley says you're drinking a lot."

A flash of guilty heat shot up the back of his neck. He picked up his glass and set it down on the floor. A sharp pain shot through his thigh as he shifted. "Helen, I don't need this, okay? She's come downstairs a few times when I've been having a cocktail to wind down the evening. I'd hardly call that—"

"And the mornings she's had to get the other kids ready for school? I honestly don't recall you ever having migraines, Isaac."

Closing his eyes, he gripped his free hand over his forehead and squeezed. "I went through a rough patch a while back. I'm through it now, okay?"

She was quiet a moment. "Are you drinking right now?"

"No. I'm not. I'm talking to you right now." He opened his eyes. "And, honestly, I don't know that you should be going through the kids to check up on—"

"I'm not checking up on you. I'm not interrogating the children about your behavior. This was volunteered information in the course of our conversation." She sniffed in a breath. "She's worried about you."

"Well, she doesn't have to be, and neither do you. I'm getting things on track here."

"Hmm."

"What, Helen?"

"Their grades?"

He squeezed his hand into a fist until a knuckle cracked. "That was months ago, and really not all that unexpected considering what they've been through. It's going to be different when school starts again in a few weeks here."

"Well, could you tell me why I'm getting calls from their dentist? I mean, I'm sure Gwen had me down as an emergency contact, but I'm hearing from some receptionist that the kids are way overdue for checkups?"

"Way overdue?" It had only been a few months. "Are those their words or yours?"

She sighed. "Isaac, I'm not trying to attack you here—"

"Feels like it."

"Well, I'm not. I'm just worried about you and the children. I remember that first year ... that first year without John. Remember when my friend Jackie moved in with me for a few months ... just to keep me company. I needed that help, that support. And I wasn't trying to raise three children while going through my grief. I'm sure you're overwhelmed."

Isaac held the phone to his chest, groped for his drink glass, and took a swig. He raised the phone back to his ear. "It is tough, but I'm getting a handle on it. I'm sure school starting again will put us into a routine. I do appreciate you thinking of me ... of us."

"Who else do I have to think about?"

He nodded sympathetically. Gwen had been her only child. John, her husband, had passed away six years ago, before Carson was even born. An only child herself, Helen's family consisted of a few cousins who lived out East. She only had a handful of friends. Still, he thought, that doesn't give her cart blanche to live up my ass.

"Isaac? I just think you might need the kind of support I received ... something to give you some time to properly mourn."

He tried to imagine it, but couldn't. Helen on the couch? There was no way. "I appreciate it," he said, "but we're pretty crammed in here as it is. I don't even have a guestroom of any kind for you." He and Gwen had talked about a bigger house, but had decided instead to purchase a vacation cabin of their own. Not long after that, everything fell apart.

Helen chuckled on her end. "No, I didn't mean ... I meant the kids could come stay with me for a while."

He looked out toward the yard. Phantom-like in the darkness, another Luna moth, or maybe the same one, hovered around the screen without landing. Isaac held his hand over the phone's mouthpiece. "I'm being nice to her," he whispered toward the insect, smiling at his own absurdity. He moved his hand. "That might not be a bad idea, Helen." School wouldn't start for three more weeks. I could use some time away from them, he thought. They could probably use some time away from me. Good five or six days, at least.

The moth fluttered away into the darkness again.

"Really? I didn't think that you'd agree so easily. I mean, obviously it would be after Emily's birthday—"

"Well, sure."

"But it would have to be soon after. I'll need some time to get them enrolled in school, and I'd—"

"Enrolled in school? What?" He swallowed. "You're not thinking I'm going to have them live with you, are you?"

Her end went silent a moment. "I don't mean forever. I just think you need at least a few months, maybe more to—"

"Forget it, Helen. That's not going to happen."

"Isaac."

He took a gulp of his drink, not caring about the sound of the ice cubes. "I said forget it. I'm hanging up now. I'll let you know about the birthday whenever I get the plans finalized." He ended the call and sat for a moment taking deep breaths, waiting for his hammering pulse to slow. Shaking his head, he noticed the moth had landed against the screen again. "Yeah, I know," he said to it, "I'm a monster, Gwen."

His phone lit up with a text from Helen: "I meant no offense. It's just something I think you should consider."

Dropping more ice in his glass, he topped it off with the remainder of the whiskey. He flipped his phone upside down on the armrest. Grimacing, he hoisted his leg back on the table. She's not wrong, he thought after a moment of staring out into the backyard's darkness. Wincing, he shook his head, not at the persistent pain in his thigh, but instead at the accuracy of his mother-in-law's concerns. Mesmerized by the rhythmic motion of the moth closing its wings and then opening them again, his mind drifted to questions he had asked himself before. What if the roles had been reversed? What if he had died in the accident, and it was Gwen that survived with only a bad leg? Even that would have been different, because she would have committed herself to physical therapy the way she did almost everything else.

He pressed his knuckles into his fiery flesh. With Gwen, the kids would do fine in school, at least better than they were with him. He knew he had used the trauma of their loss as an excuse, and it might really be the only thing that kept Emily from being held back after failing nearly every subject. The principal had made it clear to him in a late-July phone call that she was being advanced to sixth grade on an "entirely probationary" basis.

How many times had he let them stay home from school? Had he ever checked their homework? He'd walked into the living room so many times to find all three of them on electronic devices. He'd never said a word. Never monitored their screen time, which he guessed was often the bulk of their days. And he'd let Emily live in her fantasy that her dead mother was trying to reach out to her. Gwen would have scheduled therapy to make sure their middle child was processing the grief, especially after a teacher had reported her disruption to the class when, in the spring, she kept trying to open the classroom windows to let butterflies in.

He wasn't even sure if he had any idea how Carson and Ashley were doing. So much of his limited energy had gone to watching Emily, trying to discern if her magical thinking was disrupting her reality. Did he know where a five-year-old like Carson should even be developmentally? And over the past summer, Ashley could have finished her driver's training. He'd botched that too. She'd aced the written portion of the class, and had even ridden her bike six miles every day to the driving lessons with the instructor. Isaac had only done a handful of her required practice hours with her. Instead of complaining, she just kept helping out with the younger kids and doing what cleaning she could in the filthy house.

The bird detached itself from its perch and dropped down with a commotion of wings and branches into the yard. Strange for its descent not to be followed by the shriek of its prey.

Even with a chilling breeze cutting through the corridor of the porch, Isaac dragged his palm across his sweating brow. He really wasn't prepared for any of this. He had earned a bachelor's degree with an emphasis in Fisheries Management out of Michigan State University, and the U.S. Fish and Wildlife Service had soon after hired him to be a part of their Sea Lamprey Management Division. Giant leeches, the lamprey was an invasive species in the Great Lakes. They latched onto the sides of salmon or lake trout and sucked them dry. Unchecked, they could nearly wipe out the fish population, which was a huge source of revenue for the state. Fish and Wildlife worked to keep the lamprey population in check.

Gwen had struggled at first to find any kind of work with her literature degree. She eventually dabbled in freelance writing, which over the years became more steady, until she contracted with a company that paid her more than he made in salary. Coupling that with his income and benefits, they were doing well by their early forties. They'd both felt that the purchase of the cabin marked the pinnacle of their success. With Gwen working from home, she could give their children what she'd had as a child. Like herself, her own children also woke to an adult helping them get ready for school, and that same adult waiting for them afterwards.

After a childhood spent in the woods with his father, Isaac had found his dream job with Fish and Wildlife. It meant a great deal of time away from home as he and the team traveled to various rivers and streams around the edges of Michigan's Lower Peninsula. Sometimes he'd have to go as far as Upper Michigan, even Minnesota. Starting in the spring and going into autumn, they followed a schedule of ten days in the field, and four days off. Being on meant that he spent his nights in a Fish & Wildlife field camp in a trailer. During the days in the field, he helped with chemical distribution into the rivers to treat for young lamprey in their larval stage, nipping them in the bud before they could transform to their parasitic stage and ravage the fish population. When the day's treating with lampricides ended, he'd often take his fly rod out for the evening to some other nearby river. Everyone on the team knew that fishing in a river that had been treated was pointless. The dying ammocetes would come up out of the mud, providing plenty of feed for the trout population, and no reason for them to scan the surface for insects.

In many ways, the setup had been ideal, almost as though he were a bachelor, husband, and father at the same time. During the summers, he'd come home from his ten days in the field to what amounted to a war hero's welcome. Everybody was so excited to see him, and family drama was minimal because they all knew how soon he would be leaving again. For four days, he could be an exemplary father. He'd take the girls and Carson out for ice cream. Other times, he picked up a container of worms and took the kids to some inland lake to catch bluegill from the shore. He'd watch their favorite movies with them and read the younger ones stories at bedtime. Recalling those days, he knew too that he had often longed to get back out in the field by the end of his fourth day home.

When the treating season would end, he spent late autumn and winter in the office filling out reports and attending meetings, or in the shop inventorying and maintaining equipment. It meant being home every night, but once the kids were in school, they all fell into a routine that didn't ask too much of him. Even when he was home more regularly, Gwen had tended to the needs of the kids. She helped with their homework. When feverish in the middle of the night, they called out for her. She'd made each of their birthdays special with themed parties that reflected their current interests. He'd step in to help with discipline, or sometimes roughhouse with the children on the living room floor. Many of his winter evenings were spent with household repairs and touch-ups that he hadn't been able to get to during the hectic summer schedule. It had all been pretty ideal. Up until the accident. Even if the injury to his leg hadn't desked him within the Service, he had no idea how he could have gone out on any field work without someone consistent to watch the children.

Recalling his last attempt in the field, he winced. In mid-July, even though his leg was even worse than now, he'd told his supervisor that he could go on a field treatment of the Upper Peninsula's Two-Hearted River. Helen had agreed to watch the kids for a long weekend. It was a disaster. Instead of adding to their short-handed team, he hindered them, and spent most of the day on shore nursing his leg. He also nursed from a flask he'd tucked into his back pocket. They'd sent him home the second morning when they found him passed out on the field trailer floor. Isaac hadn't told Helen that the incident had resulted in an administrative leave. How long the Service would cut him slack, given the loss he'd experienced, he didn't know. He still had field equipment in the back of his SUV from the Two-Hearted trip. That alone was grounds for termination. I'm dropping the ball at every turn, he thought.

After the accident, it was as though some giant lamprey had sucked onto him with its mouth's vortex of teeth. Sitting on his porch he could feel it ... the lethargy, the lack of passion to do much of anything. His nights with the whiskey did nothing to give back to him what the metaphorical lamprey took away. Instead, the booze brought its own draining effect. He was a train wreck, he knew it, and sitting in his chair with his inflamed leg up on a table, he began to believe more and more that Helen was right. It didn't have to be forever. It didn't even have to be longer than half the school year. Given time to himself until Christmas, Isaac was sure that he could straighten out and be the father his kids needed him to be. Maybe they could enroll in online school for a few months, so they didn't have to make the awkward adjustment of being the new kids in school. There wouldn't be anything stopping him from driving down to see them every weekend. Sterling Heights was only a couple hours south. As much as he guessed that it would be good for him, he was almost certain it would be good for them. Gwen was cut from Helen's cloth. His mother-in-law would know how to see to their needs ... to see to their growth. It probably wouldn't hurt for him to talk to a therapist, maybe even a grief counselor.

Sipping on the last of the evening's whiskey, with his thoughts starting to get swimmy, it struck him that they could get started on the plan immediately. It would take an intervention with the kids, a family meeting with Helen present. It would take a lot of talking and probably some tears too, but they'd be able to understand why it was the right move. "Christmas will be here before you know it," he could almost hear himself saying to the kids. "We could just have Emily's birthday at Helen's and do the whole thing then," he muttered into the emptiness around him.

A high-pitched scream out in the yard sent a chill up his spine. He dropped what remained of his drink on the porch floor, but the glass didn't shatter. The hair on his arms lifted and his feet went cold. Two words suddenly echoed in his head. Cabin. Birthday. Very distinct, the scream combined the wail of an injured puppy with nails on a chalkboard. He knew it was a rabbit scream, but like his colleague Roger at Fish and Wildlife once said, "Nothing prepares you for hearing that shit."

After the rabbit's banshee-like death note, Isaac thought he'd heard a voice. Someone speaking, but not saying anything he could understand. Then, too, he'd fly fished enough to have experienced the will o' wisp effect of what he called "river voices." How many times had the current, going over rocks in some part of the river he couldn't see yet, convinced him that there had to be other guys out fishing? He could hear them talking. He'd swear it ... the murmur of their voices. But he'd turn bend after bend and never see a soul. The voices would just disappear, some auditory trick of moving water going over rocks. The high-pitched rabbit's scream could probably do the same to his perception, he guessed.

Birthday. Cabin. Cabin. Birthday. Why hadn't he come up with the idea earlier? The kids had never even had the chance to see the place. He and Gwen had closed on it in late November the year before. Going into a season of busy holidays, they opted to pay someone in the nearby town to winterize their vacation hideaway. Then, as a reprieve from the chaos of the Christmas season, he decided in January, just after the New Year, to take Gwen to her favorite restaurant – O'Rourke's – a farm-to-table place located on a county road. They'd had a great meal and a good time reconnecting, just the two of them. Nobody could have predicted a raven flying straight into the driver's side of the windshield as they drove home.

Located in northern lower Michigan, their cabin stood on Orphan Island in Lake Coventry about twenty miles due south of the town of Cheboygan. He'd never had the chance to get the full story, but guessed the island got its name from how it looked out there all by itself on that deep lake. The realtor had explained that it was actually a peninsula, not an island. "But given how there's no road access to the peninsula through the marsh, it might as well be," the realtor's husband had piped in. "Everyone calls it an island." On the southern shore, the Raspberry River wound its way through a thick acreage of protected wetlands. The marsh extended onto the peninsula, and it was through the peninsula that the river flowed before dumping out into the lake. As far as he knew, only one other house existed on the five-hundred-acre island, occupied by an older woman who lived there year-round. The realtor had also mentioned a few abandoned buildings from the 1940s.

Isaac thought of the woman again, his island neighbor. He couldn't imagine the isolation that must have meant for her in the winter months, not to mention the expense of paying someone from town to snowmobile her mail and groceries out to her. He wouldn't mind the kids meeting someone with that kind of fortitude. Probably a real character too.

It was perfect for a birthday, he mused, nodding. Perfect for a broken family that had spent too much of the last six months inside on screens. Taking the kids fishing and swimming, he could be the dad he used to be. They could explore, catch crayfish, and look for toads at night on the beach. Evenings spent playing board games around the fireplace. He snapped his fingers, acknowledging an idea that came into his head.

They could plant a memorial tree for their mother.

A small pinging sound drew Isaac's attention to the porch's doorway out to the backyard. The moth flew against the screen, bouncing back from it, and then flying into it again.

"You really want in here, eh?" he asked, smiling. He watched its rhythmic battering of the screen. "Slow down," he said. He took his leg from the table and planted his hands into the armrests of his chair to push himself to standing. "You're going to hurt yourself you keep that up."

When he stood, the porch floor wobbled beneath him. He felt a bit like someone had started to administer ether to him, and then stopped part way through the procedure. He laughed to himself for a moment, but stopped immediately when he put pressure on his bad leg. Walking with a hobbling limp, he closed the sliding glass door to the house and opened the screen door. The moth flew off into the darkness and then moments later returned and flew through the open door. Watching it fly past him, Isaac attempted a squat to stretch out his leg. He ended up teetering over onto his ass. He laughed again.

While he sat, his thoughts went to the rabbit out on the lawn. If it were an owl doing the dirty work, it sure was acting strange. Landing on the ground and then waiting to attack? Normally they'd survey for prey from some high branch, or even the air, locate the target, and then swoop in for the kill. Carson still liked to play in the backyard sometimes. Isaac didn't want him stumbling across the tufts of rent fur and lawn speckled with blood.

Leaving the porch, he staggered across the lawn. He sucked in a startled breath and stopped abruptly. The silhouette of what looked to be a tall man stood near the lilac bushes. Isaac's pulse beat in his ears. When he and Gwen had lived in their first house, a little two bedroom, he'd heard branches snapping in the backyard. He went to investigate and ended up chasing off a prowler. He'd waited up the next three nights with the only weapon he had at the time, the wood splitting axe he'd inherited from his father. He never got his chance to give the guy a good scare because he never came back.

Isaac stood staring at the silhouette in front of him. He swallowed. "Hey," he said. He sounded more apprehensive than threatening.

Wind stirred the branches of the lilacs, and the silhouette vanished deeper into the shadows. Had it been there at all? Isaac pulled his phone from his pocket.

Turning on the flashlight, he followed the beam in the direction of where the man had been. He took a startled step back when he spotlighted the entire body of the rabbit stretched out on the grass. After a moment, he nudged it with his foot, leaving himself no doubt that it was dead. Leaning closer and passing the light over it, he found no blood, not even at the edges of its mouth. With what his leg could give him, he bent down and scooped his hand under the animal's lukewarm ribcage. Its head lolled like its vertebrae were a bungee cord. A broken neck? He shook his head. Even through his whiskey haze, he knew something wasn't right. An owl breaking its prey's neck and then leaving it? Nothing he could put together in his mind served to explain the rabbit's strange death. Sweeping the light through the lilacs, he saw no man, but only branches and leaves. He shivered off a chill. After a moment, he tossed the rabbit body into the darkness under the bushes, guessing that some scavenger would drag it away. At the very least, Carson wouldn't spot it.

Standing again, he felt like he was being watched. He scanned his light above him into the branches of the maple. "Jesus Christ!" His phone illuminated the white, ethereal plumage of a snowy owl staring at him with yellow eyes. It stayed only a moment with its gaze locked on him until exploding from the branches and disappearing into the darkness overhead. Isaac stood, stunned, looking at the sky. His heart felt like it was beating in the back of his mouth. He shivered in a chilly breeze that seemed to follow the bird, as though it were dragging January itself in its wake. "What the hell?" he muttered.

Spending an entire winter scouting for a snowy owl still might not reward a bird watcher with a sighting. What was one doing in his backyard in the middle of August? And for that matter, he wondered, looking back towards his porch, why was there a Luna moth when they normally emerge in May or June, live for a handful of days, mate, and then die? What the hell was happening? He walked back toward the porch with a limping gait that favored his leg. Climate change is causing more havoc in the natural world than people are guessing, he thought. He wondered if it was having any effect on the lamprey runs.

Opening the screen door carefully and slipping in, he closed it immediately behind him. He picked up his whiskey glass from where it lay on the floor. As good of an insect trap as anything, he figured. Bunching the end of his sleeve over his fingers, he wiped out as much of the liquor as he could. Then, he shined his phone light over the entire porch looking for the moth. He wanted to ask Carl, his office's entomologist, if he'd ever heard of a Luna moth sighting in late summer. He knew Carl well enough to know that the man would not believe him if he didn't have the specimen itself.

He could already hear Carl. "Look, man, there are over 350 kinds of moths in Michigan. They're pretty easy to mix up. Like, just as an example, do you know how many friends I have that swear they saw a recluse spider in their garage? They'll even drag me away from a barbecue to check one out.

It's never a recluse. I mean, sure, that's spiders, but the way the light plays at night, almost any moth could seem to have that green in it. You didn't see a Luna. You just didn't." Shaking his head at Carl's hypothetical lecture, Isaac searched the porch twice for the moth. Having only the table and chair, the porch didn't offer many places for it to hide. Isaac looked under both. After ten minutes of searching and searching again, he lowered himself into his chair.

He picked up the pint bottle and shook it. Nothing left, not even a sip. He tilted the bottle to his lips, anyway. A drizzle slid to the back of his throat. The night had warmed some. He sat putting together a loose plan of what he would need to get together for the cabin trip. The big thing would be stopping at a phone retailer and getting the latest model for Emily. A guaranteed big hit. To do this right, though, he'd need a pen and paper. He'd need to be sober. Everything could wait until the morning.

He picked up his phone, slid his finger through his contacts, and then pressed a number. While he listened to trills indicating that the phone on the other end was ringing, he recalled some of the exercises the physical therapist had him doing in those early sessions. He tried to remember where he'd left his exercise bands. Nothing was stopping him from some home-grown physical therapy. His brother finally answered as Isaac lifted his leg up on the table again.

"Hey, Adam, how are you? No wait, before you even answer that, let me ask you something. What are you doing next week?"

CHAPTER 4

A cold breeze came off the lake carrying a faint odor of fish. It blew down the sidewalk where Isaac paced back and forth keeping his leg warmed up. He'd already twice gone up and back the full length of the main street, which amounted to about three blocks. Over the past few days, he'd found his exercise rubber bands and even remembered a handful of the physical therapist's instructions. He worked out a half hour each day after a few cups of coffee. Most mornings and evenings still left him in persistent pain, but he felt that during the day he was getting around better. Preparing for the trip had meant moving about, and something about getting the blood flowing really made a difference. Between watching television in the day and idle nights on the porch, he knew that he'd just been sitting too much for the last few months. Time outdoors would get him active.

"Are you the new owner out on Orphan Island?"

Isaac turned. An older woman with a bulky winter hat, fingerless gloves, and wearing a man's threadbare overcoat stood staring at him with melancholy eyes. Her tangle of gray hair stuck out from under the rim of her chook. She held a fistful of Milk-Bones.

"That would be me," he said, smiling.

She looked into his face until he had to turn away. Her eyes were too much for him ... too world-weary. "She called you here," she said. "She's been waiting a long time for you to arrive. I can only say so much."

Isaac turned his gaze back to her and furrowed his brow. "Who?" Could she mean Gwen? Would Gwen's spirit be at the cabin? Shut up, he thought. Next thing you know, you'll be going to see that charlatan, Madame Zara. He studied the woman in front of him again. She looked homeless, and he decided that what she was saying had to be gibberish.

"Just keep a lookout." She pointed at her own eyes and then at his. "You have little ones to protect."

He crossed his arms. "I'll be watching over them."

"You should," she said. She nodded solemnly. "There's maji-manidoo out there ... for hundreds of years now. Cheating time." Her lips buckled in against her teeth. "Mind your thoughts. They may not be your own. That's his way."

"What? Maji--?"

"Theresa, leave him alone, for God's sake," a bearded man said. He'd stumbled out of the Ugly Porcupine, the town's one tavern. A waft of stale beer followed behind him. He ran his fingers through his gray hair. "The man just wants to have his vacation. Just go look for your damn dogs already."

She glowered at him. "Why, have you seen them?"

"I saw them running around earlier. You know, you might think about tying them up in your yard... or getting a bigger fence."

Theresa looked at Isaac again with her mournful eyes and then turned and started across the street. "They're good girls," she called back over her shoulder. "You'll see." She stopped in the street and turned directly to Isaac. "Mind what you drink." Then she turned and finished crossing the street.

Glassy-eyed, the man looked at Isaac. "Every town has one," he said. He pointed toward Theresa. "A crazy, that is. Ours was raised by Indians." He patted his hand against his O-shaped mouth. "You know, woo woo woo. Spends half her day looking for those bitches. Just ignore her." He watched Theresa get to the other side of the street. "Stupid mutts," he slurred. He walked away with a listing gait.

Shaking his head, Isaac turned in the other direction. His body trembled. Why did his brief exchange with Theresa leave him feeling so unsettled? What did she mean by telling him to mind his drinking? She couldn't know, could she? For that matter, how did she know he had kids? Then he guessed that she'd seen them arriving together earlier. Probably everyone had ... even the drunk bigot. Christ, we just need to get out to the cabin. Enough of this stupid town. He walked on, willing the morose feelings from his spirit.

Just get a grip, man.

Glancing up, he hoped the overcast sky didn't mean rain. Isaac looked around again at the small village of Witiko, located on the northern shore of Lake Coventry. Given the age of most of the people in the village, he figured that it was some kind of unofficial retirement community. Even the realtor that had helped them close on the cabin was older, and she'd mentioned how real estate was a second career for her after retiring from 30 years of nursing.

In the past, when they'd driven down U.S. 2 in the Upper Peninsula on the way to deer camp, he remembered his father pointing out the town of Naubinway on the northern shore of Lake Michigan. He'd often say aloud, as much to himself as to Isaac and Adam, "Lots of teachers from downstate retire there." Isaac smiled. Driving with his father was often an exercise in repetition. His habit had been to comment on the exact same landmarks no matter how many times he'd made the same remark in the past. He was pretty bad as far as retelling the same jokes dozens of times, too. If they were at camp, then he might tell the same joke two or three times in one night while in a bourbon fog.

Isaac and the kids had been in Witiko waiting for their charter to the island for a half an hour. Not many people in the town looked younger than fifty. It was like a lot of small towns in Michigan north of Saginaw. Young or old, not much draw for anyone to live there as far as he could tell. Besides some storefronts that had tried to be any number of businesses, not much had changed about the infrastructure in 100 years. They had a small post office, a gas station with one pump, a diner, a quaint sandstone library, and three or four storefronts that were boarded up. The faded sign on one said Dave's DVD Rental.

The majority of the cars that were in town were parked in front of the Ugly Porcupine, notable for its cigar store Indian out front. He remembered the wooden statue from when he and Gwen had been in town the past autumn. "Not the most progressive place," she'd said as they'd walked the street, her arm looped through his. Like phantom limb pain, he could still feel her hand gripping his arm.

He walked in the direction of the small pier at the end of the main street. He passed the Lake Coventry Market, the one other establishment that had attracted a few customers. He tried to see inside, but the storefront glass only reflected his own image back to him. His brother and the kids were inside, stocking up on snacks. Isaac and the children had arrived at quarter after eleven in the morning. The guy who chartered the pontoon boat had scheduled to meet them at noon. Isaac had played coy for the last three days with his secret. It wasn't a good secret. Not in the least. Ashley was already mad at him that he wouldn't let her do any of the driving on the way up. With it being almost all highway to the cabin, he just didn't feel comfortable with her behind the wheel.

When they had finally pulled into Witiko, she started complaining about bars on her phone. Time to drop the secret. "Well," Isaac had said, bracing himself for the fallout, "get in your final texts now, because there's no cell signal or Wi-Fi at the cabin." He'd said it just as they pulled in next to their Uncle Adam's car waiting for them by the pier. "Look who's here!" Isaac had added quickly, feeling as though he needed to shout enthusiastically over Ashley's boiling silence.

Carson wouldn't really know the difference until they got to the cabin itself and none of his YouTube videos would play on his iPad. Emily had taken the news in stride. "It's fine,

Daddy," she'd said. "I want to do all the other things you talked about. The toads and stuff." Ashley had bolted from the car to her uncle. She started complaining immediately about her dad forcing them to live in an 18th century shack for the next five days. At thirty-eight years old, Adam was the closest thing she had to an ally. She whined as though to a peer about being unable to text with her friends, make social media posts, or listen to any podcasts. Isaac didn't understand it, but she was really upset about the ending of some of her longest streaks.

With a mop of curly hair, Adam wore cargo shorts, a faded Eastern Michigan University sweatshirt, and flip-flops. He pulled Ashley into a hug. "You've gotten big ... and very technologically advanced!" Carson and Emily ran to him for their own hugs. After the greetings, Adam had taken Ashley's shoulders in his hands, looked her in her mopey eyes and said, "I bet we survive this, kid ... SnapTube or no." He winked at her, but didn't get so much as a smile.

"Maybe I should have been a history professor," Isaac said. "I didn't know it meant you could look like a bum all summer."

Adam laughed. "You should see some of my colleagues. They look like this all year."

The brothers shook hands, noting that it had been a long time, but neither of them mentioned that the last time they'd seen each other was at Gwen's funeral. Isaac started taking luggage and coolers from the back of his SUV. He knew enough about the piss poor excuse for a town to get his groceries ahead of time and pack the perishables on ice. Adam must have sensed the lingering tension from Ashley because he offered to take the kids to the market for snacks. Isaac had learned that promises of junk food didn't have the same pull with Ashley as they had in the past. Still, when her uncle and the other two started for the store, she trailed along. The last thing Isaac heard was his brother asking Ashley if she thought they might have anything gluten free. She said she was more worried about the store being "glutton free."

Isaac shook his head, smiling wistfully at the memory of her clever reply. As Ashley matured into her own person, he wondered how well he really even knew her. He hoped this cabin trip would let them bond a little more. She'd been stuck in the caretaker role for too long.

Isaac arrived at the pier, which amounted to two aluminum docks that formed a corridor for a cement ramp where people could back boat trailers down into the water. As he guessed, everything he'd unloaded from the car sat exactly where he'd left it. As a town, Witiko didn't have much, but that included not having much in the way of crime. He walked out to the end of one of the thirty-foot long public docks where a pontoon boat rocked in the gentle waves, knocking against the aluminum.

A shoreline largely made up of stone cliffs descended straight into the water, making it seem more like a quarry than a lake. Evergreen trees dominated the tops of the cliffs. The lower land around the lake's southern side consisted of swamps and marshland. It's what kept it from being a more popular vacation lake. People wanted beaches and the water right outside their window, not three-hundred-step stairs down to an immediate plunge. From what the realtor had told him, he knew there were only two other vacation properties on the high cliffs of the lake. Both were owned by widows from downstate.

At the end of the dock, the black water showed no sign of the bottom. He'd heard that in the middle it was almost a half mile deep. Isaac remembered that Gwen had described the lake as foreboding, but her attitude changed when she laid eyes on what would be their property. Out past the middle, closer to the southern shore than the northern, the island almost seemed to be floating, a green oasis on that dark body of water. Where the shoreline consisted of mainly conifers, the island itself had a healthy population of birch and oak trees.

Isaac shivered in another chilling breeze. Squinting, he could just make out the small shape of the cabin, a tiny brown smudge in the green of the island foliage. He'd paid Caleb, the owner of the pontoon boat, to go out to the cabin over the past weekend and open it up for them. Caleb had also snowmobiled over a couple times to check the roof in the winter. The other property on the island wasn't visible, tucked into the trees as it was.

"Isaac?"

He turned. Caleb walked towards him following behind his pot belly. Isaac guessed he was in his early seventies. He wore scuffed-up hiking boots and overalls with a flannel shirt beneath. The few wisps of grey hair on his head shifted around in the breeze. He sported a five o'clock shadow of grey stubble.

The older man looked up as he walked. "Check out that sky ... like somebody flipped a dirty ashtray upside down over the world."

"Pretty poetic, Caleb," Isaac said. "So, what's the good word?"

The old man stood for a moment, thinking. He held up his index finger. "Bacon," he said. He pointed the extended finger at Isaac. "Now, that's a good word."

"Yeah, that's a good one."

Caleb looked back at the stack of coolers and luggage. Then he turned back to Isaac. "Bringing food up on ice?"

Isaac nodded, hoping that the old man wouldn't be offended that he wasn't supporting the local market.

Caleb crossed his arms. "Then you got lucky. I was pretty certain you were going to be going into Cheboygan looking for a hotel tonight." He nodded toward the lake behind Isaac. "Should have seen the chop on the water this morning. I wouldn't a gone out in it. And it was supposed to go all day, but then, poof," he said, snapping his fingers, "like magic, within the last hour it died down to nothing but a breeze."

Isaac looked at the water and then back at Caleb. "Cold breeze, though."

"Always cold off that lake." He nodded. "Deep water, cold winds, my old man used to say." He nibbled his bottom lip for a moment. "But then, he also used to say, 'The boss might not always be right, but he's still the boss,' so I guess take his wisdom any way you want."

Isaac laughed. Behind Caleb, he spotted Adam walking with the kids. Carson perched on his uncle's shoulders, and Emily held his hand as they walked. Ashley looked to be doing some last-minute business on her phone, but even her pouty frown had disappeared.

Behind them, farther up the main drag, a procession of three dogs walked from one side of the street to the other. He wanted to laugh at the sight of them, but couldn't. Theresa's mutts gone AWOL. He didn't blame them for wanting to be free from her. He shook his head. The dogs disappeared between buildings.

Isaac turned his gaze toward the water. "What's the word on the fishing?"

"Guys are saying it's getting worse every year. And this used to be a great bass lake around the edges."

"Any lamprey evidence?"

Caleb nodded. "Just like Bert Lake and Mullet Lake. There's been scar reports."

Isaac shook his head. The Service had been testing and monitoring a 40-mile chain of rivers and lakes near Cheboygan. They suspected a healthy and growing population of sea lamprey were thriving in the in-land waters. Not good.

"Well," Caleb said, "I captain the boat, but I don't load it. Not with my back. You get your stuff and your people on there, and we can head out."

Isaac walked down the dock to join Adam and the children. Together they began loading the middle of the pontoon boat with their luggage and supplies. Caleb said nothing the second time Adam asked, in an exaggerated sailor's voice, for permission to come aboard. Walking back to get his fly rod case, Isaac smiled at Carson dragging one of the coolers with fierce determination. Behind him, Ashley was beginning to stand from picking up a box sealed along its top seam with packing tape.

He reached a hand out toward her. "Honey, I can get that one—"

As she finished standing, the contents of the box clanged against each other. The sound of liquor bottles knocking together couldn't be mistaken for anything else.

"I've got it, Dad," she said. She walked past him. Her withering look seemed to say, "Sure, no Wi-Fi for us, but you planned ahead for your own lovely little hobby, didn't you?"

His guilt subsided over the remaining minutes it took to load everything onto the boat. He thought about the last three nights, and how between them he might have had a pint and a half... maybe less. Besides, this is a vacation, he thought.

Before starting the outboard, Caleb tossed a tarp over their luggage and supplies. He tied it in place with rope and the tarp's grommets. "Sometimes can get a little spray in the boat," he said when he saw Adam watching him. "Think you can handle that?" he asked, smiling. Adam smiled back. "Aye, aye, Captain."

A minute later, Caleb unwound the tie-off ropes from the dock cleats and stepped back onto the pontoon as it slowly drifted away from its mooring. Taking the boat at a no-wake speed, he moved them out into deeper water.

Adam stepped to Caleb at the controls as they puttered along. "So, what's this going to be at this rate, Skipper ... like a three-hour tour?" He sang the last three words.

Looking over his shoulder at Adam and Caleb, Isaac sat in the port bow seat with Carson and Emily leaning against him. Caleb glanced at Ashley's back reclined in the starboard bow seat. Seeing the captain's lip rise into a grin, Isaac looped an arm around each child just before Caleb cranked the throttle up.

The younger children shouted their approval.

The force of the sudden take-off shot Adam backwards, where he caught himself against the back perimeter fence. Isaac laughed, watching his brother find his footing and stagger his way to the control panel where Caleb had his hand on the wheel.

Adam clamped his hand on the older man's shoulder. "Okay, I take it back. This thing can really move."

Caleb didn't look at him, but just shouted into the wind, "You bet your ass it can!"

Ten minutes later, he throttled the engine back to a no-wake speed as they approached the spit of beach in front of the cabin. They slowly drifted in, and Caleb trimmed the engine before cutting it altogether.

Isaac's eyes followed the footpath up from the beach to the property's front porch that overlooked the water. It was pretty simple. Rustic, even. A one-story log cabin with a fieldstone chimney on the side for the fireplace, and a cedar shakes and shingles roof. The porch wrapped around two sides. There was a firepit about ten feet out from the porch steps. He couldn't believe that he and Gwen hadn't spent even one evening around the outdoor crackling flames. How many times had she brought up making s'mores?

"Everyone get back here in the stern, so we can get some lift on the front," Caleb said. His command rousted Isaac from his melancholy.

They made their way towards the back. Ashley struggled to tame her wind-whipped hair. Isaac put his arm around Emily and kissed the top of her head. Carson stood staring over the back of the boat at the engine's gasoline rainbow trail scumming the surface.

Caleb set his hand on Adam's chest as he tried to go past. "Not you," he said. He smiled. "I need someone in the water off the bow to guide us in."

Adam looked at Isaac who only shrugged his hands apologetically and pointed to his bad leg. Adam looked back at Caleb. "You got it, Skipper. Just don't hit me with your hat."

Caleb looked back and made eye contact with Isaac. "That one is a real comedian, isn't he?"

Isaac shrugged. "He seems to think so."

Setting his wallet, phone and keys on one of the seats, Adam walked to the gate, grabbed a length of rope tied off to the front cleats, and jumped down into the water. "It's not warm," he shouted. Before long, the first quarter of the pontoons were beached. Opening the gateway at the front of the boat, Caleb talked Adam through how to slide the walk ramp out from under it and down to the sand. Soon after, they started unloading. Isaac grabbed the liquor box before anything else and hobbled it down the ramp. He could feel Ashley watching him, and he knew that by trying to make it disappear as quickly as possible, he'd only called more attention to his booze.

In a matter of minutes, they'd stacked the last of their things on the lawn just beyond the beach.

Caleb crossed his arms and looked at Isaac. "So, tomorrow at nine?"

Isaac nodded.

"Two trips?"

Isaac explained that his mother-in-law would arrive sometime between noon and one o'clock and that he wanted to be there to meet her. Caleb could then bring them both back to the cabin.

"Small town," Caleb said, "I'm sure if I sipped on some coffee at the diner I could spot her. Could just say, 'Hey toots, I'm your ride.'"

Isaac smiled, trying to imagine it. "Yeah, that's probably not going to work for her. Her wiring doesn't really have a 'casual' setting."

Caleb shrugged. "It's your money." He pointed to a plastic beach box that sat at the bottom of a flagpole planted in the sand. At the top of the pole, a faded American flag shifted about in the breeze. "That box has a green flag and a red flag. I'll come into town with the binos every afternoon." He held a pair of invisible binoculars to his eyes. "Green flag tells me you're asking for an unscheduled pick up. Red flag means emergency pickup." He rubbed the back of his hand under his nose. "One good thing about Witiko? It's full of busybodies. Someone will usually call me if they spot either color before I do, but especially if it's red." He told a quick story about picking up the previous owner once because he needed his appendix out.

Isaac nodded. "Green flag and red flag ... in the box. Sounds good. Thanks."

Caleb started up the ramp. He stopped and cupped his hand to his mouth toward the back of the boat. "Hey, little man," he started, raising his voice, "all ashore that's going ashore!" He waited a second and then looked back at Isaac. "I think I got a stowaway."

Isaac looked over his own shoulder. Ashley was farther up the grass toward the cabin. She positioned her phone high above her in a desperate attempt for a signal. Emily sat on the edge of the lawn with her toes in the sand next to a shivering Uncle Adam.

Walking up the ramp past Caleb, Isaac spotted the back of Carson's head, and eventually all of him at the back of the boat. He stood at the stern's perimeter fence staring down into the water. "Carson!" Isaac called, "Captain Caleb has to go. Come on, pal. Chop-chop." It was like trying to talk to Ashley when she'd walk through the house with her earbuds in. "Carson?"

Isaac limped to the back of the boat and set his hand on Carson's shoulder. "You ready to do some fishing?"

Carson didn't take his glazed gaze from the water—didn't seem to acknowledge him at all. His knuckles were pale with gripping the perimeter fence. Jesus Christ, Isaac thought, did he fall asleep on the ride over? He's sleepwalking in the middle of the day now?

He shook the boy again, but gently. "Pal, we really gotta go." He glanced back at Caleb standing at the top of the ramp, looking more than ready to cast off. Isaac bent over as best he could and picked Carson up. He tried to put most of the load over his good leg. "Man, it'd be easier if you'd just walk, kid."

Carson's gaze pivoted toward him slowly. He looked directly into his eyes. "Put me down now, goddamnit." His voice registered a full octave lower.

He'd spoken it so deadpan, so authoritatively, that Isaac, shuddering, responded involuntarily and set him back on his feet, where he turned and focused on the water again. He nodded his head as though listening. "Maji..." he whispered, haltingly, sounding like someone trying to learn how to pronounce a word. "Maji-aya`..."

Isaac's forehead went cold. He looked out over the deep water. Something chilling seemed to slither up his spine. He could feel it passing each vertebra, like an ice cube being slipped up the middle of his back. He tried to shake off the deadening feeling, but a trace of the dread lingered. Lowering himself on his good leg, he kneeled down to Carson's level. "What are you saying, bud? Maji-what?"

"We shouldn't be here," Carson mumbled. "We shouldn't have brought Emily."

Isaac set his hand on his son's shoulder. "What, bud? Why wouldn't you want your sister here?"

After a moment, Carson turned to him. His eyes were clear again and innocent. "What, Daddy?" He looked around. His voice had returned to its usual pitch. "Are we at the cabin? Are we going fishing?"

Isaac smiled. "Yeah, bud." He shook his head, hoping that sleepwalking in the day wouldn't be a new routine. He didn't know how he would explain it to Caleb if Carson had christened his boat with a healthy piss.

"We all set back here?"

Isaac turned toward Caleb standing at the wheel. "Oh yeah, just adjusting from sea legs to land legs again, that's all." He took Carson's hand, and they walked toward the front of the boat.

Carson glanced back over his shoulder at the lake.

"Ok. I'll see you in the morning." Caleb craned his neck to see out beyond the prow. "Ok, Gilligan," he shouted, "when they come down, put that ramp back and give me a decent push!"

Isaac and Carson started down the ramp.

"Should I correct him that I'm the Professor, not Gilligan?" Adam asked.

Isaac said nothing.

Standing in knee-deep water, Adam watched them descend. "Everything okay?" he asked.

"Yeah," Isaac said. Then he looked back over the dark lake. He shivered in the chilling breeze. "I think so, anyway."

CHAPTER 5

I saac set the last of the perishables – the hamburger meat and hotdogs – in the refrigerator and closed the door. He could hear the others unpacking in their rooms. Wanting to air out the mustiness, he started opening some of the side windows. Carson kneeled at the front picture window that looked out over the lake. He stared intently.

Isaac grabbed the handle of one of the coolers and started rolling it toward the door. "You okay, buddy?"

Carson looked at him. "Is it too cold to swim, Daddy?"

"At your age, it's never too cold to swim."

"But Uncle Adam said his lips were blue."

Isaac made a reference to Princess and the Pea that Carson clearly didn't understand. "Just never mind him. You'll be fine, pal. But we aren't going to swim right now. Gotta have someone down there to watch you, and everyone is just settling in right now."

Carson nodded and turned back to the window.

Isaac rolled the cooler out to the porch and dumped the watery ice over the side. Leaving the lid open, he set the cooler against the side of the wall on the porch. Standing a moment on his good leg, he grabbed his left foot, pulled it up behind him, and stretched out his thigh muscle. Feels okay, he thought, nodding. After a moment, he released the foot. He looked in the direction of the neighbor's property. Given the trees, he wouldn't even know anyone lived there save for the rusty weathervane peeking through the topmost branches. He walked back into the cabin with less of a limp.

Inside, he found Carson still kneeling at his spot chasing two of his Matchbox cars back and forth across the windowsill.

Isaac smiled. "Haven't seen you play with those in a long time, buddy."

"I'm glad I brought them." He concentrated on the cars in his fingers again. "Step out slowly with your hands up. Fair warning. We shoot to kill."

What kind of stuff was the kid watching on YouTube? Shaking his head, Isaac swept his gaze around the living room. A mix of rustic furniture with knobby wooden frames and thick cushions filled the space. The rocking chair and coffee table were clearly Amish-made. An overstuffed chair near the fireplace looked out of place, but comfortable. Caleb had even brought in an armload of firewood and stacked it next to the fireplace. Isaac made a mental note to give him a good tip.

Wearing jeans instead of shorts, Adam walked out of his room. He set his hands on his hips and looked around the space. "This place is great. I could really get some writing done here, I'll bet."

Isaac remembered that his brother was writing something about the dispute between Ohio and Michigan over the Toledo territory. He'd been working on it for a few years. He often wondered what more there could be to say. "You're welcome to it whenever you'd like, little bro. Just let me know, and I can have Caleb open the place up."

"I might have to take you up on that." Adam looked around again. "Did you get the furniture this spring? I thought you said this is the first time you've been up here."

"It is the first time." He glanced around the space with a satisfied look. "No, all of this stuff was part of the deal. I guess they figured rolling the furniture into the price was better than trying to sell all of this stuff piecemeal."

Adam flipped the light switch up and down a few times, turning the overhead kitchen light on and off. "You even have juice?"

Isaac nodded. "Must have a cable running under water. I'm guessing because the other place on the island is lived in year-round." He couldn't imagine trying to keep a 500-gallon propane tank filled like their father had at deer camp. Not on what amounted to an island. "I'm still going to get a generator next summer just as backup in case the power ever goes out."

"Makes sense." Adam crossed his arms, shaking his head in disbelief. "This place is sweet. And you paid how much again?"

Isaac told him the price.

Adam whistled and shook his head. "God, that's a steal. How did you even find this place?"

He started to tell him but stopped when Emily came out of the girl's bedroom. "Hey honey, so what do you think?"

"It's really pretty. I really liked the boat ride."

Isaac nodded. "Glad you're enjoying it," he said. She walked past him toward the door. "Where are you going?"

"Out to look for butterflies."

He grimaced, but nodded his head. "Ok, just don't get too close to the water."

"I won't." She disappeared out the door.

Isaac looked at Adam who appeared to still be waiting for an answer. "Finding this place, yeah. To be continued. I just need to talk to Ashley for a second." He motioned his head toward the door Emily had just passed through. "Birthday stuff. Don't let Emily wander in on us."

"Gotcha."

Going to the open door, Isaac leaned against the doorjamb. Emily had already set a picture of Gwen on the nightstand next to her bed. He closed his eyes and swiped a finger firmly across his eyebrow to keep his eyes from welling with tears. Looking at her phone, Ashley lay on the other bed with her ears plugged up with earbuds.

"What are you doing?"

She didn't look his way. He waved his hand until she noticed him. Still holding her phone, she removed one bud.

"I just asked what you're doing."

"Looking at pictures."

"Selfies?"

Her eyebrow furrowed. "No," she said with a hint of disdain. "Just pictures of me and my friends."

He asked if he could come in, and she nodded. He took it as a good sign when she took out the other bud and set her phone face down on the comforter.

"Doing all right?" he asked. He sat on the edge of the bed.

She shrugged. "I'm fine. Why?"

"Just checking." He smiled. "So look, I wanted you to know that I got something for your sister from you. I got her a phone, so I bought a case that will be from y—"

"I already got her something," she said with a touch of pride in her voice.

"You did? How?"

"Babysitting money." She leaned over the edge of the bed and slid a backpack out from under it. "She's going to love it." As she unzipped the top and pulled it out, he recognized it immediately.

The sun. The moon. The alphabet and numbers. The fingers on the cover of the box set lightly on the plastic planchette.

He squeezed his forehead in his palm. "Oh, Ash... I don't think a Ouija board is the best idea for her."

Her face fell. Her voice rose. "Why? It's what she wants. She asked me to get her this, Dad."

He held up a calming palm and pumped it towards her softly. "I'm not mad, and I'm sure she did ask for it. I just don't think anything good comes out of her having one of these. You know how she's been."

Tears began to well along her lower eyelids. "I don't see the big deal, Dad."

"I didn't say it was a big deal. I think it's great that you bought her something that she wanted and with your own money. I'm proud of you. But whatever she has going on, I just don't think something like this helps her work through it." He slid the box from her loose grip and pushed it into the backpack, zipping it closed. "She's really going to like the phone and the case, honey."

Quiet for a moment, Ashley fixed her teary eyes fiercely on his. "Well, I guess you can drink to that."

He could feel his face blanching. "Ash."

She fit her earbuds back in. "Just go." Her voice cracked.

"Ashley."

She picked up her phone and tapped in her unlock code. "It's fine. Whatever. I just want to be alone for a while." She sniffed in a breath. "I won't give it to her."

He held up his hands in surrender. "Okay." Standing, he winced at a sharp pain in his thigh. "We're probably going to go on a hike soon if you want to go."

She didn't answer him. He rubbed his leg for a moment and hobbled out of the room.

Adam sat on the couch with the bottom of his shirt rolled up. He plunged a syringe into the roll of belly flesh pinched in his left hand. "Everything good?" Adam asked, while watching his hands.

Isaac nodded, lowering himself onto the couch and watching the needle. "Just teenage drama. She'll be fine." He swallowed. "What about you? What's this?"

"No worries, big brother. My doctor put me on these injections for my psoriasis. It's made a huge difference." He removed the needle and worked to zip everything back into a small, red first-aid kit.

Isaac recalled his brother's inflamed patches of skin from when they were kids. "Well, that's good to hear." He spotted a flash of orange and yellow. "Wait a minute, what's that on your side?"

Adam looked at him sheepishly. Saying nothing, he pulled his shirt up, exposing the flesh on the right of his ribcage. He had a tattoo of the logo for the Toledo Mud Hens, a cartoon bird wearing a baseball hat.

"Hmm, didn't know you were such a minor league fan."

"Well, I might have met a grad student at the University of Toledo while I was doing research in their Special Collections Division. I may have taken her to a Mud Hen game on our first date. We may have even dated for six months. And," he said, "to commemorate our sixth-month anniversary, we may have gotten drunk and got matching tattoos."

Isaac smiled. "I didn't know you were dating anyone. You're going to have a great story to tell your kids, I guess."

Adam pulled his shirt back down. "Well, we may have split up two weeks after we got the tattoos."

Isaac laughed and couldn't stop laughing nearly a minute later. Any time he started to get control, he'd look at his brother and start laughing again.

"All right. All right." Adam looked around the room. "So, you were about to tell me who you had to kill to get this place."

"You killed someone, Daddy?" Carson asked from his place at the windowsill. He'd traded his cars for Legos.

Isaac stifled his last chortle. "No, buddy, that's just a figure of speech."

"What's that?"

"Doesn't matter. Just means that your Daddy didn't kill anyone."

Isaac turned his attention back to his brother. Getting ready to tell the story, his first thought was to settle in with a drink. Too early, he thought. Way too early. He could only imagine the severity of Ashley's reaction if she came out of the room to find him drinking in the middle of the afternoon. "Well, we wanted a place up north for years, like a lot of people do. They aren't cheap. And we could never really agree on a property. She was insistent that it be on a lake. And well, you know, with the fly fishing I really wanted to be on a river ... or at least close to a river."

Adam smiled. "So she won."

"We both did." Isaac explained about the Raspberry River. He didn't know how big it was or if he could even fish it, but he said that didn't much matter after they saw the price for the place. "If there's trout in it, I'd bet that means the lake is probably full of rainbows too. Deep and cold as it is, I'd guess some good-sized bows if the lamprey haven't gotten to them." Isaac absently scratched his arm. "Even if the stream on the island turns out to be a dud, an outlet on the north side of the lake east of town looks promising too. It's about a three-mile run as far as I can tell, that eventually flows into the Black River. I'd bet there's trout in that stretch too."

"I hope so for your sake, bro. I remember when Dad tried to teach me to fly fish. I can still hear him. 'You don't have to flick your wrist like that. You're casting the weight of the line, not the fly. Load it up with good back cast, count to three, and then shoot the line forward.'" Adam shook his head. "I never did get the casting down."

"We don't even know what we don't know, gentlemen," Carson said. He held a Lego figure who was addressing half a dozen of the other figures.

Adam gave Isaac a wry smile. "You got yourself an old soul in that one," he said. He nodded toward Carson.

"I'll say. Half the time, I don't know what he's going on about. He's got a mind for words like Gwen's."

They listened to him pretending for a moment. A stream of dialogue continued from his mouth, muted and indiscernible.

Carson stopped playing and turned towards them. "What?"

"Nothing, buddy. Just keep going." He turned toward his brother. "So, anyway, I was in the bathroom, and Gwen started screaming my name. I'd heard that voice before when she called me out in the field to say she was pregnant with Ashley." He lowered his voice. "Besides for sex, I don't think I'd ever run into the bedroom that fast."

Adam snickered and shook his head. "Just stick to the story there, Casanova. I don't need you painting any pictures in my head."

Isaac shrugged a few fingers into the air. "The story is pretty simple, really. There was an ad for this place in her Facebook feed. It was everything we wanted, and about twenty thousand less than the budget we'd agreed on for a vacation place." He explained that she'd been so excited that she called the number that night even though it was after nine o'clock. "A sleepy sounding realtor picked up. She said that the place hadn't even been officially listed yet, but that maybe the owners had done some preemptive marketing. They're 'very motivated' she said. I guessed there must have been some kind of financial trouble."

Adam smiled. "One person's loss..."

"Yeah, no kidding. We had Helen come up and watch the kids. That was a Thursday. We'd pretty much closed on the place by late afternoon the next day. We made one more trip a couple weeks later to finish signing some of the paperwork and, boom, it was ours." He looked around the room. "Christ, Gwen would have loved staying here. I can practically see her curled up in that chair with a book," he said. He pointed at the chair.

Adam looked down into his lap. Then he looked up. "Well, you got really lucky ... I mean, with the cabin." He pointed at Carson's back. "Can you imagine the memories for him with a place like this. Even that dilapidated shack that Dad called a deer camp ... I still have great memories from it."

Isaac nodded. "I remember we'd run out in that meadow and then come back to see who had the most wood ticks on their clothes. Shit, we'd do that all afternoon. Well, when Dad didn't have us cutting or stacking wood."

Adam rubbed his abdomen where he'd injected himself. "I can still hear him. 'Always work to be done at camp, boys.'" He laughed. "Remember when we'd get home and Mom would have us strip down to our underwear in the garage? She'd leave that pile of clothes there for a week before bringing them in to wash them. God, she was neurotic about wood ticks."

"Because of Fritz."

"Who's Fritz, Daddy?"

Isaac kept forgetting his son was in the room listening. "A Golden Retriever. Just a dog we had."

"Why don't we have a dog?"

He couldn't imagine having yet one more thing to care for. "We just don't, bud."

Adam chuckled and shook his head. "Yeah, old Fritz. He got that wood tick in him in the long hair next to his belly. Thing was swollen to the size of a grape before anyone spotted it. I remember Dad spread the tines on a fork, got it around it, and backed that thing out... still alive."

Isaac could still see it in his mind. Purplish with the blood inside it, the tick sat on the linoleum of their kitchen floor. It wanted to get away, but it's little legs just ratcheted back and forth, dangling on either side of its fat body. Fritz lay in a corner next to the stove licking the exit hole. "I remember Dad pushed one of the tines into it. 'Too greedy for their own good,' he said."

Adam nodded, shaking his head. "Yup, blood everywhere." He laughed. "And that was it for both of them. No more camp trips for Fritz, and no more peace of mind for Mom."

"Daddy!" Emily's voice shouted from outside. Her feet pounded up the porch steps. She ripped open the screen door and let it slam behind her. "Daddy!" she yelled again, almost out of breath.

Adrenaline shot up Isaac's spine. His heart banged in his chest. "What is—?"

"It's Mom ... she's here too, Daddy! I got her."

Carson shot up like a popped cork to look out the window. "Where, Em? Where's Mommy?"

Isaac scrambled to his feet as best he could against the pain in his leg. "Carson, it's not … Emily, just calm down. Calm down, honey. I asked you not to do that in front of your—"

"But you should come see! It's a monarch. It's Mo … it's her, Daddy."

Isaac pumped his palms at her and pressed a shushing finger to his lips. "Shh, I'll go see. Just don't with the … just calm down and don't say anything else for a second."

She stood, her lips tightly closed, going up and down on her toes like a piston. "Hurry, Daddy," she hissed.

Adam stood and walked to the window. "I got him, bro." He negotiated Carson back down into a kneeling position. "Show me what you've got going on here. What's that guy doing?"

Carson said the figure in question was the hero getting ready to shoot the bad guys. He said the bad guys didn't know what they were in for. "They underestimated him."

"I'll bet they did." Adam ruffled Carson's hair.

Isaac followed Emily out the door where she ran down the steps and across the lawn. A jolt of pain shot from his knee through his thigh and into his hip. "Goddamn it." He grabbed the porch railing to keep from falling down the stairs. He stood a moment catching his breath and letting the sizzling spasm subside.

"Daddy?!" She stared back at him from some 10 yards away.

"Daddy can't go that fast, hon. You're going to have to calm down, for Christ sake," he said, the last of which he muttered under his breath. Using the railing, he finished the steps and started hobbling across the lawn.

"Hurry," Emily shouted from down near the shore. "I don't want her to run out of air."

"What are you—" he started, but then he noticed the beach bucket flipped upside down in the grass right next to the sand.

Emily kneeled next to the bucket. She recalled the event to him with her hands flipping around in front of her. "She was flying all around my head and landing on my arm and then she landed on a flower and I didn't want her to fly aw—"

"Honey, take a breath," he said. He finally reached her. "Just calm down. You're going to make yourself pass out."

Her face turned from smiling frantically to instantly fearful. "I am?"

He sighed. "Well, no, but you need to calm down. Clearly the butterfly isn't going anywhere."

"It's her. I know it's her, Daddy. Just the way she was so comfortable around me. I could just—"

"Emily, seriously. Take a breath." Something lingered in the corner of his vision. He turned. The lanky silhouette of a man stood about a quarter of a football field away. When Isaac craned his neck for a better look, the man turned and disappeared up a path through a stand of pine trees in the direction of his neighbor's place. He wondered if maybe the old woman had a son who was visiting. Or maybe a caretaker. The way Emily had been shouting, it didn't surprise him that someone would come to investigate. He figured that half of Witiko was looking out toward the island, wondering what in the hell was going on.

"Okay," he said. He inhaled a deep breath. "Let's see your butterfly."

Emily nodded, smiling. She set her hands on either side of the bucket and tipped it gently, revealing nothing but grass and a single black-eyed Susan. Emily looked inside the bucket. "She disappeared, Daddy."

"I'm sure it just flew away."

"How?" she asked, her voice high-pitched and desperate.

He offered his hand to her until she took it. He pulled her to her feet. "It's pretty hard to get a bucket like that to sit flush on the grass. I'm sure there was just a space where it could get out."

He gave a little pull and got her walking in the direction of the cabin. He looked toward the pine trees again. No silhouette. The neighbors probably weren't used to hearing shouting children. He looked down at Emily's forlorn face. "Honey, what would you have done with it ... with her? You wouldn't want to keep it from being able to fly, would you?"

She shook her head solemnly.

He opened the cabin door to find both Adam and Carson kneeling at the window. They were in the middle of some involved play-acting with the Legos.

Emily went and flopped on the couch. She crossed her little arms.

"Honey," Isaac said, "we are here for five days. I bet she'll be back to check on you."

Her face brightened. "Probably for my birthday!"

He nodded, holding up a calming palm again. "Probably, but for now, since we're all unpacked and settled in, I say we go for a walk and see what this island has to offer. I need to get some blood flowing into this leg."

Carson looked at him. "You don't have any blood in your leg, Daddy?"

"No, it's just a figure of ... never mind." He waved a dismissive hand at him. "Let's just get ready for a little hiking."

Adam held up his first aid kit. "Let me put this away," he said. He stood and walked towards his room.

Emily and Carson tied their shoes.

"Double knot them like I showed you," Isaac said.

Emily tied her laces and then helped Carson with his. "You just tie the loops together," she said, just like Isaac had explained it to her.

"Hey, Isaac," Adam called from his room. "Come here a minute."

"Sit tight, kids." Isaac walked into Adam's room where he found his brother pointing to a frame on the wall. Isaac stepped in front of the picture. Either taken from a drone or an airplane, the image was an aerial photograph of the island. More than anything, it showed nothing but the olive green of the leaf canopy. Around the island, the deep water appeared almost black under the overcast sky of the day that the photo was taken. A strip of marsh connected the island to the swampy shore.

"That's a pretty cool view of the place," Adam said.

Nodding, Isaac leaned in for a closer look. He could make out the roof of his place, the lawn, and the beach and flagpole. Just beyond a small grove of pine trees, he picked out the shape of the neighbor's roof. Surrounded mainly by forest, the neighbor's place did feature a spit of lawn on its west and south sides.

He shook his head. "Man, they're only like a hundred yards away." He pointed to the evergreens, which had clearly been planted as a natural wall. "You wouldn't even know we're practically on top of each other with these trees here."

"Daddy, let's go," Carson called. "Chop-chop."

"Be there in a minute, bud," Isaac called back. His eyes flicked over the picture and stopped on a light discoloring of the water along the shoreline. He pointed. "I'll bet that's where the mouth of the river empties into the lake." The spot looked to be about 300 yards east of the neighbor's place. South of the mouth, he spotted a ribbon of sparse foliage trailing back through the canopy. "Here," he said, tracing with his finger, "is where the river flows through the woods. Good sign that it's wide enough to show up in a picture like this."

Adam leaned in. "What do you think this is?" He pressed his fingertip to another thinning in the canopy leaves, more circular than linear.

"Daddy?!"

"One second!" Isaac studied the area where Adam had pointed. "Almost looks like a pond or a meadow." He wondered if maybe a beaver hadn't built a dam across the stream. Beaver ponds were well-known for holding nice, fat trout. "Well, maybe we'll come across it on our walk," Isaac said. He smiled. "Let's get going."

CHAPTER 6

Ahead of them, Carson and Emily's footsteps crunched in the leaves and fallen sticks of the forest floor. They'd followed a nearly overgrown path from behind the cabin out to the timberline where the woods abruptly started like a wall at the edge of the grass. Isaac buttoned his shirt as they stepped into the cool shade of the old-growth trees. He nodded to himself, glad that he'd told the kids to get something warmer on. Between the breeze off the lake and the shadowed forest, it couldn't have been much more than 50 degrees.

"Never understood why people feel they need to have grass around places like this," Adam said as they made their way into the forest. He bent for a fallen branch and started using it as a makeshift walking stick.

"I don't know," Isaac said. "People just can't relax. Why would you want to come here and walk behind some goddamn lawnmower? It's like people look at a property like this and think, 'It's so peaceful. I wonder how I can turn it into endless work?'"

Adam hummed his agreement in his throat.

Isaac had done some stretches on the porch while the kids were inside getting sweatshirts and jeans. His leg felt tolerable, and a few intermittent steps landed pain-free as though the limb had never been broken.

He'd asked Ashley to go with them, but decided it best not to push it when she said she wanted to stay at the cabin and maybe even take a nap. The hike would be better without her glowering. He wondered, after this trip, if he'd ever get her to come back.

"I didn't expect such as an easy walk."

Isaac pointed above them. "It's the canopy," he said. "Hardly any sunlight getting down here for any kind of undergrowth. It's sunny right now, and I challenge you to find any light making it through."

"Right there, Daddy," Emily said. She pointed.

A shaft of light had broken through, illuminating a troop of mushrooms at the base of an oak. He half expected her to say the light was Gwen, but she didn't.

"Good catch, Em."

Adam looked at him and smiled. "Man, I gotta remember that they're always listening."

"Always," Isaac said. He looked to his left and strained to hear anything that sounded like the singing current of a stream. He wasn't sure how far east he'd have to walk to get some fishing in. He started to steer them in a more easterly direction.

Adam stopped and crouched down to his knees in front of a rotted log. He called the kids over to him and told them what to do. Declining, Emily instead watched while Adam and Carson pulled off pieces of the decaying wood.

Adam looked up at Isaac. "Remember busting these up as kids and finding salamanders?"

Blue-spotted salamanders. Isaac remembered them. An hour of breaking up and turning over wet, rotted logs usually yielded one, sometimes two. He could picture his own young hand holding the length of the amphibian's black, slick body spotted with robin-egg blue spots.

Adam dug his fingers into the middle of the log.

"That's too dry," Isaac said.

Adam brushed his palms over his pant legs. "Still might be one down near the bottom. Feels like it might be getting damp."

Down on his knees, Carson pulled at a section of the log that was slowly breaking away from the rest. It finally gave way and rolled toward him. He screamed and started brushing at the carpenter ants scattered on the thighs of his jeans.

Dumbfounded, Adam stared at his distraught nephew.

Isaac reached down, grabbed him by the hood of his sweatshirt and dragged the boy back from the colony. Hundreds of worker ants scurried over the ground, scrambling to snatch rice-like eggs and move them to shelter. "I think we got them all, bud," Isaac said. He swiped his hand, knocking one more from the boy's knee. Staring at the ground twitching with insects, Carson looked ready to cry.

Adam used his foot and nudged the log into place over the ant nest. "I'm sorry, Carson. Uncle Adam has bad ideas sometimes."

He sniffled. "It's okay."

Emily stepped over and took her brother's hand. They started walking again. "That was our fault," she said. "We have to respect creatures in nature. We're in their home."

Isaac and Adam gave each other a surprised look. "It's gotta be stuff Gwen said to her," Isaac whispered.

"She's not wrong," Adam said. He picked up his walking stick.

They trekked for another ten minutes. Ahead of them, a ribbon of sunlight came down into the forest and stretched for some distance both south and north. The stream, Isaac guessed. He nodded hopefully, liking the fact that the river was wide enough to make a crack in the canopy of leaves and branches above.

"What's the hurry, man?" Adam asked.

Isaac didn't realize how much his pace had quickened. Carson and Emily were practically jogging to keep up.

"I hear voices, Daddy," Carson huffed, catching up to his father's slowing pace.

Isaac looked down at him. "I bet you do, buddy, but it's not what you think."

"There's a stream!" Emily announced as flashes of the sun-dappled current came into view through the trees.

He smiled, nodding. "I know, honey." There was just something about coming upon a new stretch of moving water for him ... the hope of possibility. It felt the same every time, and never lessened in its intensity. "I know."

A moment later, they stood on the bank of a stream Isaac guessed was at least fifteen feet across. With low hanging branches over the surface, fishing it would mean unfurling roll casts over traditional casting. Still, it was a beautiful stretch of water with a bottom mixed with gravel, sand, and dark mud near the bank. In the middle he guessed it was a foot and a half deep. Logs lodged in the river bottom near the shore seemed like they would make good trout cover. Stones sticking up throughout the middle created scum lines downstream that might hold trout too. The low land around the river rolled with northern hardwood and hemlock ridges, and cedar, spruce, and balsam rills. Isaac wondered if it grew even wider as it made its way to the lake.

"You look like you're pleased with what you're seeing," Adam said. He set his hand on his brother's shoulder.

"I am." Isaac smiled.

Carson announced that he could still hear people talking. "It sounds like they're whispering. Sounds like girls."

Isaac explained to him that it was just an illusion, a trick of the current making its way over rocks and rounding bends. "I call them river voices."

Seemingly satisfied with the explanation, Carson picked up a flat stone and tried to skip it. It hit the water and disappeared with one splash.

Isaac went down on one knee as best he could and plunged his hand through the cold water into the dark silt near the bank. He knew he was likely too far upstream, but he let the current sift a handful of the muck from his palm. There were no lamprey larvae.

"Hey Isaac, what do you think that is?"

Isaac looked up and followed his brother's pointing finger with his eyes. On the other side of the river, about twenty yards away, patches of sunlight came through the canopy, shining down on what looked like a small clearing. Overgrown with ivy, juvenile maple, and weed trees, a ten-foot high cyclone fence with barbed wire affixed across the top encircled the parcel of land.

"No idea. Let's check it out," he said, even though the sight of it unsettled him. What the hell could that be? Most likely something bad.

A number of years back, he'd been fly fishing at night on the South Branch of the Au Sable River. Going onto the bank to take a leak, he'd heard it. It wasn't like any sound he'd ever experienced before in the woods. It droned and hummed with a measured, consistent rhythm. His rod caught against branches as he clawed his way up the hillside, following the beam of his headlamp up toward the sound. When he had crested the top, the mechanical noise was still there and louder. In the distance, through the woods, a pale light glowed ghostly. He headed for it.

He had stumbled out into a sudden opening. An acre of timber had been clear cut around the well site, and a dirt road disappeared toward the south into the darkness. They'd squared a twelve-foot high chain-link fence around the pumping station, and a street light glowed down on it from a freshly planted light pole. The pump made a racket resonant of the sounds that would wake him when he and Gwen were young and living in an apartment near a rail yard. It looked futuristic and prehistoric at the same time—the steel, birdlike head dropping down and coming up. Down and up. Down and up. Endless in its hunger.

Even though the stretch that he had been fishing was protected by the State from ever being developed, a company in Traverse City owned the mineral rights to the land around the South Branch. Natural gas or some other resource, they were pumping it out of the ground, setting their pumping stations just close enough to the protected property line and then drilling at an angle. He'd heard the arguments about the risk of brine or chemical spills into Singer, Sanger, and Sauger Creeks—all three of which fed right into the South Branch. The company didn't care. They were leeches, taking what they wanted to take, pristine trout stream be damned.

Cyclone fencing in the woods was never a good sign. Jesus Christ, he thought, is someone drilling on this island?

Isaac held Carson in his right arm, putting most of his weight above his good leg. In his left hand he held his pants, shoes and socks. Adam stripped down similarly and gathered a wary Emily into his arms. They waded across the shallow stream.

Carson leaned his lips near Isaac's ear and whispered. "Daddy, you're in your underwear. They'll see you."

"Who?" he asked. He laughed. "Your sister and uncle?"

"No."

"That's a touch cold on the feet," Adam said.

Isaac nodded, knowing that a cold stream usually meant a trout stream. Reaching the other side, they set the children down, dressed again, and then walked toward the fence. Through spaces where the foliage wasn't completely grown together, they could make out a compound of weatherworn limestone buildings. The roofs were bright green with moss, and tree branches poked through the spaces where glass windows had been. Much of the exterior wood under the roof edges was rotted and sagging away from the buildings. Not far from where they stood, Isaac spotted the fence's gated doorway. It was secured with rusted chains and locks that looked like they could be antiques.

Shit, not a beaver pond. Not a beaver pond at all. "I'd bet this is that clearing you saw in the aerial photo," Isaac said.

"Those look like dormitories." Adam pointed toward two rows of one-story buildings.

Isaac nodded when the memory came to him. "You know, the realtor did say something about some abandoned buildings."

Carson mumbled something.

Isaac looked down at him and ruffled his hair. "What, bud?"

"Nothing. I just said 'leave me alone'."

"To who?"

"I don't like it here, Daddy." Trembling, Emily's voice came from behind them. "I don't like it here," she repeated, her volume rising. "We shouldn't be here."

Isaac turned toward her some twenty feet away from them. Still retreating slowly backwards, she stared at the fence, wide-eyed.

"It's just some old ..." He could already tell there'd be no talking her down. "Okay, honey," he said. He smacked Adam in the arm with the back of his hand. "We can go."

Adam lingered, peering curiously into the compound of buildings. "There's a stone sign. It says 'St. Fran...' and then the word on the second line starts with 'Ch'." He stepped back from the fence. "I'll bet that says St. Francis ... you know, like Assisi. I wouldn't doubt if that's an old monastery."

Isaac pulled his sleeve. "Ok, but come on. We have to go." He pulled on Carson's hood. The boy peered thoughtfully through a chink in the leaf-covered fence. "We're leaving, little man. Chop-chop."

Carson looked up at him. "Not in boats it didn't happen, Daddy. Not canoes, they said."

He smiled. "All right, then. You hear that, Uncle Adam. No boats. We are stripping down again."

"You sure, Carson? I wouldn't mind crossing the stream by boat."

Carson shook his head solemnly. "That's not how it happened. It was her."

"Her? Her who?"

"I don't know."

Adam grinned. "Fair enough. Well, anyway. No canoes. We're wading again."

They walked back to Emily, and Isaac pulled her into a hug. She trembled against him. "It's okay," he said. "They're just old buildings, honey." He explained that they put the fence around the place to keep people from exploring and maybe hurting themselves.

"I just want to go back to the cabin."

He set his hand on her back and with a gentle push got her started in the direction of the stream. "That's what we'll do then. No sweat, sweetheart."

As they walked, Emily looked back over her shoulder a few times. At the stream's edge, the brothers stripped down again and carried the children across the water. A mix of sand and gravel in the river's bed pushed up between Isaac's toes. It was good trout habitat. While they crossed, he glanced downstream to watch for rising fish.

"This is the worst part," Adam said. He pulled his silt covered foot from the stream bottom near shore. The greasy, black mud dripped from his toes.

Isaac shook his head. "You'd never survive out in the field on a treatment. Sometimes they don't even let us bring our sleeping masks."

"Oh, shut up." Adam sat in his underwear on the bank with his feet dangling in the current, letting the flowing water wash them clean.

Isaac felt something silky sliding along his thigh. When he looked, Carson was lightly touching the vertical scar on his leg.

"Does that hurt, Daddy?"

He let his son take his hand away before stepping into the leg of his pants. "Nope, doesn't hurt at all." As he thought about it, he realized it'd been a good ten minutes since he'd thought about the leg. I just need to keep getting in walks, he thought.

Almost halfway back to the cabin, near the log where they'd found the carpenter ants, Isaac stopped the kids and pointed. "See anything about this tree, kids?"

They studied it a moment.

"It's wearing a ribbon!" Emily said. She pointed to a strip of hunter's orange nylon tied around one of the branches.

Isaac nodded. "That's right. Any time I go in the woods, I bring a few pieces of bright material like that." He explained that when they left the cabin, they'd been going in a southeast direction. "Here we turned due east, so I marked this spot so I could find it again."

"What's due east?" Carson asked.

Adam chuckled. "It's your daddy's very manly way of saying 'east'."

Isaac ignored him.

Emily reached toward the ribbon, but couldn't get her groping fingers to it even on tiptoes. "Aren't you going to untie it?"

Isaac shook his head. "No, this way if I want to come back to the river, I just find this spot and turn east."

"Oh no, no, no... *due* east," Adam said, smiling.

"You know, bro, you can be pretty funny sometimes, but then there are those times when you're awake."

Before Adam could respond, something landed in the branches above them.

Emily gasped a startled breath.

They looked. Some twenty feet above, a raven perched on a branch looking down at them. Isaac stared, feeling a cold chill crawling up his spine. What the hell was it with him and ravens? After a moment, he bent down. Coming up, he threw a piece of fallen branch at the bird. It flew away and then up and out of the canopy.

"Daddy, don't! Why are you scaring it away?" Emily asked.

He thought for a moment. "I just didn't want him to poop on us. They'll do that sometimes."

When they started walking again, Emily scanned the branches above them vigilantly. Watching her, Isaac shook his head. She'd be occupied with the thought of crapping birds for the rest of the way back.

Carson walked up and fit his little hand into Isaac's. "They say that's a good idea, Daddy ... the thing you do with the ribbon."

He looked down. "Who does, bud?"

"They do."

"Well, it's pretty standard advice to keep from getting lost in the woods, so I guess, yeah, a good idea." Smiling, he reached into his pocket and brought out two pieces of the orange material. He gave a piece each to Emily and Carson. "Now you guys can mark any spot that you want to remember."

Carson said he wanted to go back and tie a piece to a branch where they crossed the river. "In case we ever need to go back to the buildings."

Isaac looked to make sure Emily wasn't within earshot. "You don't need to do that. I'm sure we can find that place again if you ever want to go back. It was kind of neat, eh?"

"No."

"Come on, it was a little neat." Isaac squeezed his son's hand and they kept walking. It wasn't long before they came out of the trees and onto the small stretch of lawn behind the cabin.

"No!" Ashley wailed from inside. Wordless shrieks followed.

Isaac shot an urgent look at his brother. "Take these guys to the beach," he said. He ran toward the cabin, ignoring the pain that sizzled in his leg with each sprinting footfall.

"Daddy, what's wrong?"

"It's fine, Em!" he hollered as he went up the back stairs. "Everything is going to be fine!"

Ashley screamed again.

What the hell was I thinking leaving her by herself?

He found her sitting in her bed sobbing into her hands. Her hair hung damp, and the blankets were twisted around her legs.

He bolted to the bed. "Honey, what is it? What's wrong? What happened?"

Near hyperventilating, she continued to sob. When he was able to pry her hands away briefly, her reddened face shined with tears.

Isaac pulled her into his arms and held her against him. He kept repeating to her that everything was okay. As far as he could tell, she didn't seem to be injured. "Are you hurt? What's going on? Did you have a dream?"

Her head nodded violently against his chest. "It was ... I saw ... I saw Mom!" She started sobbing again.

He gripped her to him tighter. "It's okay," he said. "Those are hard dreams when they happen."

Her sobbing slowly subsided. She drew in staccato breaths, trying to get air. "I was ... I was ... I was swimming in the lake." Her voice cracked again.

"Just catch your breath. You have to calm down, sweetie. Just take your time and settle down. Remember, it was just a dream. It's over now."

Holding her for several minutes, he listened to her slowing breaths. He stroked his hand over her hair. He kissed the top of her head.

"Is Ashley okay?" Carson asked.

Isaac looked at him standing big-eyed in the doorway. "Go back with Uncle Adam, pal. Everything is going to be fine. Just a bad dream."

"Love you, Ashley."

"I love you too, Carson," she said. She sniffled. Her voice sounded nearly normal, if not slightly raspy. She peeled back from Isaac's embrace and lay back on her pillow. Her fingers swiped repeatedly across her cheeks. She breathed in short, quick breaths through her nose.

"Doing a little better?"

She nodded and looked into his eyes. "It was so real, Dad. I was by myself, and I wanted to see how deep the water was so I dove down toward the bottom." A residual sob shook her, but she collected herself again. "I could hear voices, but I couldn't understand the language. Then I could feel something coming toward me, and I looked, and it was Mom. She was swimming underwater toward me." She hid her face in her hands. "She was so pale, Dad. Her hair was full of seaweed, and her forehead was bleeding. Her fingers were really long and white and she grabbed my arms. She was trying to tell me something. The way her mouth was moving, I could tell she was trying to talk. The voices were chanting."

He took her hands from her face and set them on her lap. "All right, take a breath."

She shook her head. "I could read her lips. She said, 'Don't drink—' but then something behind her, I don't know what, just ripped her away. It got so cold. Her face looked like it was screaming, and she just disappeared into the darkness."

Isaac sat stunned. "Well, it was just—"

"No, but then I couldn't breathe. It was just all black around me. Cold and black ... and those chanting voices. I didn't know the way to the surface. I was drowning, Dad. That's when I forced myself awake." She covered her face with her hands again and wept softly. "I miss her so much."

He pulled her into him and held her. "I know, honey. I know. We all do." A tear broke from his eye, and he wiped it away.

When Isaac rose from the bed a few minutes later, Ashley was on her phone.

"You going to be okay?"

She nodded.

He left the room and, closing it behind him, he leaned against the door. Don't drink. Had she made that part up? Did it mean him? If she hadn't been so earnest, so clearly shaken, he would have guessed she was joking as a way to rib him about his box of booze. He couldn't escape the feeling that the dream, Gwen's message, was somehow meant for him.

Not drinking. He nodded his head slowly to himself. It was something he could address just as soon as they got home from the cabin.

CHAPTER 7

Sitting on the porch, Isaac looked across the lake at the small constellation of lights that was the village of Witiko. The red and green sidelights of what Isaac guessed was Caleb's pontoon boat puttered along the northern shore. Caleb had mentioned that he made some side cash by taking the occasional tourists out for rides. On Isaac's own shoreline, two flashlight beams zigzagged across the beach. Giggling and shouting to each other, Carson and Emily were looking for toads. It had been one of those strange Michigan days where the evening ended up being warmer than the afternoon. Rather than the sweatshirt and maybe even jacket that he'd imagined, he wore one of his old, long-sleeved Fish & Wildlife shirts. Ashley had stayed up after her bad dream, ate a hamburger, played three rounds of Uno with them, and then went back to the bedroom. She seemed to be okay. When Isaac checked on her, she was scrolling through pictures on her phone. He lifted his second drink to his lips, the perfect mix of whiskey and melted ice.

After dinner, he'd let the younger kids cast out worms that he'd dug from the soil behind the cabin. Forty-five minutes later, without even a nibble between them, they changed into bathing suits and swam until they were too cold. Isaac hoped that he'd do better fishing the stream than they'd done in the lake.

Adam pushed open the screen door and then guided it closed behind him, keeping it from slamming. He sat in the porch's other chair on the opposite side of a small table. He took a sip from his beer can.

"You want a couple fingers of this?" Isaac asked. He wiggled his whiskey glass, sending the ice cubes tinkling against each other.

Adam set his beer on a coaster. "No, a beer or two is more my speed."

"Suit yourself." With his mind already loosening, Isaac took another sip.

They sat for a moment, listening to the joyful soundtrack of Emily and Carson on the beach.

Adam rubbed his hands on his cheeks and then brought them palms together in front of him. He tapped his index fingers lightly against his lips. "Hoo boy, I'll say this much, big brother, you've got your hands full."

Isaac toasted him and took another drink. "It sure as hell hasn't been easy."

"They're each kind of wound up in their own way, aren't they?"

Isaac nodded. "Problem is I don't know if it isn't me that's doing the winding. Kind of watching myself fail every day ... at least it seems like that."

Adam picked up his beer can. "I don't know, I job shadowed you today. You looked like a father in his prime." He swallowed a sip and set the can back down.

Isaac shrugged. "Maybe moving the whole operation to the cabin has put me on my best behavior, I don't know. I just feel like this has to be a good trip, like maybe I'm trying to make up for the last six months. I'm not up for going into details, but I've dropped the ball more than a couple times." He held up his whiskey glass. "This hasn't always been the most helpful."

Adam looked at Isaac's amber drink reflecting the cabin's light behind them. "Then why have it?"

Isaac took a drink. The last slivers of ice went down his throat. "Because sometimes it *is* helpful." He reached to pick up the fifth, deciding that he would get up for more ice on his next refill. If I even have a next refill, he thought defensively. But he knew he would.

Adam watched him pouring the liquor. "You can drink it straight like that?" He shook his head. "Tastes like kerosene to me."

Isaac shrugged.

"Well, I'll join you for one, but I'm getting some ice." Adam stood from his chair and headed through the screen door.

Taking a wincing drink, Isaac called for Adam to bring him some ice too.

Returning, he dropped three cubes afloat in Isaac's glass. He held out his own tumbler half-filled with ice. "How about just a finger-full for me... just a taste."

They sat for a moment. Isaac took sips of his drink. Adam sat holding the glass in front of him, but seemed to be waiting for the ice to melt a bit. The flashlights continued roving the sand. The kids called each other's names and ran back and forth to see what the other had discovered. Isaac remembered his own childhood, and the hours chasing behind flashlights on beaches not too different from this. It was all easier then.

He set his glass on the table, topped it off, and then told Adam about Helen's offer to take the kids.

"Whoa, that's pretty bold."

Isaac snorted a little chuckle. "That's just Helen being Helen. I already told her no." He picked up his glass, took a drink, and set it down again. His cheeks tingled. The sides of his mouth pulled into a permanent whiskey grin. "I'm really starting to think, though, that she might be right in this case."

Adam took a tentative sip. He made a face. "Whew, that's strong." Then he looked at Isaac. "You really think things are going that poorly?"

"I don't know," he said. He rested his palm against his cheek. "They aren't going well. And, when I think about it, you know, them with her for a while, it's like I can feel a weight lifting, like I can take a full breath, you know? It just feels like I'm always waiting for the next tragedy. Even coming into the yard and hearing Ashely screaming like that today. I swear, I'm waiting on a stroke or a heart attack." He shrugged his hand into the air incredulously. "And it was just a bad dream she'd had. A goddamn dream," he said. He chuckled half-heartedly. "I just don't know if I have any fuel left in the tank for what all this is asking of me. I mean, it wouldn't be for good. Just a few months to recharge, you know, and I guess mourn properly, like Helen said. Right now, it just feels like everything is turned up to eleven, like there's never a break from—"

The brothers were suddenly lit up and shielding their eyes. Emily stood halfway up the lawn with her flashlight on them. "Daddy! Come here, quick! There's a fish with little lobsters on it. It looks hurt!" She turned and ran back down to the beach. Carson's light shined fixedly on the water's edge. "Daddy!" she shouted.

Still squinting, Isaac looked at Adam and gave a resigned smile. "Case in point."

The brothers followed their phone lights down to the beach. Isaac stopped once to knead his knuckles into his rigid thigh muscles. He pushed his glasses back into place.

"Daddy, hurry!"

"We're coming," Adam said. "Give your dad a second."

When they arrived to the beach's edge, Carson had the fish spotlighted in his beam. Just beneath the surface, an eighteen-inch rainbow trout with pale eyes undulated in the gentle motion of the soft waves.

"Look at the little lobsters!"

Isaac smiled. "Those are crayfish, honey." Nearly a dozen of the crustaceans crawled over the body. He didn't want to tell the kids that they were eating the carcass. Now and again, spooked by the light, one would shoot backwards into the darker water out beyond the halo's edge.

"Can we help the fish, Daddy?" Carson asked. "It's still moving."

"That's just the motion of the water. That fish is dead, guys. It happens." He bent down a little closer. "But, Emily, go up on the porch and grab Uncle Adam's walking stick. I want to see something. It's just inside the porch door leaning against the wall."

When she returned with the branch, Isaac used it to scoot the fish onto the wet sand of the shore. The crayfish scattered, though two were still clinging to the body with their claws. Hitting the sand, they released their grips and started back for the water.

"They'll pinch," Isaac said as Carson bent to grab one. "You gotta pick them up just right."

The boy drew his hand away and took a couple steps backwards.

Isaac wedged the stick under the fish and flipped it to its other side. "Goddamn it, I knew it."

"Oh, Daddy, something hurt it." Emily put her hand over her mouth and stared at the fish with big doe eyes.

Lamprey wounds. One of the marks, a perfect circle ringed in bruised black with a bright red center, sat near the fish's head. The other showed longer parasitic activity, ripped open as it was through the white and pink flesh. Isaac pushed the end of the stick into the wound and the wood tip disappeared into the body.

"He's sticking his tongue out!" Carson squealed.

The tail of a crayfish backed out of the trout's mouth, and then the rest of the scavenger's body followed behind it. It fell onto the sand and retreated into the water.

"Yuck. Why was he in his mouth?"

Adam set his hand on Carson's shoulder. "That's a dentist crayfish."

He glanced at Isaac who shook his head and rolled his eyes.

"That's not a dentist, Uncle Adam. That's silly."

Isaac looked at his brother and smiled. "You tell him, Carson."

A pungent waft of rotted fish rose up to them from a ground-level breeze coming off the water.

Emily held her nose. "Oh, it stinks so bad."

"The goddamn things are relentless," Isaac said. He shook his head. "They practically suck the soul right out of them." Using his phone, he took a few pictures of the scars. Afterwards, using the stick, he nudged the body back into the water.

"What sucks the souls, Daddy?" Emily asked. Her voice trembled.

Isaac swallowed. "Nothing, honey. I just meant boat motors. I think this fish got too close to the propellers and was clipped."

"Captain Caleb's boat?"

"I don't know, honey. Maybe."

Carson shined his light on the body. A few crayfish were already crawling towards it again. "Poor fish."

Isaac looked at his phone. It was after nine o'clock. "All right, everybody, did we find any toads?"

They shook their heads.

"Oh well. If it's warmer tomorrow, they'll probably be out. For tonight, though, it's time for you guys to get to bed."

He figured all the fresh air and exercise had worn them out because neither grumbled a complaint. They walked back toward the cabin following Emily's light.

"Brush your teeth first," Isaac called to them as they went through the screen door. He picked up his glass and took a long drink.

"Well, they're good about going to bed," Adam said.

"That helps." Isaac toasted his glass in the air.

"A boat propeller, eh, Mr. Fish & Wildlife?"

Isaac smiled. "I guess no worse than telling the kids that crayfish go to dental school." He took another quick sip. "And, do you see any of them going swimming again if I tell them that the lake has what amounts to three-foot-long leeches with mouths like electric can openers?"

"Good point." Adam took a sip of his own drink. "Do lamprey ever attach to people?"

"It happens, but it's really rare. Their prey is cold-blooded, and that's what the biologists say the suckers are drawn to." He shook his head. "I can't believe our lake is infested, though." He took another drink. "If they're spawning in that river on the island, no amount of treating downstream from the lake is going to do anything." Even he heard how he'd slurred the s in "downstream."

Adam held his drink out toward him. "You want the rest of this?"

Isaac looked at the melted ice cubes floating in an almost clear liquid. "No thanks. You can just dump it out."

Adam stood with his glass. "I'm going to get some water. You want some?"

"No, but bring me some more ice."

Listening to his brother in the kitchen, he stretched his leg out in front of him. Grimacing, he wondered if maybe he needed an x-ray to see if everything had healed properly. Somewhere on the island a band of coyotes started making a yowling racket. Their short howls rose and fell in pitch, intermixed with yips and barks.

Adam dropped a handful of ice into Isaac's tumbler. He took his seat again. "That's a little unsettling," he said. "It sounds like they're on the island."

"They probably are," Isaac said. He took a drink and then explained that they'd easily be able to cross the ice in the winter, or even make their way through the marsh.

"That doesn't worry you?"

Isaac laughed. "Coyotes? They're skittish as hell."

"Sounds like there's a lot of them."

"Nah, even a small family can make enough noise that it sounds like a hundred of them. They're harmless." Isaac combed his fingers back through his hair and shook his head. "I still can't believe Gwen never got to spend even one night here."

The brothers sat in silence, looking over the dark lake. More lights had gone out in Witiko. Isaac sucked on his drink, refilled it, and then drank again. He remembered the image of Adam down on his knees playing with Carson at the windowsill. I need to do that, he told himself. That's why we're here.

"I'm gonna get a dock, and then a boat, and then no more pontoon Nazi for me," Isaac said.

Adam looked at him. "I don't know, Caleb seemed nice enough."

Isaac shook his head and waved a hand toward his brother. "No, he is. I'm kidding." He took a long drink. "So, yeah, anyway, Gwen found this place on Facebook. It was just some random ad in her feed thing. We called that night to—"

Adam laughed. "You told me all of this already."

Isaac tilted his head and looked at him. "Are you sure about—?"

"Daddy!?" Carson's agitated voice carried from his room out to the porch.

Isaac set his glass down. "Goddamn it," he hissed. He wondered if the coyotes had the kid spooked.

"I can check him," Adam said. He started to stand.

"Sit down. Sit down." Isaac lumbered to his feet and met his brother's eye. "Why's everybody got a bug up their ass about taking care of my kids?"

Adam cocked his head. "What? I was just trying—"

"No, man. No. I'm sorry." Isaac held up an apologetic palm. "It's just ... I mean, thinking about Gwen just now and her not being ... I just get angry. It's fine." He patted Adam's shoulder. "But, sit down. I can check him."

"Daddy?! Chop-chop!"

Isaac cupped his hand to his mouth. "I'm coming, bud." He looked down at Adam. "He's using my own phrases against me, bro."

Staring out at the lake, Adam said nothing.

Isaac touched his shoulder. "S ... sit tight. I'll be right back."

"I'll be here," Adam said in a flat voice.

Going through the screen door, Isaac listed to the right. He gave his head a quick shake and righted himself again. Reaching it, he opened Carson's door and found him sitting in his bed in the glow of his lamp.

"What's up, big dude?" He smiled broadly.

"The girls won't be quiet, Daddy. They're in here talking."

Isaac furrowed his brows. "They're coming in here? I don't think so."

"I can hear them," he said. He crossed his little arms. "They aren't here now, though. They left when you came in."

Isaac smiled. "Well, I can see that, bud." He looked around the room and spotted an air register. "See that," he said. He pointed to the vent. "I bet their voices are coming through there."

"They won't leave me alone. They're whispering to me about doing bad things."

"Bad things, eh?" Isaac remembered sharing a room with his brother. They could hear almost everything their parents would say in their bedroom through the cold air return. Sometimes they heard things they really didn't want to hear. Using his foot, he pushed Carson's little suitcase against the grill. "That should block it. If you hear them later and it's bothering you, just come sleep in my bed. You'll be in there tomorrow anyway when your grandma gets here."

"Ok."

Isaac started to close the door.

"Daddy?"

Sighing, he opened the door wide again. "Yeah?"

"Love you, miss you, see you in the morn!"

It was a bedtime phrase he'd picked up from Gwen. Overcome with emotion, Isaac swung lumbering into the room and sat on Carson's bed. He pulled him into a hug and then gave him a kiss on each cheek. "I love you too, little man. So much."

Carson wrinkled his nose. "You smell like medicine."

"I do? Well, you smell like crayfish."

Carson looked at him a moment and then grinned. "You smell like that dead fish."

Isaac stood and pointed at him. "Well now, I can't top that, mister. And, besides, it's time to get some sleep. Another big day tomorrow."

"Daddy?"

He stopped again with his hand on the doorknob. He took a calming breath. "Just this one last thing, bud. It's getting late."

"One of the girls said that smell is hooch. What's hooch?"

Hooch? How the hell was Ashley coming up with this stuff? A sickly, shameful heat burned along the back of his neck. "Nothing. Don't worry about it."

"Okay."

"Turn your light off now."

Carson looked at the lamp and then back to Isaac. "Can I please leave it on? I promise I'll sleep."

Isaac nodded. "That's fine. Goodnight." Leaving the room, he closed the door and padded his way to the girls' door. He listened for a moment. If they had been talking about doing "bad things" they'd certainly clammed up. Sneaking out for a midnight snack drawer raid after everyone went to sleep was likely the extent of their mischievous plotting. He couldn't imagine Emily agreeing to anything that was truly bad. He thought to check in on them. Guessing that Ashley would be able to tell that he'd been drinking, he instead listened a moment longer and then returned to the porch.

"Everything ok?" Adam asked with a wavering voice. His head lolled a moment on his neck.

Isaac snickered. "Yeah. Everything okay out here?" He rolled his head in an exaggerated circle, mimicking his brother.

"I'm fine. Just the Ambien is kicking in ... you *know*, 'the nighttime sniffling, sneezing, aching, coughing, stuffy-head, fever, how the hell did I end up in the middle of the kitchen floor in my underwear, so you can rest medicine.'"

Isaac laughed and dropped back into his chair. "Shit, I'll drink to that." He poured three fingers full over what remained of his ice.

"I'll say this much," Adam said. His voice sounded dreamy. "I think the kids should stay with you. That's too jarring getting moved around like that ... and I'd think, confusing. Just work on whatever you need to work on while they're with you."

Isaac took a drink and nodded. "I think you're right. I think letting them go with Helen would be a copout."

Adam staggered to his feet. "Well, I am cashing in my chips while I can still make it to the bedroom."

"I'm probably not long behind you." Isaac took a gulp of his drink. "I'm going to sit a minute though and make sure the kidss tay ... the kids stay put in their rooms."

Adam said nothing else. He wandered through the screen door mumble-singing something about not minding other guys dancing with his girl. It wasn't until he was in the kitchen and belted out a Roger Daltry-inspired "The kids are all right!" that Isaac recognized the song. He shook his head, smiling.

After a moment, he settled his gaze upon the distant, dwindling lights of Witiko. He thought about Gwen, and what it would have been like if she were there with them. He pictured her on the beach, walking in the forest, and sitting on the porch with him holding a glass of wine. He gripped his forehead in his hand and squeezed his eyes closed to keep the tears from coming. The inside of the cabin remained quiet as time passed. He refilled his drink several times after finding he'd emptied it. Now and again, he'd snicker the word "hooch" and shake his head. "Little snitch," he'd mutter. "Where does she get off talking to Carson like that?"

He was still drunk when the falling temperatures finally woke him. His head drooped to one side, leaving him with a kink in his neck. His leg felt as stiff and aching as it ever had. He shivered. Finding it face down on the floor, he checked his phone. Almost three thirty in the morning.

While he'd slept, a nearly full moon had risen over the trees. Its reflection wavered leisurely on its back on the water between Witiko and the island. Beyond the porch, everything was washed in a blue-black luminescence. Where he couldn't earlier, he could distinguish between the darkness of the water and the lighter darkness of the island's shore.

It would have been beautiful to look at for a while if he didn't feel like vomiting as soon as he stood. He took gulping breaths in through his mouth and released them the same way until the sickening feeling waned. Opening the screen door, he stumbled into the cabin. He knew that if he could get in bed on his back, breathe through his mouth, and keep his head turned to the left, he wouldn't throw up.

He started for his bedroom, keeping an eye on the less than familiar surroundings. Stumbling between the couch and the coffee table, he had to look twice to believe what he saw on the table top. Holy shit. He stood over it shaking his head in disbelief. While he'd slept, the girls had snuck out of their beds and set up the Ouija board right in the middle of the living room. He could picture them on their knees, fingers hovering lightly, whispering their questions to keep from waking him. And this, even after he'd made his wishes absolutely clear to Ashley.

Yes, she was stuck without Wi-Fi. Yes, she'd been excited to give the gift to her sister. And, yes, she was a little too aware of his drinking habit. None of it gave her a right to defy him.

"What a little shit," he mumbled. Was this the "bad things" Carson had been talking about when he'd said he heard the girls whispering?

He looked again. The eye of the planchette magnified the number four, and the tip of the heart-shaped piece pointed to the Good in "Goodbye." Well, at the very least, the spirit had the manners to say goodbye. He imagined Ashley getting tired of the pretend seance after a while and shifting her fingers so the ghost made a hasty retreat. Why the hell didn't they even try to hide this from me? he thought. It's like she wanted me to know ... as though she were saying, "I don't even respect you enough to care if you're disappointed." His fists clenched at his sides.

When he reached for the planchette, it slid backwards away from his grasp. It magnified the word "No." He took a step back and blinked his soupy eyes. He shook his head, trying to rattle some focus into his cotton candy brain. When he looked again, the planchette rested again over the number four with its point fixed on "Good." He stepped closer to the table. When he reached again, the planchette veered from his fingers and fell onto the floor.

"What the hell?" Isaac glanced down. Was he that drunk? Not seeing the game piece immediately, he crawled on hands and knees, flashing his phone light under the couch. He found nothing but dust bunnies. Getting back to his feet, he swallowed the acrid bile rising up his throat. He stood just breathing for a moment. Big breaths through his mouth.

After a moment, walking behind the couch, he spotted the game piece some six feet away in the middle of the floor. "Slippery little twat, aren't ya?" he slurred. He stalked towards it, waiting for it to move again, almost expecting it. It stayed still. Standing directly over the planchette, he bent down for it. Then, he picked up the game board from the table. Staggering his way out the screen door, he crossed the lawn down to the beach. He ignored his throbbing leg. The moonlight illuminated his way.

He held the planchette close to his mouth. "Monkey with a drunk, you get dropped in the drink." Laughing at his accidental alliteration, he repeated the phrase. He laughed again until he coughed. Then, he retched. He swallowed hard to keep from vomiting.

Reaching the water's edge, he threw the game piece out as far as he could. Then, wristing it like a frisbee, he sent the board out into the lake. He didn't know what would happen with them. They might sink. They might drift to shore and rock back and forth in the waves like the dead fish. Let the girls find one or the other or both. It didn't matter. They were going to wake up in the morning and discover the game gone. Emily would ask after it. Or would Ashley have to keep her from blowing their cover? Would she tell her, "Oh, we weren't supposed to be playing with it before your birthday. Don't tell Dad that we did." How far would she take her deception?

He settled his hands on his hips and stared at the dark water. Ashley could take her lying all the way to her grandma's house as far as he was concerned. He didn't seem to be getting anywhere with helping her mature into a young adult. And then "hooch"? What the hell did she think she was doing talking to the younger kids about his drinking? She knew better. He'd been as direct with her as he could, and her response was to rebel blatantly. Was she gaslighting him about what she was and wasn't doing with her friends? Let Helen deal with that for a few months if she's got a bug up her ass to parent them.

Turning from the water, he spotted something lingering in the moon's luminescence to his left. He blinked for focus and adjusted his glasses. A man's shadow stood some thirty feet away. Tall and thin, he seemed to be watching Isaac.

Isaac tremored in a sudden chill. Some memory. "Hey—" he started, but the insides of his cheeks suddenly tingled and seeped with warm saliva. It was going to happen. It was happening. The drop to his knees sent an electric shock of pain through his bad leg. He threw up into the sand, and then, after some moments of convulsing breaths, threw up again. And again.

When his stomach finally stopped spasming, he thought about Helen's arrival – the kids coming down to greet her, and then the fly-covered stain of vomit on the beach. That could not happen. Still on all fours, he pulled his palms from the sand and rose to kneeling. His head swooned for a moment. Starting to dig a hole with his fingers, it wasn't long before he dug into the wet sand beneath the sugar sand surface. Glancing to his left, he wasn't surprised to see that the man's silhouette had departed. Who would stay to watch a forty-something-year old father with three kids dig a hole to bury his own drunken vomit on a moonlit beach at four in the morning?

He was making quite the impression on his new neighbor. Turning his head from his task, he threw up again.

CHAPTER 8

Isaac woke to a pounding. In his head. In his ears. He squeezed his eyes shut and massaged his fingertips into the lids. His mouth was cotton and sticky. The muscles at the back of his throat strained against the dryness when he swallowed. He had a dull pain in his side, but he knew that calling it his "side" didn't hide the fact that it was his liver. He'd felt it before.

Coming in from burying his mess on the beach the night before, he'd found the fifth bottle next to his chair. He'd poured the rest—what amounted to a generous shot—into his tumbler. He'd hoped downing it would wash away the aftertaste of having been sick. Instead, it almost made him sick again. Taking the emptied bottle into the kitchen, he'd stuffed it deep into the trash beneath the other refuse. Then he went to his room and threw himself diagonal across the bed. He'd realized only moments after landing on the mattress how lucky it'd been that Carson had stayed in his own bed.

The pounding came again into his half-sleep, followed by the sound of his door creaking open. "Isaac?" Adam said. "Caleb is here ... with the boat."

Isaac bolted up into a pain that might as well have been the butt-end of a two-by-four hitting him between the eyes. He grabbed his head, rubbing his thumb and fingertips into his temples. "Can you tell him I'm going to need ten minutes?"

After a moment, Adam walked over and sat on the bed. "I don't think ten minutes is going to do it. I don't see you getting on a boat."

Isaac settled his throbbing head back onto the sweat-soaked pillow. "Maybe if I just had some water."

He closed his eyes. He woke a few moments later to the sound of a water glass being set on his nightstand.

"Isaac?"

He blinked open his aching eyes. "Yeah?" The stench of his own body odor overwhelmed him.

"I brought you water, but this is a wash, man. You can't go into town like this."

"I gotta be there when Helen gets there," he mumbled. He tried to reach for the glass, but the idea of swallowing anything got the inside of his cheeks watering lukewarm and sickeningly. He pulled his hand away from the nightstand and took a few hard swallows to keep himself from retching. Closing his eyes again, he let his mouth hang open. "I'll be all right."

"Look," Adam said, "I'll go into town and meet her. I'll just say the kids were more comfortable staying out here with you than with me. I mean, that makes sense."

"They still sleeping?"

"Out like lights."

Isaac nodded his head slowly. Even that hurt. "I think you'll have to go. I feel like shit."

"It's no problem. There's a half a pot of coffee out there when you're ready to warm some up." He started for the door.

"Adam?"

"Yeah, bro?"

"When you're in town, will you grab the gear from the back of my car. You can't miss it. It's all marked with Fish & Wildlife logos. My keys are on the kitchen table."

"You got it. If she'll be here in the early afternoon, I'm guessing you have about three or four hours to pull yourself together."

He closed his scratchy eyes. Three or four hours seemed generous. Helen's tendency was to be early, not late. "I'll be fine," he said.

"I hope so. Try to get some of that water in you." He closed the door behind him.

Isaac set his head deep into his pillows and arranged his position in such a way for the least pain and discomfort. Even as he felt like he might be able to sleep, he couldn't. Every little sound reminded him that his kids were in the cabin. They could wake and start moving around at any moment. He didn't want them to find him in his room. Not the way he was. He could only imagine what it would smell like when they opened the door.

He fumbled his glasses from the nightstand, put them on, and checked his phone. Twenty minutes to ten. Swinging his legs over the edge of the bed, he sat for a moment, just breathing. He stared at the top of his hands dangling like pale, dead spiders between his legs. He took a cautious sip of the water, waited, and then took a longer drink. Keeping it down, he opened his side table and grabbed the aspirin he'd unpacked into it the day before. Three tumbled out into his sweaty palm. Popping them into his mouth, he took another long drink and got them down.

The shirt he'd worn the day before reeked of sour sweat. He unbuttoned it, peeled it from his damp torso, and threw it to the floor. He stared at the shield of brighter shirt material on the shirt's shoulder where the U.S. Fish & Wildlife patch had been, like an army officer's shirt stripped of its stripes. Gwen would have called the sight something ... symbolic or metaphorical. An omen, maybe. She wouldn't have been wrong. He wasn't long for the job at the rate he was going.

Using his toes, he snagged the shoulder strap of his luggage bag and dragged it to him. Bending to look into it made him nauseous. He lifted it onto the bed and, eyes closed, rooted his hand through it like someone trying to draw a slip of paper from a hat. He came up with underwear and then a pant leg before finding a t-shirt. It was nearly ten o'clock by the time he stood tentatively in the middle of the floor mostly dressed. He reached down and zipped up his fly. You can do this, he thought. You don't have a choice. He grabbed a polo shirt and shorts to change into after a shower. He knew if he could get into the bathroom and clean up, he'd feel better. There was little chance of him feeling any worse.

Forty minutes later, he sat on the porch with a tepid cup of coffee. His hair was still wet, but felt good against his neck in the morning breeze. When he had come out of the bathroom, Carson had been at the table eating a bowl of cereal. He seemed in good spirits and reported sleeping well. Isaac adjusted himself in his seat. Behind him, the muted sounds of his son came through the glass where Carson kneeled again at the windowsill with his toy cars.

Taking his second cautious bite of a plain piece of toast, Isaac looked over the lake. It was the calmest he'd seen it. The sun had risen over the eastern side of the water and lit the stone cliffs of the western shore. Two fishing boats floated near the northern shore. He guessed they were fishing for bass. It's going to be warmer today, he thought. Nice day. He hoped the kids would get the chance to do some more swimming.

"Hey, Dad." Ashley came out onto the porch holding a cup of coffee. "I made a fresh pot. Do you want a refill?"

He shook his head. She had a lot of nerve waltzing out to him after the bullshit she'd pulled with the Ouija Board.

"Do you think Carson is okay?" she asked.

"What? Why?"

She took a sip of her coffee. "He's just mumbling to himself a lot. It's creepy. He sounds like he's talking with someone about murdering people in their sleep. You should hear him."

He sniffed in a breath. "He's just playing ... just using his imagination. That's what happens when you finally get away from screens. You should try it."

She rolled her eyes. "I'm just saying, you could be raising a little serial killer."

"So, how long have you been drinking coffee, anyway?"

Blowing over the rim of her cup, she sat down in the other chair. "Like a year. I don't drink it all the time ... just mainly when I'm out with friends. A cup sounded good this morning."

He looked towards her. "Why? Were you up late last night or something? Carson said he heard you guys whispering." He wondered if she'd fess up about her little deception. He didn't understand how she had walked past the empty coffee table and then come out to join him on the porch, cool as a cucumber. She had to have seen that the Ouija board wasn't there. Was she getting that good? That devious? A year of drinking coffee without him having a clue? He wondered what else she and her friends were doing.

"He must be hearing things. Emily didn't say anything when she came to bed. I was reading a magazine, and at one point I looked over at her, but she was out."

He took another bite of toast. "That's pretty early for her. She didn't get up any time later? Not even for the bathroom?"

Ashley shrugged and then swept a few strands of hair from her face. "Maybe. I slept with my music in, so I wouldn't know."

Bitter, he bit into another piece of toast and then sipped his coffee. Lying right to my goddamn face, he thought. He decided that he wouldn't bring up the game, just to see how long she'd let the charade play out. Plus, he didn't want any kind of blowout with the kids just before Helen arrived. He checked his phone. 11:00. "Your grandma will be here soon," he said.

Ashley stood. "I know. I think I'm going to read until she gets here."

"Good plan," he said, nodding.

She lingered a moment. "Everything okay, Dad?"

He kept his eyes fixed on the lake. "Yup. Just having my coffee." He scratched his forehead. "Speaking of which, go easy on that stuff. No reason a kid your age needs all that caffeine."

She didn't say anything as she opened the screen door and disappeared inside. She let the door slam behind her. Good, be pissy, Isaac thought. He set his head back against his chair. The aspirin was working. He still felt rung out, but on the mend. Should be fine by the time she gets here, he thought. He took a sip of coffee, set the cup down, and closed his eyes.

"Good morning, Daddy."

Isaac opened his eyes groggily. He smiled at Emily. "Morning, Mrs. Almost-Eleven-Year-Old." He checked his phone. Already past noon. He could feel how the little catnap had done him some good.

"Two more days," she said in a sing-song voice. "Is Grandma almost here?"

"Should be soon." He attempted his coffee. "You think you could get me a little more?" he asked. He held out his cup. "It's cold."

She took it from him and returned with it refilled. Steam rose from the surface.

He took a drink and then adjusted himself straighter in his chair. "How'd you sleep?"

"Good."

"Why'd you say it like that?"

She sat down in the other chair. "Because Mommy didn't come see me."

He took a longer drink. More and more he felt better. "Ashley said you went to sleep pretty early. Maybe the moths weren't even out yet."

She shook her head. "No, I meant she didn't come see me in my dreams. I don't think I had any dreams at all."

"So you just slept all night, eh? Didn't do anything else?" He studied her side-eyed while she looked out at the water. Of any of his kids, she would break under pressure.

"I didn't wake up once."

Her deadpan face gave nothing away. Unbelievable, he thought. It wasn't like Emily to lie. She just didn't have it in her. The paranoia always got to her. The few times she'd fibbed over the years, she always ended up ratting herself out within a half an hour. He raised his cup to his lips and glanced back at the placid lake. Maybe they hadn't both played with it. He couldn't imagine Ashley playing with it by herself. Maybe she'd left it out hoping that Emily would wake up first and find it. Underhanded, true, but not a bad plan. How could he have taken the gift away after a surprise like that?

Still, what was she thinking? The game was gone when Ashley had woken. Emily hadn't burst into their room thanking her profusely. She had to know something was wrong. Someone other than her sister had to have found it. Ashley had to know that. What the hell is going through her head right now? he wondered. Maybe she'd woken earlier in the morning to use the bathroom. Did she see that the game was gone, but just assumed her uncle had put it away because Isaac was still sleeping? When she'd brought her coffee out to the porch, perhaps it was a test to see if he'd say anything.

Since he didn't, maybe she guessed that she was out of the woods.

She wasn't. Not by a long shot.

"I always have dreams," Emily said dejectedly. "Always."

Isaac set his cup down. He reminded her that she'd had a lot of fresh air and exercise. "That will make you sleep hard."

"I should have had more dreams then, not less. REM is the deepest sleep. That's when dreams happen."

He wondered how much time she spent online. "Don't know what to tell you. I heard we forget most of our dreams."

She wrinkled her nose. "It's just really weird."

He slapped and rubbed his palms together. "So, what do you think you want to do today when Grandma gets here? Feels like it could be decent swimming weather."

"That'd be fun," she said. She looked at him and then looked out toward the water. "It's sunny. Warmer."

He took a bigger bite of cold toast. He was relieved that she didn't mention boat propellers, crayfish, or any other reason she might have for avoiding the water. "Hey, I'm going to make some sausage patties and some of those frozen hash browns. You want some?"

She shook her head. "I'm not hungry right now. I'm going to take a shower and get ready for Grandma."

He followed her inside. Rummaging through the drawers, Isaac found a frying pan and a cookie sheet for the hash browns. Starting to feel even better, he knew a good hangover breakfast would move him a little closer to feeling normal.

"What about you, Carson? Want a sausage patty or hash browns?"

He didn't turn from his playing. "Yes, please. Both."

Isaac set five hash brown rectangles on the pan and slid them into the oven. The sausage started to simmer in the frying pan. His mouth watered.

"I'll take some hash browns and a sausage patty too, Dad," Ashley called through the open bedroom door. "Thanks for asking."

"Sorry. I thought you were all involved with your magazine."

"You know, you're right. Reading and eating can be a lethal combination, I've heard." She paused a moment. "I'm going to take the risk, though."

Grinding his teeth, he dropped a hash brown on the sheet and tossed another patty into the frying pan. Just too clever for her own good, he thought. He wasn't sure how he'd bring up the Ouija board, but her plan of just letting it blow over like it never happened wasn't going to work for him.

"How long do I have to strangle the windpipe for?"

Isaac felt like someone had poured ice water over his spine. He looked at his son's back at the window. "Carson, what are you talking about?"

He froze with his fingers on the windowsill. "I'm just playing," he said, meekly.

"Well, I don't like that kind of playing. No more about hurting people or anything, you understand?"

Carson nodded.

Isaac flipped the sausage patties, trying to forget the sound of absolute sincerity in his son's voice when asking about the nuances of windpipe strangling. He listened for anything else, but Carson only raced his cars back and forth in silence. Not so much as a "vroom" out of him.

After giving each of the kids their plates, Isaac took his own out to the porch. He held one of the sausage patties pinched between his teeth. Sitting down, he snapped off a bite, nodding. It was the kind of meal that was going to hit the spot. Nothing like a little grease, heat, and fried potato to polish off a dying hangover.

Finishing the last few bites of his meal, he could hear the motor coming his way. His plate was empty and sitting on the edge of the little table when Caleb's pontoon boat came into view cruising across the water. The kids burst out the screen door one at a time—Emily, then Carson, then Ashley. They shouted and waved from the beach. Helen stood at the front of the boat with a blanket pulled tightly around her and a kerchief tied over her hair. As a ship's figurehead, she looked like the product of a woodcarver inspired by the visage of his overbearing mother. Not that her frown needed to be explained (she was always frowning), but he wondered what she and Adam might have talked about. When it came to himself, he knew there was no limit to the issues that they might have delved into. As it was, Adam sat at the back of the boat, seemingly as far from her as he could get. Seeing the children on the sand, she finally let a hand emerge from her melodramatic blanket to offer a serious, single wave of greeting.

CHAPTER 9

Isaac stood on the beach taking luggage and whatever else Adam handed him from the ramp. "Take your time," Caleb said. "I'm in no hurry. Was hoping to go to the Ugly Porcupine for a burger tonight, but the wife informed me that she's roasting a turkey breast." He shook his head. "Not enough water in the world to wash down the dry that meat will be."

Adam and Isaac laughed.

Helen didn't. "For myself," she said, "I would appreciate anyone putting in that kind of effort, no matter the results. Simple gratitude."

Caleb didn't say another word. He retreated back by the boat's steering wheel, waiting to cast off.

Ole killjoy strikes again, Isaac mused.

Adam handed him his Fish & Wildlife gear.

He laughed, shaking his head. "You didn't need to bring the lampricide," Isaac said. He shook the quarter-full plastic container. The dark brown chemical clung to the insides like molasses. He set the container on the sand and turned back to the ramp.

"I didn't know. You said to grab your gear ... the stuff with Fish & Wildlife markings on it." He handed Isaac the electrofishing backpack, a long net, and a small duffel bag. "And you're welcome, by the way."

Within an hour of her arrival, Helen was lounging in a beach chair on the sand, supervising the kids while they swam. She wore a red, floppy hat with a wide brim. Her chair was positioned directly over the spot where Isaac had laid his vomit to rest. Ashley reclined in a two-piece bathing suit next to her to "work on her tan." Helen had been cordial enough to Isaac, and even complimented the cabin's interior as he gave her the tour that ended at her room. Maybe she knew that he hadn't done the decorating, and so felt okay with making some approving remarks. She'd had nothing overtly negative to say, and he breathed a sigh of relief, thinking that maybe Adam had been able to keep the topic of conversation off of Isaac.

Adam sat bent over in one of the porch chairs, tying his hiking boots. His mop of hair was still damp from a recent shower. Isaac stood at the edge of the porch with one hand on a support post and the other on his hip. Smiling, he watched Carson and Emily enjoying the water. His hangover was largely behind him. As undesirable as it had been, all of his throwing up the night before had gotten a lot of the booze out of his system. That always made for a speedier recovery.

"You ready?" Adam asked.

Isaac nodded and then cupped his hand to his mouth. "Helen," he called, "Adam and I are going to take a hike. We shouldn't be longer than an hour."

Without turning around, she raised her hand in the air and waved it back and forth.

"Bye, Daddy!" Carson called.

Isaac waved to him. He spotted Emily in mid-dive. She was still swimming under the water when he turned and walked inside through the screen door.

Adam grabbed his walking stick and followed Isaac through the cabin and out the back door. Walking for a time in silence, they followed the same route they'd taken the day before. Their feet crunched in the fallen branches and leaves. The sweet odor of the leaf litter breaking down permeated the air.

Isaac reached up and pulled a leaf from a branch. "She have anything to say?"

"Not really." Adam sniffed in a breath. "Small talk more than anything. She was pleasant enough."

"She mad that it was you coming to get her and not me?" He dropped the leaf and watched it twirl to the ground.

"Nope, but it was an enlightening trip."

Isaac glanced at him, and then back to the woods ahead. "How's that?"

"It was only a smidge after ten o'clock when Caleb got me to the pier. I took a walk to their little library and did some research."

Half listening, Isaac stopped walking. "It's gone," he said.

"What?"

He pointed. "The ribbon I tied around that tree branch yesterday." He rubbed his fingertips over his stubbled chin. "Squirrel must have taken it for its nest." He reached into his pocket, extracted another strip, and knotted it tight to a thicker limb.

They turned easterly toward the stream and started walking again. "I was hoping we'd go this way," Adam said. "That's not a monastery like I thought."

Isaac glanced at his brother. "What is it?" He noted how little pain his leg had been giving him. The hikes were good.

"Get this. This is wild." Though they weren't visible yet, he pointed with his walking stick in the direction of the fence and the compound of buildings. "That place was an orphanage."

"An orphanage?"

Adam nodded. "Yup. St. Francis' Children." As they walked, he explained that the orphanage had been constructed during the Great Depression by a Detroit philanthropist named Alistair Boyles. As a boy, Boyles and his sister had been orphaned in Dublin. As the son, he'd inherited his father's meager life savings. Despite the hardship, Boyles had done okay for himself through hard work. He eventually emigrated to the United States at 17 years old. He'd worked religiously, lived lean, and saved money for years, adding to the inheritance that he'd never touched. His eye was always on opportunity. Making small but astute investments into the burgeoning auto industry, he'd amassed a fortune after twenty years in his adoptive country.

At eleven, his sister had stayed in Dublin with a friend's parents who'd spoken confidently of adopting her. It was the only reason Boyles had felt comfortable enough to go abroad. He found out only years later that the adoptive family had fallen on hard times. The mother had died of tuberculosis, and the father, a drunkard, took to beating the children, including Boyles' sister. She ran away and turned to prostitution. At nineteen she was found dead in an alley from multiple knife wounds.

"Jesus," Isaac said. "That's not much older than Ashley."

"I know." Adam shook his head. "It's sad, but I think there's a book here, or at least an article. I mean, the whole thing's pretty fascinating ... historically, anyway."

Isaac smiled. "As fascinating as the bloodless Toledo War?"

"Bloodless?" Adam crossed his arms. "Tell that to Deputy Sheriff Joseph Wood. He was stabbed with a pen knife by Two Stickney while he was arresting Two's father, Major Stickney. Wood recovered, but I'm sure it hurt. A lot. Have you ever seen a pen knife? Oh, there was blood spilled, mister."

Isaac stopped at the edge of the babbling creek, looking up and then downstream. "The guy's name was Two? Like the number?"

Adam nodded.

"Come on, you're making this shit up."

Adam sat on a fallen log and started unlacing his boots. "It's true. And without the Toledo War you might not even have your precious Upper Peninsula, so put that in your pipe and smoke it." He started unlacing his other boot. "Look, if my advisor hadn't put the idea in my head that I could try to get my dissertation published, I wouldn't even be trying to rewrite the thing. Now I'm kind of stuck with it. I need a book to get tenure."

"But you won that Collins thing last year ... that teaching award."

Adam smiled. "Good teaching doesn't get you tenure." He stood and unzipped his pants. "Barely gets you noticed."

"I don't understand your work," Isaac said. He looked at his brother with his pants down to his ankles. "What the hell are you doing right now, anyway?"

"Fording the river." He pointed. "I want to check that place out again."

Isaac shook his head, but then sat and started unlacing his shoes. "Fording? You can't just say crossing?"

"Nope, I'm fording ... *due* south."

"Oh, shut up."

The brothers held their clothes as they had the day before and waded into the water. Isaac looked downstream for any rising fish. He wished he'd brought his fly rod. He could have fished a few bends while his brother checked out the orphanage. Then again, he thought, he'd be fishing it soon enough. Moments later, they sat on the opposite bank tugging their pants over their wet legs.

"But this Boyles guy..." Adam's animated gestures made him look as though he were lecturing to a classroom. "... whatever happened to his sister must have really haunted him." He explained that Boyles began to hear about a lot of orphaned Irish Catholic girls in Detroit. With its mix of poverty, sickness, and hopelessness, the Great Depression saw many Irish fathers abandoning their families, either from work, drink, desertion or death. The condition of the orphanages in the city appalled Boyles. "He called them 'the purgatory before Hell' ... the Hell being the streets of Detroit where they would find themselves at 16." Boyles instead had envisioned the young girls of St. Francis' Children orphanage having an upbringing according to nature, thereby developing a more rugged individualistic attitude before tackling the challenges of the world on their own. "Did you ever hear of the Greenbelt towns?"

Isaac shook his head.

"They were these towns owned by the federal government that were called Utopias at the time. They were specifically designed to foster community. They were surrounded by 'greenbelts' of forest and farmland rather than the urban sprawl of a city." Adam mentioned that this was right around the time that B.F. Skinner was writing his utopian novel, *Walden Two*.

"This Boyles guy had it in his head that he could give these children a utopian upbringing. 'Mother Nature is the Providential Parent.' That was the motto of this place," Adam said. He stopped at the foliage-covered fence. "He bought property on this island, paid to have the buildings constructed, and some of the first orphans arrived in 1938."

Isaac nodded slowly. "That's gotta be why it's called Orphan Island."

Adam held his fingers in the fence and pressed his eye closer. "It was originally called Majeen Island. That's what the Ojibwe called it. Where Witiko is now used to be the site of a temporary Chippewa fishing village. They'd stay here taking trout during the summer months. Locals started calling it Orphan Island after the drowning."

"What drowning?" Isaac turned toward his brother.

Adam explained that in 1947, seven of the orphan girls took canoes out on the lake. They were between the ages of eight and thirteen. One of them was celebrating a birthday, and the canoe trip had been part of the celebration. When they hadn't returned by that evening, the staff had gone looking for them. "They didn't find them anywhere," he said. Scanning the compound through the fence, he told Isaac that one of the staff members never returned from the search either. "After a couple days, two of the four capsized canoes ended up beached against the island's shoreline. Without any other evidence, local officials deemed it an accidental drowning." The missing staff member was counted among the assumed drowning victims.

"Wasn't long after that the State came in and shut the place down." He snapped off some of the branches on the fence and then pressed his eye to the links again. "I'm serious, I think this could at least make for a great article. Maybe a book ... I don't know. Just the way the whole thing represents the progressive thinking of those times, but then like most of the experiments from that era, the orphanage was a failure. I might still be able to find someone who spent time here ... you know, to interview. Do you have anything at the cabin that could cut through these chains? There could be some primary documents in one of those buildings."

Hearing something, Isaac looked into the branches of the trees behind them. A crow sat on a branch some twenty-five feet in the air watching them. Isaac bent for a rock and hurled it at the bird. "Get the hell out of here!" Instead of flying away, the crow side-stepped the rock, stretched its wings, and then resumed its observation.

Adam looked at Isaac.

"What? I hate those goddamn things."

"I know."

Isaac joined Adam closer to the fence and pried away branches for his own peephole. He looked at the moss-covered buildings. "Anybody alive for you to interview would be up there by now, like mid to late eighties. You think they'd have memories of the place?"

"I don't know." Adam shrugged. "Maybe." He turned away to lean his back against a tree trunk. He crossed his arms. "I went to that Porcupine bar after the library for a bite to eat. Heard an interesting story there, too."

"Yeah?"

Adam nodded. "About your place."

Isaac crossed his own arms. "My place? What about it?"

"Just about the last owners." He took the end of his walking stick and twisted it into the ground as he spoke. "I was sitting at the bar next to this older guy. He asked me where I was staying, and I told him."

Adam explained that the old timer had told him that the previous owners were an older couple in their sixties. They came to the cabin once a month during the summer and stayed for three or four days. It was always just the two of them. They came into town on Fridays for the fish fry at the Ugly Porcupine. They talked about how the wife had just one year left at her job, and then they were going to retire to the island permanently. "Then, last summer, they came up with about a dozen people. Looked like their kids and maybe their grandkids as far as my new friend could tell. He said he guessed it was some kind of celebration because he saw wrapped presents amongst their luggage. Said it took Caleb two trips to get all of their stuff across the lake, and they cleaned the market out of ice cream."

"That's a big crew," Isaac said. "They must have brought tents, I'd imagine. Cabin wouldn't sleep that many."

"I would guess. Whatever they had arranged, it didn't last long. Early on their third morning, they put up the red flag." Adam said the guy remembered it specifically because he was the one who spotted the flag and called Caleb. "He figured maybe one of the kids was hurt or someone had a medical emergency, but then here came Caleb's boat riding low in the water with all of them and all of their stuff jammed on it. He said they didn't talk to anyone in town. They just packed their stuff, drove away, and the next thing the town knew, the place had brand new owners."

Isaac shrugged. "I don't mean to sound cold, but I don't care what happened. It made them offload the place, and that's enough for me."

Adam walked back to the fence. "Doesn't it seem a little strange to you? One minute they're talking about retiring here, and the next they're abandoning the place?"

Isaac pushed his fingers through his hair. "Look, I don't know what happened. Maybe the family is toxic. Maybe they had some big blowout and said things they can't take back. Maybe they'd filled the place with bad memories. All I know is—"

"The guy at the Ugly Porcupine thinks the island is haunted ... that the spirits of those orphan girls are still out here roaming around."

Isaac shook his head. "Ghosts? Are you serious? I always thought you were the smart one of the two of us."

Adam looked at him and then looked back through the fence. "Well, he said some nights he's seen the silhouettes of two empty canoes just floating out on—"

"That's enough, man. Seriously." He crossed his arms. "And do me a favor and just keep these stories to yourself. The drowning ... all of it. That's the last thing Emily needs to be thinking about while she's here. You know what I'm going through with her."

Scratching his fingernails up and down his arm, Adam stared at the ground.

"Look, I'm sorry. I know you're excited about the history and everything, but I just don't have the headspace for bullshit right now. I'm trying to straighten things out, not make them more complicated."

Adam held up his palms in surrender. "All right. All right. I won't say anything."

"Not even to Helen."

Adam held an invisible key to his lips and turned it.

"Thank you."

"But," Adam said, "if we are making suggestions to each other, I have one of my own."

Isaac tightened his crossed arms over his chest. "Fire away, little brother."

"Go easy on the booze."

"Are you kid—"

"No, I'm not kidding." He exhaled breathily. "I mean, last night I was in the guestroom dead to the world on Ambien. What if something had happened? What if they needed someone all of a sudden?" He crossed his own arms around the butt end of the walking stick. "I bailed you out with Caleb this morning, and I was glad to do it, but if one of those kids had been hurt or they were just scared, would you have been in any condition to help?"

Isaac stared at his brother.

"Just think of Dad, man, and his drinking. Have you thought about that? It's in the blood, and your kids really need you right now."

Isaac's guilt washed through him. His mind started to entertain what could have happened to one of the kids. Carson could have slept walked right into the lake or Emily could come searching for him after a dream. He fought those thoughts away. "Point taken."

"I'm not trying to be an assho—"

"Not at all. You're right." He looked at the ground. "Just being here, without Gwen ... it was a hard night last night. I don't even know why I haven't just sold the place. The kids don't care one way or another ... not really. This was always my dream ... me and Gwen."

Adam set his hand on Isaac's shoulder and squeezed. "I know. I love you, brother."

"I love you, too."

Adam squeezed his shoulder one more time and then shuffled down toward the gate of the fence. He took a link of rusty chain into his hand. "So, you think you have anything at the cabin that might cut through this?"

The crow shrieked above them and flew away.

"Jesus Christ," Isaac said. He held his hand over his heart. "Goddamn birds." He took a moment to recover and then looked at the fence. "I didn't bring anything that would cut through that, but you can look around. Who knows what the previous owners left."

Adam crouched down and examined the chains nearer the ground. He slapped his palms together, wiping away the stain of rust.

Isaac scanned his eyes over the gate. "Very funny," he said. He looked at a strip of hunter's orange ribbon tied to the fence.

Adam glanced to see where his brother was looking. He slowly stood, still staring at the strip of material. "I didn't put that there. I swear."

Isaac reached up and fiddled the tag ends. "Well," he said. He looked at Adam skeptically. "Someone did."

Wiggling his fingers, Adam waved his hands back and forth in front of his face, warbling the Twilight Zone theme song.

"Oh, shut up," Isaac said, unconvincingly.

CHAPTER 10

Returning to the cabin, Isaac went to the refrigerator and took out a two-pound package of ground beef. "Hey, bro," he said, "you up for shucking some corn?"

Adam stood at the screen door looking down toward the beach. "You've got company."

Walking over to join him, Isaac looked at the beach. A large umbrella had been planted in the sand, and Helen and an older woman were sitting in beach chairs underneath. The kids were sitting on the sand around them, listening to the two women talk. "That must be the neighbor," Isaac said. "I was hoping to meet her."

"I wonder if she knows anything about the orphanage?"

Isaac slapped an open palm into his brother's back. "Whatever it might be, you're not going to know because you're not going to bring it up."

Adam sighed. "Okay. Okay."

Isaac tucked in his shirt and smoothed down his hair with his palm.

"You can play 'Meet the Neighbors.' I'll start shucking the corn."

"Coward," Isaac said. He exited through the screen door.

The woman was the first to turn and look at him. She wore something that almost looked like a kimono with flashes of glossy purple. Thin and frail, she hunched more than sat. Like his mother-in-law, she wore a broad-brimmed hat. She also wore wrap-around black sunglasses that he remembered his grandmother had worn for her cataracts. The woman's bony fingers were covered in rings with turquoise stones. Isaac guessed that she was in her early to mid-eighties.

"This must be your son-in-law," the woman said. She looked at Helen and then back to Isaac.

"Hi, Daddy," Carson said. He held a dreamcatcher in his hands.

Helen turned. "Yes, that's Isaac. Isaac, come and meet our special guest."

He smiled broadly. "On my way to do just that." He held out his hand.

She lifted her fingers to wave his hand off. "I'm sorry dear, I'm not a toucher. One of the beauties of living on this island is less exposure to germs. One has to be careful at my age."

"She's 84 years old!"

"Carson!"

The woman chuckled. "He's done nothing but speak the truth, Helen. I'm proud of my age. I've been told I don't look a day over 80."

Isaac took back his extended hand. She's already a character, he thought. "Well, like you heard Helen say, my name is Isaac."

"And I am Evelyn Cameron."

He returned her smile, glancing again at the dreamcatcher Carson was holding.

"I hope you don't mind, but I brought gifts for the children," she said, following his gaze. "Dreamcatchers are one of my hobbies." She'd learned it as a young girl from an Ojibwe friend. Using a willow hoop and nettle, she formed the frame and wove the interior netting, sliding in beads and adorning the frame with feathers. "Those are Screech Owl feathers. I was fortunate enough on one of my walks to find the ground under which a parliament of them had gathered." She stopped for a moment. "I love that ... a parliament of owls." She smiled as if musing for a moment before continuing. "My nephew helps me with the deer hide strips from which the dreamcatchers dangle. He has the meticulous nature necessary to work with the skins," she said. "Too many people rush the process out of impatience or squeamishness."

Helen shuddered. "That wouldn't be something I could do."

"We are able to retrieve the hides from deer that die on the island during the winter. Every spring turns up a carcass or two that are generally well-preserved because they've been frozen. Unless, of course, the scavengers get to them before my nephew can." She tapped a finger against her chin. "Did you know that squirrel hide actually has more tensile strength than that of deer?"

Helen and Isaac shook their heads.

"Various skins have a variety of purposes," Evelyn said.

"Asabi ... Asabikesh ..." Carson spoke haltingly.

"Asabikeshiinh," Evelyn said.

"Yeah, that," Carson said. He held up his dreamcatcher. "That means spider. These can catch bad dreams like a spider web catches bugs. You have to hang it above your bed."

Isaac gave him a thumbs-up. "Pretty nice present. I hope you thanked Ms. Cameron."

"I did."

"They all did," Evelyn said. "You really have such splendid children. Emily is the picture of health from what I can tell."

Isaac thanked her. "Knock on wood, they've all been quite healthy." He smiled at his neighbor. Not being able see her eyes made him turn away and look out over the lake. She definitely had a personality. Dreamcatchers. Knowledge in the tensile strength of squirrel hide. Parliament of owls. It was exactly why he had hoped the kids would get a chance to meet their neighbor.

Evelyn picked a drinking glass out of the sand with a straw standing in its contents. The beverage itself looked like the consistency of canned clam chowder, though it was green in color. She pursed her withered lips around the straw and drank.

"Yuck, what are you drinking?" Carson asked. His eyes went wide.

"Carson!" Helen scolded.

Evelyn laughed. "It's okay, Helen." She turned to Carson. "This, my dear, is a smoothie of kale, dandelion and yogurt, among other herbs. Indeed, not very tasty, but a woman my age must do anything she can to keep her body young." She fit her glass back down into the makeshift sugar sand cupholder.

Emily looked up from her dreamcatcher that she'd been studying. "Ms. Cameron, can you make a dream maker?"

Oh boy, Isaac thought.

Evelyn looked at her. She offered a thin-lipped smile. "My dear, you want to have nightmares?"

Emily shook her head. "No, not nightmares. Just dreams. My mom comes to see me in my dreams, but I didn't dream last night."

"Emily, Ms. Cameron doesn't want to hear about—"

"No, Isaac," Evelyn said. She raised her pale palm to him. "Helen told me about ... well, about your recent hardships. Your loss." She placed her hands over her heart. "My sincere condolences."

"Thank you."

Evelyn turned her attention back to Emily. "Dreams are indeed a portal for the dead. My late husband, Joseph, would visit me while I slept. I used to think they returned out of longing or sadness. But, through research I learned that the dead are not sad. They are in a much better world. They come to us for a time to ease our mourning. They are there for us, not themselves. And, they will visit less often as they feel our growing strength. Your mother must see that your own resilience is growing, and so will visit you less."

Emily studied Ms. Cameron. "I haven't seen a butterfly all day either. Those are her, I know it."

"Honey—"

"More evidence of your inner strength, young lady," Evelyn said, smiling. "Even if you don't feel strong, the dead know best when we are ready to move on without them."

It was heavy talk, but Emily looked convinced. Isaac's mouth ticked up into a small grin. Well-played, Ms. Cameron. Well-played.

"What if I still want her to come sometimes?"

Helen touched her shoulder. "Emily—"

"It's okay, Helen. It's fine. People don't talk about the mysteries enough." She turned again to Emily's attentive eyes. "All the more reason to hang your dreamcatcher. We have only so much dream space each night. The catcher will filter out the dreams you don't want to have, making it all the more likely for you to dream the dreams you wish."

Emily smiled and held up the dreamcatcher. She studied the webbing of nettle in the sunlight and then looked at Isaac. "Daddy, can I have Uncle Adam help me hang this up right now?"

"Me too," Carson said.

He nodded, smiling. "Go ahead." Before he could remind them to, they each said goodbye to Ms. Cameron and thanked her again.

She watched them run up the grass toward the cabin. "Really, such lovely children. Active minds and very healthy." Evelyn spun a ring on her left hand's middle finger. "Three children and, if Helen is to be believed, not a debilitating illness between them."

"Nope, very lucky on that front." Isaac glanced around. "Where's Ashley?"

"Inside." Helen motioned toward the cabin. "I think she had too much sun. She said she was tired."

"All right. I'll check on her in a minute."

Ms. Cameron brushed her bony hands down her thighs. "I think it's time for me to pardon myself as well." She looked at Isaac's offered arm. "No, no, I'm fine. Fiercely independent, you might even say." Using the armrests of her chair, she pushed herself into a stoop-shouldered standing position. She bent slowly for her smoothie glass and retrieved it from the sand. "I hope I haven't taken liberties that I haven't earned, but I've invited Helen and the two younger children to my porch for iced tea and finger sandwiches tomorrow."

Isaac smiled, nodding. "That's a generous offer. Works out, too, because I wanted to take my rod over to the river tomorrow and see what the fishing is like."

"I have nothing to tell you about the fishing. I only know it is a lovely stream to walk along."

Isaac thought of the man's silhouette from the night before. "So your nephew stays with you? I saw a man—"

"Yes, that's Silas. He's my caretaker of sorts." She nodded her head slightly. "He asked me to tell you that he hopes you're feeling better."

Oh shit, he thought. If he told her about me throwing up on the beach, what must she think?

Helen's head pivoted on her neck. She set her gaze up at him.

Evelyn smiled. "He said he heard coughing. I just hope you're not battling a cold while getting ready to celebrate a special birthday."

Isaac breathed in an exaggerated sniffle. "Just allergies, I think."

"You have allergies now?" Helen asked incredulously.

"I—"

"This is an old peninsula," Evelyn said. "Largely untouched. There's flora and fauna here that one doesn't always encounter." She raised a knowing, solitary finger. "That could be the culprit."

"Must be," Isaac said. He gave Helen a quick look. "If we end up going back into town, I'll pick up some allergy medication."

"Stinging nettle," Evelyn said. "It grows abundantly near the stream. It is a natural anti-histamine. Do you know it?"

"I do," Isaac lied. "I'll look for some when I go fishing tomorrow. Thanks for the tip."

Evelyn nodded. She explained that Silas would pick up her umbrella later in the evening. Offering a final goodbye, she shuffled off and disappeared into the trees that surrounded her property.

"Well, she certainly was a pleasant surprise," Helen said, watching her depart.

Isaac looked in the direction of Evelyn's property. "She's a character, all right."

"She's simply an interesting person." Helen cleared her throat. "Why is it when people get older, we refer to them as caricatures rather than people."

Isaac sighed. He looked to the side of Helen's leg. A dreamcatcher lay on the webbing of the beach chair. He nodded toward it. "She give you one too?"

"No, this is Ashley's. She left it when she went in."

He held out his hand. "I'll give it to her. I'm going to check on her."

She handed it to him. "She made quite a show of not taking it with her. On the whole, she was very rude to our guest."

Isaac shrugged. "She's in a mood. She's fifteen and stuck here with no internet."

"I'll have a talk with her."

"No," Isaac said. He swiped his hand through the air in front of him. "Just let it go. The kids are here to have fun, not talks."

She stared at him for a moment. "If you don't nip that kind of behavior in the bud immediately, you'll—"

"Just," he started, holding his palm towards her, "just enjoy the beach, Helen. Okay? Let it go."

With a huff, she reclined back into the lounge and stretched her legs out in front of her. She picked up her book and snapped it open.

He started toward the cabin. "I'm making burgers and corn in a bit," he called over his shoulder. "Are you hungry?"

"I've brought my own food. I'm off red meat for good."

Of course you are, he thought. Going inside, he walked towards the girls' room. Emily sat at the kitchen table pulling stringy threads from a corn cob.

She smiled. "I'm helping Uncle Adam."

"Well, that's nice of you." He glanced into his own room to see Adam standing on the bed with the dreamcatcher dangling from his fingers. That's right, he remembered, Carson is in with me tonight. He heard Carson tell his uncle to put it "more above my side."

Leaning into the door frame of the girls' room, he looked at Ashley stretched out on her bed. As before, as always, she had her earbuds in and was messing around on her phone.

"What are you doing?" he asked in a raised voice.

She didn't look up from her phone. "Editing pictures I took today."

He walked over and sat on the edge of the bed. He looked at her until she looked at him.

"What?"

He pointed to his own ears. "Can you take those out?"

She pressed something on her phone and the murmur of the tiny concert in her ears went silent. She left the earbuds in.

"Grandma said you got a lot of sun. You feeling okay?"

She rolled her eyes. "I'm fine."

He reached and set the dreamcatcher on her night table.

"I don't want that."

He shrugged a hand into the air. "You don't have to hang it up, but she gave it to you. It'd be a little rude not to—"

She reached with her hand and pushed the dreamcatcher to the floor. "I said I don't want it. She was creepy, and kept staring at me, and that Silas guy was like Slender Man."

"Like who?"

She shook her head and rolled her eyes again. "Doesn't matter. I'm just saying that I didn't like her. She was asking Grandma questions about us, and if we struggled with any 'chronic' health issues."

He shrugged. "Don't know what to tell you. Old people think about health problems a lot. It's kinda what they mostly talk about." He bent for the dreamcatcher and picked it up to his lap. He smoothed one of the feathers between the pads of his finger and thumb.

Ashley glanced sneeringly at it and then back to her phone screen. "I'm surprised you let Emily keep hers." She pointed at her sister's dreamcatcher dangling above her bed. "Isn't she going to become obsessed with the occult or something? Or is that just when I get her something?"

Isaac exhaled breathily into his palm. He guessed that she'd put two and two together. She had to know that he'd found the Ouija board and taken it. She probably didn't know that he'd scuttled it in the lake, but she knew that it was gone. What the hell did she think was going to happen after that stunt?

He picked up Ashley's dreamcatcher and held it out in front of him. "Hon, this is just a little trinket ... something to make her feel good when she's trying—"

She snapped fierce eyes on him. "And what about what I got her? You don't think she would have felt good thinking that she was talking with Mom? That's all she wants, is a way to think she's talking to her."

His lips buckled in against his teeth. He glanced back at the partially open door. "We just disagree on that one," he mumbled.

"Yup, we disagree, which means you're right and I'm wrong. Got it."

She tapped the side of her phone. The whisper of her music leaked into the room again. He took in a deep breath and then sighed it out. He went to pat her knee poking up like a little mountain under the comforter, but then thought better of it. He stood, and something along his femur gave a twinge, making him wince. Make up your goddamn mind, leg. He looked back at Ashley. "Well, dinner should be ready soon," he said. He rubbed his thigh.

A portrait of determined indifference, nothing about her face said that she'd heard him. Her finger slid up the screen of her phone.

Before leaving, he set the dreamcatcher on the night stand.

Ashley's hand shot out and pushed it to the floor again. "Are you deaf? I said I don't want that stupid thing."

He turned on her swiftly with his finger pointing inches from her face. "You know, I'm about tired of your bullshit. You think I don't have feelings? You think you can just do or say whatever?" He pulled his finger back. "Just, forget it. I don't care anymore. Do whatever the hell you want, Ashley. That's what you do anyway, right?"

Her shocked face stared at him. Tears welled along the rims of her lower eyelids.

Good, he thought. Some tears. Some emotion. Maybe he'd broken through her tough exterior. Maybe she'd think about how she'd been talking to him ... how'd she been behaving behind his back. He turned from her and limped to the doorway. Coming into the main room, he slammed the door shut behind him.

Emily's gaze snapped up from the corn cob in her hand. "Everything okay, Daddy?"

He took a breath and glanced at the box of booze on the floor. One belt, he thought. Just a quick shot. His mouth watered at the idea of whiskey.

Outside on the lawn, Adam and Carson were spread out prone on the grass. They were looking intently at something in their fingers. Either cars or Legos, he guessed. Beyond them,

Helen reclined stiffly in her lounge with her book. Sunlight shimmered here and there off the lake's small waves. After a moment, he turned away from the box of whiskey and instead sat down at the table opposite Emily. The guilt of snapping at Ashley weighed on him like a waterlogged sweatshirt pulling him down into a drowning. "Everything's fine," he sighed. "Just a little disagreement. That happens." He forced a smile. "How's the corn coming?"

CHAPTER 11

Squinting, Isaac held the blurred phone screen close to his face. He moved it nearer and farther, but the numbers wouldn't come into focus. Trying to keep quiet for Carson, he groped his hand over the nightstand until his fingers found one of the temples of his glasses. He fit them into place, and the numbers glowed back at him plainly: 2:46. He set his head back deep into the pillow and stared up into the darkness. Again.

He'd been drifting into a half-sleep after hours of tossing and turning, and then something had woken him. What, he didn't know, but he felt certain that getting even close to sleep again would be impossible. The evening had gone well enough. He'd grilled, the family had eaten, and then they'd settled into a marathon game of Uno. Mostly because of Helen's feigned exasperation and claims of being "ganged up on," Carson and Emily loved playing their +2s and +4s against their grandmother. The game became less about winning, and more about piling as many cards as possible into her hand. Frustrated at first, Isaac finally realized how much fun they were having. He'd tried a few times to play cards that he knew Helen needed, but she only retorted, "I don't need your pity." Her tone was playful enough. She seemed appreciative that he'd agreed to her request to build a fire in the fireplace, which he got up to stoke from time to time. He didn't tell her as much, but he'd enjoyed the exercise and sweat of splitting some wood.

Adam had sat in the corner with a pen working through one of the chapters in his manuscript. After cards, the kids roasted marshmallows and made s'mores right in the living room. None of it—the food, the games, the desserts—had lured Ashley out of the bedroom. He'd brought her a plate at dinner time, but his soft rapping on the door was met with a cold, "I'm not hungry."

He listened for a moment. Was that what had woken him ... Ashley rummaging for a snack after her hunger strike during dinner? If she had made something to eat, she was done and back in her room. Nothing stirred in the interior of the cabin, though he was certain that the noise that had woken him had come from there.

He'd done well all evening, hadn't so much as looked at his box of liquor. Even when Adam had offered him one of his beers, Isaac refused. It wasn't difficult. It was some heavy IPA that didn't even smell like beer, but more like potpourri. Isaac preferred Miller Lite and usually only to chase his whiskey. The night had ended around 10:30 with everyone yawning, including Isaac. He looked out at the beach one last time. Evelyn's umbrella was still there. He'd crawled into bed next to Carson, certain that he would sleep, only to fall into a bout of insomnia.

Lying in the darkness, trying not to wake Carson with his endless shifting of positions, Isaac couldn't recall a time from the last six months that he hadn't passed out on whiskey to go to sleep. He'd soaked the sheets with sweat, and he didn't have to look to know that his hands were trembling. He recalled how after his mother was diagnosed with cancer, his father decided to quit the bourbon cold turkey. His withdrawal from the booze was bad, including hallucinations. He swore the phone was ringing when it wasn't, and he'd pick it up and shout into the receiver, "Who is this? You have to stop calling here. You have to stop!" The doctor said the worst of the hallucinations would be over within 48 hours. His father was self-medicating again way before he'd ever reached that milestone. He continued drinking for another year until the end of his life at 63 years old. Isaac's mother passed the year after.

He carefully pushed the damp covers off of himself. Slipping into his shorts and sandals, he pulled his t-shirt over his head. He was wide awake. If I don't get to sleep right now, he thought, tomorrow will be a wash. He padded into the kitchen and took a tumbler from the cupboard. He closed the utensil drawer someone had left open. He wouldn't be able to risk getting ice. Just a couple of shots, he thought. Just something so I can sleep. As much as he wanted a drink, he sat on a stool at the counter staring at the box on the floor. His tumbler was empty between his fidgeting fingers. The compressor on the fridge hummed.

He imagined any one of them coming out of their rooms and finding him drinking at three o'clock in the morning. Helen's suspicions would be confirmed. Adam's look would be withering. And Ashley's glare? Satisfied and damning. Emily would have thought nothing of it, but the idea of her ignorance brought him no comfort.

He pulled a sheet from a roll of paper towel and dabbed at his beading forehead. A shot or two would end this. A third or fourth shot, and he'd be able to sleep. It wasn't only the idea of being caught by the others that made him hesitate. In all likelihood, they'd all keep sleeping, even if he took the risk for a handful of ice. With the tumbler pinched between his fingers, and a bottle under his arm, he could turn the knob on the door silently, slipping the latch from the strike plate. He could whisper the door open, slide through the screen door, and close the main door again just as quietly. Then, he could settle into a chair on the porch, drink, and look out into the darkness of it all as he had so many times over the last half of a year. In forty-five minutes, he'd be able to crawl into bed, pass out, and sleep until noon.

He remained on the stool. He found himself squeezing the tumbler so hard he was surprised it hadn't shattered in his grip. Sixty-three years was all his dad got. A self-imposed early death. If Isaac went at the same age that would mean Carson would be 22, just like he'd been when he'd lost his own father. It's not like you don't still need a father in your twenties. Hell, even your thirties, he thought. As it was, Gwen had only met the man once, and that had been a slurring embarrassment.

He wasn't going to do it. Even if it meant he'd stay up the rest of the night staring into the half-darkness above his head, he was done. At least for tonight. He remembered the mantras his mom would relay to their father during the times when he was trying to quit. The man refused to try AA, but she did pick up some of their literature. "I can't promise that I won't drink tomorrow," she'd read aloud, "but I'm not drinking today. I like that one, Charles. Don't you like that one?" He'd just nod to her and try to smile, but he sweat like a cornered man who knew he'd be drinking again, and soon. And never stop.

Isaac liked the saying. It was too much to imagine a life ahead without whiskey. The idea of it—of saying "never again"—felt like too much pressure. Too much responsibility. The crush of it was enough to see the futility in even trying. But just this one day, this one dark night of the soul? Tomorrow was tomorrow, but tonight was tonight. He could do it. "I'm not drinking today," he whispered aloud into the silent kitchen.

He stood and went to the refrigerator. Setting his tumbler on the counter, he took out the milk and poured himself a full glass. He wasn't sure how long it'd been since he'd had a glass of milk. Setting it in the microwave, he warmed it for twenty seconds. He wasn't being cautious anymore about how much noise he was making. Let them come out and find him. He'd be like one of those perfect fathers from the old sitcoms he used to watch. A child would be up late struggling through some personal conflict. The dad would come downstairs in his crisp bathrobe, claim that he couldn't sleep, and then pour himself a glass of milk. Sitting at the counter, he'd drink his milk and share some homespun wisdom that would right the child's world. Drinking his own milk, he half hoped Ashley would come out and find him. He wondered what he might say. Maybe it too would be profound in its simplicity. Christ, what wisdom do I even have? He wondered.

It ended up that nobody joined him. Instead, his only company was the continued hum of the refrigerator's compressor. Isaac finished his milk and poured himself a second glass without heating it. He drank about half of his second helping, and poured the rest into the sink where it clung to the stainless steel before sliding down the drain.

Tiptoeing back into the bedroom, he undressed and then crawled into the sickly wet and chilling sheets. He edged himself toward the dry middle of the bed. Reaching out with his arm, he wanted to pull Carson to him and hold him against his chest. He wanted something solid to anchor him until he finally fell asleep. And if he didn't fall asleep, he'd at least be holding his boy when the sunshine lit the windows. A new day. He reached and kept reaching.

Carson wasn't there.

Isaac sat up and turned on his lamp. The other side of the bed was empty. He guessed that his restlessness had driven Carson to someone else's room. While he dressed, he spotted the dreamcatcher lying on the floor. He shook his head. The physics of the task must have escaped Adam. "As a repair man, you make a pretty good demolition crew," their father used to say, teasing Adam any time he'd try to fix his own bike or help out with a household repair.

Enough moonlight lit the girls' room for him to see that Carson wasn't bunked in with either one of them. Snoring lightly and wearing a sleeping mask, Helen didn't stir when

Isaac slinked into her room and swept his phone light over her bed. The careful way she'd crawled in, the other side of the bed was still made with the pillows tucked under the comforter.

No Carson.

Isaac closed her door quietly behind him. As he thought of it, his brother's room made the most sense. Over the course of the day, Adam and Carson had become quite close, especially with Adam getting down to ground-level and playing with him. He started for his brother's room. As he walked across the living room space, a cool breeze whispered over the tops of his sandaled feet. The creaking front door blew open even farther. Staring at the threshold, he gasped in a sharp, painful breath.

He burst out onto the porch. The full moon had the landscape cast in varying shades of darkness. The semi-dark of the lake, slashed here and there in luminescence, transitioned into the black of the westerly cliffs, topped with the dark outlines of evergreens against a blue-black sky behind them. Isaac scanned the beach. Evelyn's umbrella was gone. Surely walking into the water would have woken Carson if he were sleepwalking.

The lawn was a blue-green shimmering. He spotted the trail of darker splotches of footprints across the dewy grass headed east in the direction of Evelyn's property. Heart banging in his chest, Isaac followed the prints until they ended at the tree line where he'd seen Silas' silhouette disappear the night before. A winding path weaved through the tree trunks, and Isaac staggered along it. "Carson?" he called. His heart hammered his ribs. Coming out on the other side of the trees, he stood on lawn again. The little splotches of footsteps reappeared trailing toward the residence.

Evelyn's looming place, a two-story Victorian with a wrap-around porch, was more a house than a cottage. All of the windows were dark. He spotted Carson standing within yards of the dwelling, luminescent in a pool of the nearly-full moon's light. He looked to be mumbling to himself.

"Carson!" Isaac called in a hissed whisper. He kept on towards his son. "What are doing?" The boy stood staring intently at the house. Was he holding a knife? Isaac remembered the open utensil drawer. Jesus Christ. Isaac approached cautiously with his hand out in front of him, fingers splayed. "What are you holding, pal? Be careful."

The rusty weathervane creaked back and forth in a breeze above them.

Carson looked at his hand, and the steak knife dropped from his grip and stuck in the ground inches from his bare foot. He turned and looked at Isaac. "You wouldn't understand," he said. Tears streamed down his cheeks.

The boy looked pale, in shock even. "Are you okay? Are you hurt? Why don't you come to me?" Isaac pleaded.

Carson turned back toward the house. "I can't do it," he said.

Isaac lowered himself to one knee. Was he talking to him or was this just more sleepwalk babble? "Yes you can, buddy," he said. He held open his arms. "Just come here. You're not in trouble."

Carson tilted his head. "Just go to him?" he asked. His smooth skin glowed alabaster in the moonlight.

Isaac nodded. "Yes, just come here. Are you waking up? You were sleepwalking." He scanned the house, but the windows remained dark. "Come on, we need to go."

"Daddy, they said ..." he started, but stopped. "I'll shhh, then. I'll shhh."

Isaac motioned him towards him with a beckoning movement of his fingers, like encouraging a toddler just learning to walk. "I just want to get you back to the cabin, buddy. You're not in trouble at all. Are you awake?"

Carson turned towards him, as though truly hearing him for the first time. Then he broke into a run right into his father's arms. The impact knocked Isaac off balance and onto his back with Carson sobbing on top of him.

"Goddamn it," he hissed against the spike of pain through his thigh. He twisted himself around trying to get to his feet.

"I'm sorry, Daddy ... I'm sorry. They said—"

"It's fine ... it's just my leg. Come on, buddy. It's okay." He gripped the boy to him while trying to right himself. "You gotta shush, though. Shush. Okay? You gotta let Daddy get up."

He idled back to a whimper. "I'll shush. I'm sorry. I'll shush." He sniffled.

A few branches snapped in the trees on the other side of the house.

Isaac got to his feet and lifted Carson in one arm over the solid foundation of his good leg. "All right. There we go. Let's get you back to the cabin ... back to bed." He took a few steps forward and managed to crouch. Snagging the steak knife from the grass, he limped back over the lawn toward the trees. "What were you doing, huh? What were you doing?" he whispered into his son's ear while kissing the tiny lobe.

"I can't tell, Daddy. They ... I can't—"

Isaac kissed the side of his son's head again. "I know, buddy. I know. We're going to get a handle on this sleepwalking. We will. I'm sure it's scary waking up like that."

More branches snapped in the distance, and seemed as if they were getting closer. Isaac quickened his pace as much as he could. Getting into his own yard, he glanced back a few times, but nobody came out of the trees.

By the time Isaac opened the cabin's main door, Carson lay almost asleep on his shoulder. Closing the door behind him, he spotted the chain lock and slid it into place, guessing that it wasn't within the kid's reach. He set the steak knife in the sink before retreating to his own room. His good leg had gone numb when he finally set Carson down on his side of the bed. The boy's eyes snapped open.

"Daddy, can you put the dreamcatcher back up? Please?"

"Right now, bud?" Isaac asked. He tried to catch his breath, and wiped the sheen of sweat from his brow.

Carson nodded with little shakes of his head, his eyes pleading.

"Okay."

Isaac picked up the dreamcatcher by the strip of deer hide lace from which it dangled. The thumbtack Adam had used was still pressed through the skin. Standing on the bed, with Carson watching him closely, Isaac used a clinch knot to tie the dreamcatcher to the hoop on the overhead light's finial. He climbed back down and looked at Carson, smiling reassuringly. "That's not going anywhere now," he said.

Carson smiled his approval and then rolled on his side. "I won't," he snapped. "Leave me alone."

"What, bud?" Poor little guy was still half out of it.

"Love you, miss you, see you in the morn."

Isaac smiled. "Love you, too."

By the time Isaac had undressed and turned out the light, Carson was asleep again. He hoped the same for himself, but after twenty minutes he stared, hopelessly awake, into the darkness. A little shot of the ol' rot gut would help bring him down. A little something to offset the jolt of adrenaline he'd just experienced. Then he thought about if he had decided to have the shots he'd contemplated earlier. Would he have been able to spot the little footprints? Would he have even noticed that Carson was missing? The tragic possibilities were too much to consider.

He rolled on his own side and pulled his son against his chest. Even in sleep, the boy's smooth fingers found and clung to Isaac's wrist.

Isaac kissed the back of Carson's head and closed his eyes. His heart slowly idled into a resting rhythm. He hoped for sleep to come soon.

CHAPTER 12

I saac lay in bed for a moment after waking. He already felt better than he had any other morning in months. No headache. No grogginess. He sat on the edge of the bed, and even his leg felt less painful than in his usual waking moments. He remembered his doctor had said something about alcohol contributing to inflammation.

Sunshine lit up the blinds. Looked like another beautiful day. He worried that it was maybe too bright for fishing, but then figured that the trees would provide shade on the stream. He glanced to the other side of the bed. It was empty. Slipping on his glasses, he checked his phone. Almost 11:30 in the morning. He remembered that Helen was taking the kids to Evelyn's for some kind of afternoon get-together. Carson must have been fine when he woke up. Helen would have rousted Isaac if not, he was sure of it.

Slipping on swimming trunks and a t-shirt, he walked out into the cabin's main room. Earbuds in, Ashley sat at the counter with a cup of coffee. Hunched over a bowl, she ate dripping spoonsful of cereal. She looked at him and then back down to her phone. What she was doing on it yet again without Wi-Fi, he didn't know. Probably staying on a screen just to spite me, he guessed.

He walked to the coffee pot and poured himself a cup. "Coffee smells good," he said. He took a sip. "Tastes good too."

She didn't acknowledge him.

He tried not to care, not to think about it. He'd be on the river soon. That, for a few hours, would be enough. He walked his cup out toward the porch.

"Uncle Adam is gone," she said.

He turned and looked at her. "Out for a hike?" He guessed that maybe he'd found something to cut through the chains at the orphanage.

Standing up with her cereal bowl and phone in one hand and her coffee in the other, she started for her room. "No," she said. She talked around a mouthful of cereal. "He left."

"Left? What are you talking about? When?"

"He was gone before anyone even woke up. There's a note on the counter," she said. Then she closed her door with her foot.

Isaac walked to the piece of paper. It was brief, saying only that he couldn't stay any longer and that'd he'd explain when they returned. He scratched the back of his neck, furrowing his brow at his brother's blocky handwriting. Nobody from his work could have even reached Adam if they'd wanted to. And if they did, what kind of emergency could a university history department have that would require the immediate presence of a junior faculty member? Had the Toledo War started anew?

The surface of the lake was chopping with small whitecaps. He took his coffee out to the porch and sat. The American flag snapped in the wind at the top of the flagpole. At least Adam had swapped out whatever of the signal flags he'd used to have Caleb come get him. He stared at the water for a moment, stroking his chin. Was he that anxious to get started on more orphanage research? Didn't seem likely that he would skip his niece's birthday party for that.

Isaac snapped his fingers. Maybe it's the grad student ... that girl in Toledo, he thought. Maybe things weren't quite as over as Adam had made them out to be. If a man is rehashing and regretting something that ended, something romantic, those can make for long, fretful nights. They can make for desperate early mornings too. There'd been enough feelings between them to get those matching tattoos. Drunk or not, Adam wasn't one for impulsive decisions involving permanently inking his body. Taking off like that out of the blue ... it had to have something to do with a woman. Isaac sipped his coffee.

Almost eleven months into their relationship, he had broken things off with Gwen. He'd gotten it into his head that he was too young to be committing to one person. She'd been confused and in tears when he left her apartment. The decision only felt right for about a day. Then he missed her. He'd dumped her on a Wednesday. Calling her that Friday, he found out from her roommate that Gwen and some friends had gone to Mackinaw Island for a *Somewhere in Time*-themed weekend they were having at the Grand Hotel. Isaac had spent that night staring into the darkness of his ceiling, imagining her meeting some Christopher Reeve-looking dude and forgetting all about him.

It was 4:30 in the morning when he had climbed into his car. By ten, Isaac stood on the upper deck of a Shepler's ferry heading to Mackinaw Island. He stopped in a few of the shops before walking to the Grand Hotel. When he had found her on the lawn watching the time travel movie projected onto an outdoor screen, he had flowers for her and a promise ring. His desperate, romantic gesture along with a profuse apology had worked. They spent the better part of Saturday and Sunday morning in her room. He smiled fondly at the memory.

If Isaac were up early enough the next morning, he'd raise the green flag, buzz into Witiko, and give his brother a quick call. Or maybe not. Adam had ended the note with "No worries." Isaac could do just that ... he could just not worry about it and focus the next day on Emily's birthday. Maybe it was for the best. He didn't begrudge his brother, but he was a little jealous of the fast bond he'd created with Carson. With Adam gone, Isaac could focus on bonding with his son.

Sipping his coffee, looking out on the sunshine, he rejoiced momentarily in not having drank the night before. Just the same, he craved to spike his coffee with a shot ... or skip the rest of the coffee altogether and just make a drink. It would be that easy. A little pre-fishing celebration. Isaac wiped his arm across his brow and looked at his sleeve dappled with wet spots. Underneath everything, he sensed a slight sick, as though without much effort he could throw up. Each drink of coffee seemed to be making him feel worse.

The river. He just needed to get out and move around. He needed to fish. His body needed time to adjust to a state of not being possessed by booze. In the last six months, he doubted if there'd ever been a time that some amount of alcohol wasn't processing in his system. How many mornings had he woken up and poured himself a generous shot from the hair of the dog? Then, in the afternoons, he usually had a drink or two. Sometimes three. At work, it had been from a flask. At home, it was on the rocks while he was out in the garage pretending to be working on something. If he was honest with himself, the whole idea that he only drank a pint of whiskey a day was bullshit. Most of his days over the past few months had been spent partly buzzed before he even began his evening drinking.

Rising from his seat brought another wave of nausea. He stood for a minute, balancing himself with his hand on the back of the chair. When the feeling passed, he started the task of gathering his gear.

He rapped on the door frame to Ashley's room to tell her he was leaving for a few hours. She didn't look up from her phone, but just raised her hand in a half-hearted wave. He didn't care. Let her be pissy. She was the one in the wrong. He walked out the back door into the trees and turned immediately east. Going in that direction, he'd eventually come to the stream and closer to its mouth.

Moving around had done him good. His waves of nausea had largely passed. He sweated, but it was the good sweat that came with getting the blood going. The day, or at least part of the day, was going to be about what moving water and fishing had always given him – time to think about nothing but the stream, its likely good spots, and the rising of trout.

There'd be plenty of time soon enough to work through what he had to do. He had to have a heart-to-heart with Ashley, and let her know that he knew what she'd been doing. The betrayal with the Ouija board couldn't go unaddressed. He would apologize too for the way he'd been over the last months. He'd let her know that things were going to change, and were already changing.

And then Carson. The doctor had said to come back in if his sleepwalking ever became a danger to himself. Sleepwalking barefoot in the middle of the night while carrying a steak knife across slick swaths of lawn and through woods weaved with exposed roots seemed like a clear and present danger. They might just have to look into the short-acting tranquilizers the doctor had mentioned as a last resort.

Of all of them, he worried the least about Emily. She seemed good while at the cabin. Not much talk of butterflies or moths since the first day. He didn't believe she'd mentioned her mother much at all the day before. No talk of dreams and no lamenting dreams that hadn't materialized. Well, other than her brief conversation with Evelyn which, as far as he could tell, had actually brought Emily some helpful perspective. Watching her swim and splash with her little brother, Isaac had witnessed a ten-year-old girl that seemed as well adjusted as any. Her appetite was the best it had been since the funeral. He had gladly slid a second hamburger patty on the grill for her. He'd smiled while watching her eat her third cob of corn.

It was her birthday celebration, and at last she seemed to be thriving.

Isaac adjusted the straps of the electrofisher on his back. He'd wanted to travel as light as possible. Wearing rubber hip waders, he carried only the backpack, a small duffel bag, a long net, and his fly rod already rigged up. He didn't bring his vest, so snapping off his fly would mean the end of the fishing for the day. He'd tied on an Adams, which was considered a pretty universally productive dry fly on most Michigan streams. It wasn't meant to imitate any specific insect, but instead had traits that could be taken for several different bugs, opening up the possibilities for a strike.

He was almost more curious about what his electrofishing would turn up, versus his fly fishing. Electrofishing was standard practice for Fish & Wildlife in determining if lamprey were spawning in a river. The backpack generated the power, and the end of the handheld pole sent electrical currents into the stream bed. If there were lamprey larvae, the charges would get them up and out of the mud.

The river murmured in the distance before coming into his field of vision. It was an insistent churning muted somewhat by the steadily-increasing wind whipping through the branches overhead. He hoped the gusts wouldn't throw off his casting too much. Coming to the river's edge, he quietly celebrated a stretch of stream some twenty-five feet across. If he was careful, he wouldn't be limited to just roll casts. The river wasn't any deeper than it had been upstream – an easy wade in hip boots. The stretch downstream toward the mouth was winding, and the bend he could see seemed ideal for a hungry trout to be hunkered down in its depths. He hoped for more bends just like it.

As much as he wanted to get in and just fish, he stuck to his agenda. Taking out a strip of hunter's orange, he tied it to the branch of a tree and set his fly rod at the base of the trunk. His plan was to walk along the bank and get closer to the mouth. He'd do his work with the electrofisher and then leave it on the shore downstream. He'd then walk back upstream and fly fish his way down to retrieve the backpack and head home to the cabin. Couple hours tops.

Walking the bank downstream, he started to see flashes of the choppy lake surface through the trees. A quarter mile to the west, Evelyn's weathervane turned frantic circles in the wind. He was getting close to the mouth. Stepping into the water, he found a branch dangling three feet above the surface. He tied a marker to it.

The stream was still shallow, and the streambed's fine sediment looked ideal for sample testing. Isaac crouched down to the electrofisher and set the instrument to its dual channel setting. He adjusted the primary channel setup to 125 volts. Afterward, he set the duty cycle to three bursts at a burst frequency of four Hertz with a burst duty cycle of 25 percent. Then he pressed through on the menu to the secondary channel. That he set to 125 volts with a 30 Hertz frequency.

He took a pair of rubber gloves from the duffel bag and pulled them on. Hoisting the backpack onto his shoulders, he picked up the yellow pole and then powered on the pack. Usually when he was out with a Fish & Wildlife crew, someone would say "Heat 'em up" at this point in the process. Stepping into the river, nobody missed the opportunity to jump on the line, "See you on the other side, Ray." Usually two or three people would answer, "Nice working with you, Dr. Venkman." They were tired *Ghostbusters* references, but all part of the field routine. Isaac stood for a minute in reminiscence. He missed his work, his co-workers, and the sense that he was doing something positive by keeping the sea lamprey population in check in the Great Lakes.

Wading out into the water, he set the pole's anode down near the stream bed. He held his net flush against the river bottom and flipped the switch on the electrofisher. The familiar high-pitched beeping pulsed from the pack. He pushed his way upstream against the current. If there were any ammocoetes, the three staggered bursts from the electrofisher's primary channel would get them moving out of the sediment. The secondary channel's longer waveform would stun them in the water and send them tumbling into his net ... at least a few of them.

He knew that he was working sloppily and inaccurately. Normally, he'd be with a team, including three or four people with electrofishers, and another team forming a line of gathering nets. They would have sectioned off a portion of the river with upstream and downstream block nets running bank to bank to keep any lamprey from escaping. He knew too that what he was doing was far from protocol. It wasn't as if he could go back to his supervisor and say he'd done some electrofishing on his own and turned up some juvenile lamprey.

"With what?"

He imagined himself saying. "Oh, with some equipment I was supposed to return to the shop three weeks ago." He shook his head.

Switching back and forth between the channels, he'd worked twenty-five yards upstream. He stopped and lifted the net from the water. Along with some small branches and two crayfish, there were six or seven stunned lamprey larvae, each about three to five inches in length. Goddamn, he thought, shaking his head. Sure enough. He flipped the anode off, and its high-pitched beep was replaced instantly with the riotous racket of bird calls above him. He looked up. A gathering of ravens, more than a dozen, were in the tree branches over him, cawing their gurgling croak. The wind-blown branches seemed to try to shake them, but they held steady to their perches. They sounded as though they were laughing at him.

"Jesus Christ!"

One stooped from its branch and flew directly at him, a flash of black wings, gaping maw of beak, and dead gray eyes. Isaac swung the net reflexively, causing it to veer off to his left. Most of the contents of his net flew through the air and back into the river. Seeing another raven break from its branch towards him, he scrambled for shore, kicking up arcs of water as he ran. He dove flat onto the ground, tossing the net out in front of him. He contorted out of the backpack. The cold breeze of something flying just inches above the length of his spine chilled him. "Jesus Christ! Jesus Christ!" Freed of the backpack straps, he rolled onto his ass and elbows. His breaths were frantic. He shielded his face with his right arm.

After a moment, he moved his arm to see into the trees. The birds were gone. Not even a straggler or two remained, as though they'd never been there. The wind, more squalls now than gusts, continued through the branches. He listened for a distant cawing from the birds but heard nothing.

Isaac sat with his elbows on his knees and stared at the flailing branches where the birds had been. His bare skin was hot and sticky against the insides of his hip boots. Moments later, he had to stretch out his throbbing leg. He wiped his left hand over his sweating brow. "What the hell?" he murmured to himself. Sure, ravens will protect their nests, but it was too late in the summer for them to be nesting.

He wondered too if the birds had been there at all. Had it been just more of his now dry whiskey-soaked brain? How many phones that weren't ringing had his dad answered in the two days he tried to quit? How many times had he gone to the front curtain, looked out on the porch, and announced that someone was at the door. His mother would open it every time to find nobody there.

If the birds were there, Isaac had done something to seem a danger to them. Given the secluded island, he imagined that he probably looked threatening and out of the ordinary with his bulky backpack and net. Or maybe the elecrofisher's beeping had triggered them. That could be it, he guessed.

It wasn't the first time birds had seen him as a threat. He'd been fly fishing once a few years prior on the Pigeon River. A large tree had fallen across the stream, forcing him onto the bank. Finding his way back to the water downstream meant following a rough path that other fishermen had blazed through the tall grass and tag alder. As he did, he'd heard a commotion above him. Cedar waxwings were dive bombing him. At that time, he'd laughed and waved the end of his fly rod at them, feeling like a musketeer fending them off. He could hear their babies peeping in the branches around him. The adults were clearly being protective.

But ravens? Isaac took a breath and exhaled it. Had to be ravens of all birds, he thought, shaking his head. Goddamn things.

CHAPTER 13

I saac climbed to his feet and gathered the electrofisher, net, and duffel bag into a pile at the base of the tree that he'd marked. He peeled off the rubber gloves. Kamikaze birds or no, he was going to fish the river. He walked back upstream along the bank, shooting glances from time to time at the overhead branches. No ravens, but the wind was increasing steadily. The trees on the opposite side of the river plunged and bucked. He could feel the wind even at the forest floor level. Casting was going to be a trick. Coming to it on the bank, he picked up his fly rod. Taking a bottle of floatant from his pocket, he squeezed a few drops on his fingertips, and smoothed it over the Adam's hackle.

He could still hear Gwen. "It's kind of cruel, isn't it? Out of instinct, the fish comes up expecting something good to eat, but then gets a mouth full of barbed thorax."

She had been describing the fly. Hackle, dubbing, and materials representing a tail and wings were tied around a fishing hook. The hackle made the fly float and the other materials augmented the deception. Some flies were shockingly accurate in their representation of their living counterparts. Using a fluid back cast, the fly fisher then shoots the line forward, where the fly touches down on the surface like any other insect on the water. If the angler is lucky, a fish rises from the depths to gulp the artificial fly off the surface. Even with Gwen's protests of cruelty, Isaac couldn't help but love everything about fly fishing.

Stepping out into the water, he worked his way to the middle. He studied the branches behind him. The space above the water was wide enough to use a standard cast. Downstream, the current riffled into the left bank, where over time, it had hollowed out a space under the roots of a cedar near shore. The darkness of the water there suggested that the hole was two feet deep or more, rather than the foot of water that he waded in. A root from the tree extended its touch out into the current, creating a scum line of small bubbles. Everything about the bend suggested promise. Isaac stood for a moment studying the hole, waiting for any sign of a feeding fish. He stole a quick glance at the branches above him.

The timing with the wind was tricky. He tried a few casts to the upstream side of the hole, but the gusts kept downing his fly feet away from where he'd wanted it to land. He had to wait in between the gusts for the eye-of-the-storm moments when everything would go temporarily still. Landing a cast near the bank, he let the Adams drift through the hole's upstream riffle, and then into the darkness under the roots. Anticipating, his fingers twitched on reel and rod. Over the course of ten minutes, he'd landed the cast he wanted several times with a perfect drift. Nothing rose out of the hole. He wondered if the wind had any kind of impact on fish and feeding. No other bugs were hovering around the water to give a trout a reason to look up. Then too he wondered if the river was just dead ... a spawning ground for lamprey with nothing else to offer.

He took a few careful steps closer to the hole, watching that his feet weren't kicking up too much silt. Within striking range, he cast to the downstream scum trail. A gust took his line nearly all the way across to the right bank. He brought it back in and waited. Then, he cast again during a brief break in the wind. The Adams landed just upstream from where the root tip touched the surface. Isaac pulled back slightly on the line, keeping the tippet from tangling around the root, and then watched the fly drift right through the scum and bubbles.

A fish rose and sucked the fly off of the surface. Isaac pulled up slightly and the weight of the fish tugged tension against his grip. He was hooked up. Holding the line against the rod with a finger of his right hand, he reeled in his slack with his left. He'd trained himself to always play the fish on the reel rather than stripping in the line. When the last of the slack wound onto the reel, the fish broke the water in a desperate jump above the river. Rainbow, he guessed, watching its brief, silvery flight before it crashed back down through the surface. Back in the stream, it swam hard toward the left bank. Isaac shifted his rod tip to the right and cranked the reel, keeping the fish from getting under the tree where it would have likely tangled the leader around submerged roots. Without his vest, he didn't have his fishing net, so he kept the fish on longer than he would have liked to tire it out. It leapt into the air two more times before he had it reeled into the shallow water. Using his boot, he edged it onto the pebbly shore.

He crouched down to it. Dipping his hand clean in the water first, he picked up the rainbow, pinched the Adams between his fingers, and pulled the barbed hook from its lip. He guessed it was somewhere between ten and eleven inches. He took the gasping fish out into the middle and, kneeling, set it in the stream. It drifted in the current, slowed by the break wall of Isaac's hips in the water. The fish rolled on its side. "Come on," he mumbled. He scooped the fish back to him, righted it, and held it loosely between his palms. He'd resuscitated many fish this way, holding them in the oxygenating current until, recovered, they'd swim away.

Waiting, he looked into the tree branches above, tossing in the wind. No ravens. He hoped that they wouldn't lose power at the cabin, but guessed that they were relatively safe with the bulk of the powerlines running underneath the lake. Of course, if they lost power in Witiko, they'd lose power on the island.

When he checked on the fish again, it was gone. Instead, a three-foot long lamprey slithered between his palms holding against the current, its whorl of a mouth and file-like tongue latched onto his wrist. The slimy, black, eel-length of it snaked against the gravel bottom as it fed. Slapping at the parasite, Isaac jerked his hands from the stream and scrambled to his feet, kicking chaotically. The water turned opaque with swirled up sediment.

He took long strides out of the river and collapsed onto the bank. Holy shit. What the hell was a lamprey that size doing in the river? It was long past the time that they should be spawning. He turned his hand to examine his wrist, expecting blood. Pale and striped with faint blue veins, it was untouched. He sat shaking his head. His heartbeat pulsed behind his ears. From upstream, what sounded like the chattering of teenage girls came off the current's auditory play in the wood's acoustics. He rested his forehead against the palm of his hand. I'm never touching a drop of whiskey again, he thought.

Catching his breath for a moment, he spotted debris coming around the upstream bend. With the wind, he expected broken off pieces of branches. He stood speechless when, seconds later, he recognized over half a dozen rainbow trout between eight and thirteen inches long floating dead on the surface. Their eyes were white, and their normally brilliant bodies were pale and muted. Isaac took a step back, scanning for scars, but saw none.

"What in the hell?" He glanced back upstream in the direction of the ethereal, river voices. Then, when he looked downstream again, the fish had vanished.

A chorus of withered, child-like voices whispered in the wind. "She's coming..."

A feeling of dread washed over Isaac, both chilling and heating him like a fever. This was wrong, he thought. Coming to the cabin was a mistake. They could pack up. They could wait for the late afternoon to see if the wind would die down. They could signal Caleb. It would just be better. Isaac wouldn't have to worry so much about Carson's sleepwalking in an unfamiliar place. He could patch things up with Ashley. Back in Witiko, he could call his brother and find out why he'd left so abruptly. He had a feeling that whatever was happening with Adam couldn't be good. Maybe he needed a big brother more than ever.

Isaac dropped his face into his hands. He pressed with his fingertips, massaging the ache in his forehead. Or maybe I'm just losing it, he thought. Seeing things. No better than the old man.

He turned over the math in his head. It hadn't even been thirty-six hours since his last drink. The doctor had told his mother that hallucinations were rare with withdrawal, but if his father had suffered from them, it seemed likely that Isaac could too.

Holding his fly rod, he started trudging back downstream along the bank. A sickly sweat dripped from his forehead. Tomorrow, he thought. Tomorrow I'll be better. By three o'clock in the morning, I'll be out of the woods. He slung the electrofisher over his shoulders. Then he gathered the net and duffel bag. He figured he could try fishing the river again on Friday, the day after Emily's birthday. By then, he guessed, most of the withdrawal symptoms would be behind him. Christ, I hope so, he thought as he trekked back through the woods towards the cabin. The wind howled overhead, seeming only to increase in intensity. He quickened his pace.

Arriving, he walked in through the back door. The front window looked out on the roiling lake with waves getting close to two feet high. The sunny skies of the morning had become dark gray with threatening storm clouds. Audible from inside, the flag snapped and whipped on the pole. If the wind hung around until the next day, he wouldn't be going into town to call Adam. Caleb would never take his boat out in that kind of weather.

Isaac found Helen, Emily, and Carson sitting around a puzzle at the kitchen table. "We found these pieces in a drawstring bag in one of the drawers," Helen said without looking at him. "So I guess the picture will be a surprise." They had about half of the border pieces done. The colors were mainly muted reds, whites, and flesh tones. Emily asked him about his fishing, and he told her the part about catching the rainbow trout and how it had jumped out of the water. He kept the hallucinations to himself.

"I need to talk to your father for a moment," he heard Helen say. "Keep looking for the pieces with flat edges, Carson."

When he stood up from storing his gear near the front door, Helen hovered next to him. She pointed with her finger, indicating that he should follow her out onto the porch. Closing the door behind him, he joined her where she stood at the porch's edge. Helen pulled her sweater tight around her torso. One of the teetering beach chairs finally fell over in the wind.

"I need you to take care of something," Helen said. She explained that when they were coming back from Evelyn's they stumbled upon a dead rabbit in the yard. With her back to the window, she lifted her hand to her sternum and pointed, so he could see but the children couldn't. "It's over there, on the lawn next to the trees. Emily found it, and she was very upset. I told her that it was sleeping and that we should leave it alone." Helen sighed. "She keeps asking if she can check if the bunny has hopped away. It's all I can do to keep her inside."

"Got it. I'm going to pick up some of the beach stuff, and then I'll take care of it."

She nodded. "I'll keep them busy with the puzzle." She took a few steps and then stopped. "Did you ever find out what happened with your brother?"

"Not without a cell connection, I didn't."

She looked out over the water. "Hmm. Very strange."

Walking past her towards the steps, Isaac shrugged. "Nutty professor, I guess." He was at the bottom of the steps when he heard her behind him.

"Or, maybe something happened here that wasn't sitting well with him. He could have felt that staying would have been, in its way, condoning it."

He turned, but her back was already to him going through the door. The brief camaraderie he'd felt from their shared deception regarding the dead rabbit vanished. She and Adam must have talked. Was his brother that worried about his drinking that he would offer up his observations willingly? Or, had Helen grilled him to such an extent that he'd let bits and pieces of the truth come out? Was Ashley somehow involved? She could have shown Helen the box of liquor. Two remaining fifth bottles of whiskey didn't help his case that he was getting on top of his drinking.

Anyway, he told himself, I'm not drinking, so the hell with her. Let her think whatever she wants. He folded the beach chairs, collected the plastic pails and little shovels, shook out the sand-covered towels, and slowly brought everything to the porch. He took one final walk down to the beach and started lowering the flag. The way it whipped in the wind, it sounded as though at any moment the fabric would tear free of the grommets. He folded the flag and set it in the beach box with the others. Standing on the sand with his hands on his hips, he surveyed the wind-whipped water. Enclosed as it was by dark stone cliffs, the lake looked like a cauldron someone had set to a high boil. He hoped it would die down by Friday so Caleb could come get Helen. Then he and the kids would finally have a day to themselves.

Turning in the direction of the rabbit, he spotted the canister of lampricide he'd tucked under the porch. He thought about how easy it would be to treat the river himself. He'd done it enough times before to do it in his sleep. He also knew, though, that what he had already done with the electrofisher would have leap-frogged him from administrative leave to termination. Administering lampricide on his own could very well land him with legal troubles beyond just being fired. The best he could do would be to contact his supervisor when they got home and show him the pictures of the scarred fish from the lake. He could mention, too, his suspicion that the lamprey might be spawning in the island's stream. The Service would eventually make the same discovery of lamprey larvae that he had made on his own.

Just at the edge of the trees, Isaac found the rabbit's body. His own body shivered in a feverish chill. Was his withdrawal getting worse? The way the rabbit lay, it did look like it was simply sleeping in the grass. He crouched down to it the best his leg would allow. Like the rabbit he'd found in his yard the week before, there wasn't a mark on it. He picked up the rigid body and held the little face between his fingers and thumb.

He moved it back and forth. He couldn't be certain with the rigor mortis, but it felt like its neck, too, was broken. He furrowed his brows. Even if there were owls on the island, this wasn't their work. They would rend and tear. He couldn't think of any predator that would break a rabbit's neck. If there were, it certainly wouldn't just leave its kill. With a palm resting against his cheek, he stared at the carcass. It didn't make any sense.

Standing, he looked back through the cabin window. Unaware of him, all three still had their heads bent to the puzzle. The wind raged, whipping his hair around his face. He walked around the side of the cabin and took the body out into the woods in the back. Going some fifty yards into the trees, he used the heel of his good leg to kick out a shallow grave. Isaac dropped the body into the hole and then used his foot to slide the dirt back over it. He knew that most likely some scavenger would come along, dig up the body, and drag it away. Either way, buried or scavenged, Emily would never see it.

He turned to head back to the family. Behind him, a colossal cracking sound was followed by the crash of a large branch hitting the ground. Hustling back to the property, he scanned for any suspect branches above the cabin. He noted that the trees had been cut down or trimmed back to the point that no branches hung over the building's roof. He wouldn't have to worry about storm damage at least.

He walked through the screen door and then sat at the table with Helen and the kids. He pushed his fingers through the pieces, looking for flat edges. "How was your little brunch up at Evelyn's?" he asked.

"Wonderful," Helen said. She pointed to the counter. "There are a few sprigs of stinging nettle there that Evelyn picked for you this morning. She said you should use it while it's fresh."

"I think I'll take a pass," Isaac said.

"Tallick," Carson said without looking up from the scattered pieces. "The tea was tallick."

"What's that, bud?"

Helen cleared her throat. "That's my fault," she said. "Metallic, honey. And Grandma shouldn't have said that. It was rude to say about our host's efforts."

Emily held her stomach. "The iced tea was so gross, Daddy. She made it with blood oranges!"

Helen cleared her throat. "It was unlike any iced tea I've ever tasted. An acquired taste to be certain. Evelyn said the metallic taste was saffron, except not pure saffron." Their host had explained to them that saffron was good for her cataracts, so she put it in the iced tea, which usually added to the sweetness. She'd also said that getting pure saffron could be challenging, and that the owner of the market in Witiko wasn't exactly an herbalist. "The cheap imitations can have a strange taste. That's all that happened. She was kind enough to make us sandwiches and brew the tea, and I'm proud of both of you for drinking as much as you did. That was very polite."

Emily held her hands down near her pelvic bone. "My stomach really hurts."

Helen looked at her. "You didn't eat much at Ms. Cameron's. Maybe you're just hungry?"

"I can make you something," Isaac said.

Emily shook her head. "I don't want to eat."

"Well, when you're ready, I can throw something on the grill." Isaac found an edge piece and snapped it into place. He looked across the table at Emily. Tears were streaming down her face. "Honey..."

"Daddy, my stomach really, really hurts," she sobbed.

Helen looked at her and then at Isaac. Her face showed recognition. "I think I know what this is," she said. She stood from the table and touched Emily's shoulder. "Let's go in and see Ashley, okay? If you lie down, I think you'll feel better." Walking the hunched-over Emily out of the room, Helen looked back at Isaac. She mouthed the word "cramps."

He nodded. A cold chill passed through him.

"Come on, now," Helen said. She opened the door to the girls' bedroom. "We're going to get you comfortable, and then you can have a nice talk with Grandma and Ashley."

"Oh, Em, what's going on?" Ashley said sympathetically from inside the room.

Helen closed the door before Isaac could hear anything else. He was left only with the sound of the wind roaring past the windows. He ran his fingers through his hair. Cramps? What the hell else could go wrong on this trip? Grabbing the stinging nettle sprigs, he stuffed them down in the garbage.

CHAPTER 14

It had been a long afternoon and early evening. The door to the girls' room had remained largely closed. Helen had come out to run cool water over a washcloth. She'd come out again an hour later after Emily had been sobbing and wailing. Each time she came out, Isaac looked up from the puzzle pieces he was sifting through with Carson. Helen told Isaac that they'd explained to Emily what was happening with her body, and she hadn't taken the news well. "She's just a little overwhelmed," Helen had said before closing the door. Isaac put in a couple of frozen pizzas that he'd brought. When he announced that they were done, Helen came out, made herself a salad, and then slid a few pieces on a plate for Ashley. Emily still wasn't hungry.

"Do you think I should go in?" Isaac had asked.

Helen shook her head. "This is a situation for big sisters and grandmas, I'm afraid."

He nodded. When Carson finished eating, Isaac cleaned the kitchen. Afterwards, he stood for a time at the front window. Somewhere around six o'clock the sky had opened up and drizzled a steady rain on the wind-tossed lake.

Carson announced that he was bored with the puzzle. He took his Legos in front of the fireplace. Isaac paced the cabin, using the time to check for any leaks. The realtor had mentioned that the only issue with the cabin was that it would need a new roof in the next year or two. Old roof or no, he couldn't find any place where water was getting inside. It was a small blessing in what had turned out to be a stressful evening. When he spotted Carson lying on his side to play with his figures, Isaac asked if he was tired. He sat up, nodded, and then went into the bathroom to brush his teeth.

After a few minutes, Isaac sat on the edge of the bed tucking Carson in.

"Are you going to bed too, Daddy?"

It was just after nine o'clock. "No, bud, it's a little early for Daddy." He squeezed Carson's knee through the comforter. "I haven't been sleeping very well here, so I think I'm going to sleep in Uncle Adam's room. I don't want to keep you awake with my tossing and turning."

"It's okay. I don't wake up."

He squeezed his knee again. "Nah, we're both big guys. We should be in our own rooms." He stood and pointed at the dreamcatcher. "I bet that works better with just one person in the bed, anyway. I mean, what if it messed up, and you got my dreams and I got yours?" He smiled. "I don't want to dream about Big Bird farts."

Carson crossed his arms. "I don't dream about that! How would that be a good dream?"

Isaac squeezed his foot. "I know you don't. I was teasing." He walked to the door and set his finger on the light switch. "The night light is plugged in."

Carson looked at the light in the outlet and then looked back to Isaac. "I miss Uncle Adam."

"I wish he could have stayed, too. I'll play cars with you tomorrow if you want."

Carson nodded.

"And maybe before school starts we can go down to Ann Arbor and visit your uncle. They have some neat toy stores downtown."

"That sounds fun."

Isaac listened to the wind roaring outside the window. Heavy, intermittent rain drops pelted against the glass. A low, drawn-out thunder rumbled in the sky above the cabin. "If you need to later tonight," he started, looking at Carson's apprehensive face, "you can get in my bed ... but no Big Bird farts."

Carson laughed and then rolled to his side. "Goodnight, Daddy."

"Night. Love you." Isaac turned off the light and shut the door.

He trudged out to the living room and collapsed onto the couch. After a moment, he stretched his aching leg onto the coffee table. He'd sat too long working on the puzzle with Carson.

Lounging, he thought about making one drink, but knew that just one drink had never been his strong suit. He didn't know if in the last six months he'd ever had just one drink.

But *that* night I wasn't drinking, he thought. Not that night. I knew the roads were going to be icy, he assured himself. I didn't even have a glass of wine with dinner. Even with that crazy raven, if he'd been drinking anything and had to live with the idea of being partly to blame for Gwen's ...

He stood and poured himself a glass of milk. Then, he sat staring at the charred logs in the fireplace. Every now and then a rain drop came down through the chimney and poofed into the ashes. The thoughts started coming to him as they always did if he was idle for too long. It was like when he sat for hours, and his leg, through its pain, reminded him of the loss he'd been through ... was going through. Closing his eyes, he pictured just the five of them at the cabin. With the kids finally tucked away, this would have been their time. Holding each other in front of the fire, or sitting on the porch listening to the hushing of the waves. Or maybe skinny dipping—making love by the lake in the shadow of this dream that they'd bought for themselves.

"Goddamnit, Gwen," he sighed, closing his eyes and scratching his forehead.

He shook his head and pushed the thoughts away. Sipping on his milk, he waited for anything that felt like sleepiness. Outside in the western distance, he spotted something he hadn't seen before. Two different spots of light on the high cliff bank. They were maybe a half mile apart. The widows had certainly picked a terrible stretch of weather for spending time in their cabins. He wondered if maybe there weren't new owners.

Helen opened the door to the girls' room and closed it quietly behind her. "Finally," she whispered. "She's asleep."

Isaac bent forward and set his glass on the table. "Well, that's a relief."

Helen draped a washcloth over the faucet of the sink. Opening a cupboard, she took down a wine glass and then filled it from the bottle of Chardonnay that she'd brought with her.

"No nightcap?" she asked. She sat in the overstuffed chair to the side of the couch.

Isaac raised his glass of milk. "Just this." He took a drink and then held the glass between his hands on his lap. "That was a long night. How's she doing?"

Helen took a sip of her wine. "That poor thing. I don't know if schools just don't talk about it anymore, or if she didn't pay attention, but she had no idea about puberty." She explained that each detail that they shared with her only made her more panicked. "She was inconsolable."

Isaac rubbed a finger and thumb over his chin. "She's pretty innocent."

Helen snapped a look at him. "Innocent? She's anxious, Isaac. I would be surprised if she weren't diagnosed with generalized anxiety disorder. She should really be seeing a counselor."

He nodded. "I've thought as much."

"And?"

He looked at her expectant face. "Well, I just need to ask around. You know, find somebody good. I've heard that with kids, a bad counselor can be worse than no counseling at all."

She took another sip of her wine. "And so you've asked around?"

He looked into his lap. "I said I need to."

For a moment they sat in what would have been silence, save for the soundtrack of the relentless wind going past the windows.

"What do you think," he started, "want me to make another fire?"

"No, thank you." She cleared her throat. "I was wondering though if you'd given any more thought to our last phone conversation?"

God, this again. He pulled his leg from the table and twisted a knuckle into the tightening muscle. "I haven't had time to give much of anything more thought, but I know I already gave you my answer."

She nodded and took a longer drink. "I think you should reconsider. It's been an eye-opening couple of days for me."

He looked at the glass of milk and imagined it as ice and whiskey. Just the idea of it ... the steadying effect. He could feel what was coming. She had crap to say and she was going to say it. "Yeah?" he said. "What are you seeing differently, Helen?"

She leaned forward and set her glass on the coffee table. Sitting back, she laced her fingers together and set her hands in her lap. "I'm not trying to be hurtful. You need to know that. But I suspected this, and now it's been confirmed for me." She looked into his eyes. "Isaac, you have a drinking problem. You just do." Lips tight against her teeth, she smiled sympathetically.

He looked at her posture and thought about the way she'd delivered her lines. It was as though she had watched instructional videos on how to have an intervention. "Helen—"

"I'm very serious."

He fished his phone from his pocket and looked at the time. "Just so you know, it's been almost 40 hours since I've had a drink."

She smiled again. "Do you hear yourself? People who don't have drinking problems don't keep track of how long it's been since they've had a drink. Certainly not in hours." She cleared her throat. "And, don't you think this sudden sobriety might have something to do with me being here? Perhaps this is you being on your best behavior?"

Grimacing, he lifted his leg back onto the table. "Helen—"

She shook her head. "No, Isaac, I won't have you gaslighting me anymore ... not with—"

"Gaslighting you?"

"Keep your voice down." She looked at the girl's door and then back to him. "Migraines? Allergies? Goodness, I don't know what to believe anymore. I learned today from Evelyn what Silas witnessed on the beach at three o'clock in the morning. It's shameful. She must have wanted to spare you in front of me with all that talk about you coughing."

A feverish guilt washed through him. "Yeah, well what the hell is he doing creeping around our property at that time of night? That's the question."

She reached for her wine glass and held it between her hands. "You really think that's the question in this circumstance? What Silas was doing?" She shook her head. "What you were doing – what you were thinking – is the question."

He stared at her, trying to keep his anger in check. "I'm trying to do better, I told you that."

"And I want to help you do that. You are incorrectly making me the enemy here."

"I don't think that making the kids adjust to a new school is exactly the best way to give them more stability."

She laughed incredulously. "Stability? I'm sitting on Evelyn's beautiful porch eating a cucumber sandwich when Carson tells her, 'Me and my daddy were in your yard last night while you were sleeping.' Do you have any idea what that sounds like? Is it true?"

He could feel himself blanching, the blood rushing out of his face. "It's not true in the way it ... he was sleepwalking. I woke up, and he wasn't in the bed, and I found him in her yard." He knew better than to mention the steak knife.

"Hmm," Helen said. "Well, when Evelyn asked him why you were in her yard, Carson only shrugged and said, 'My daddy likes hooch.'" She reached and set her wine glass down again. "Such a precious moment. I really wish I would have had it on video."

He glared at her. "You think that helps? Think trotting out your goddamn high horse helps?"

"I suppose you're right." She looked down into her lap. "It doesn't help. But I also suppose that I've moved from being worried to being angry." She looked up and crossed her arms. "If you've known that he sleepwalks, how could you come here and not take precautions? Even just chain locks high up on each door to keep him inside? I mean, you know that Gwen was a sleepwalker as a child. And do you know what can trigger it? Do you? A sudden change in sleeping environment ... like going to a cabin on a secluded island."

"It's not an island." As he stared at her, his nostril twitched involuntarily. "There's a lot to navigate here. I can't—"

She lifted her palms into the air. "And that's what I'm offering you ... a break from all the navigation."

He sat for a moment staring into the maw of the fireplace. He remembered the good things Adam had said of his fathering. "You know," he started without looking at her, "all in all, I think I'm doing okay."

"Then you're lying to yourself."

Pulling his leg from the table, he stood and hobbled into the kitchen. "Here, I'll show you something. Right now." He reached into the box and pulled out one of the fifths of whiskey. Opening it, he held it above the sink and poured it down the drain. Finishing that one, he drained the next. The odor made his mouth water. He let the water run for a time to cut the ethanolic smell rising from the drain. Then he turned back towards Helen who had been watching him over the rim of her wine glass. "That was about sixty dollars' worth of booze." He crossed his arms. "I'm telling you, I'm done."

She stood next to the overstuffed chair holding her wine in one hand and with her other hand on her hip. "It's really not that easy," she said.

"Now, come on. What more—"

"Do you know how many times," she said in a raised voice, "that John would hold nearly full packs of cigarettes up and crush them in front of me? The first few times I was actually impressed by his bravado. He seemed so determined." She took a sip of her wine. "Of course, he died of lung cancer at 65 years old, so I've learned to ignore bravado."

Isaac threw his hands in the air. "I don't know what I'm supposed to do here. I really don't, Helen."

"For one, stop lying to yourself."

He hobbled back to the couch in front of the fireplace and sat. It was farther from the girls' room, in case one of them was still awake. "We're just going to agree to disagree on this. I'm done talking about it."

She sat in the chair again. "I would like to finish talking about it."

He lifted his leg back onto the table. "We are finished."

"You need to see someone, Isaac ... if not about your drinking, then at least about your grief. You need a grief counselor. And the kids, for right now at least, need someone who can give them one hundred percent."

He stared into the fireplace. If he stopped responding, maybe she would stop talking.

"Isaac?"

He sighed and turned to look at her.

"Let me just ask you this," she said. "Do you think it was a good idea to leave a despondent teenager alone in this cabin while you went fishing?"

He snickered. "Got lucky, I guess. I'm surprised she didn't end up falling in with the local street gang."

She smiled, but it was damning. "Your snark aside, do you think it was a good idea to leave her here distraught?"

"I don't know what you're talking about."

She crossed her arms. "And that's the problem. You don't know enough about what's happening with these kids. Ashley thinks you hate her."

"That's teen talk."

"Fair enough, but she does feel that you are disappointed in her, and she doesn't understand why. She says you've been distant with her since the first night."

Isaac thought about trying to explain what happened with the Ouija board. He already knew that the telling of it would make him look bad in Helen's eyes. Hearing about tossing the game into the lake, she'd wonder aloud if maybe he didn't need anger management classes on top of substance abuse counseling. And then too, she'd wonder why he wasn't just honest with his daughter. Why not just tell her that he'd discovered what she'd done. Why not try to understand her motivation or perspective? Talking, they might have reached a better understanding. Why turn it into some kind of juvenile challenge to get her to confess and apologize? Those would be Helen's questions. And he knew, too, that they were good questions. They were the kind of questions for which he didn't have answers. Ashley had been his right hand around the house over the last three or four months, and he was silently punishing her over one misstep. He was in the wrong, but it wasn't anything he wanted to get into. Not with Helen.

He took his leg off the table again. There was no positioning it to where it didn't ache. "Look, we had a little falling out. I'll smooth it over tomorrow."

"A falling out? Over what?"

"It doesn't matter."

She nodded slowly, her face thinking. "And you don't think perhaps you're punishing her for texting with me ... for being forthcoming with me about her concerns?"

"What? No, that's not it at all."

"Hmm."

He hated it when she'd purr like that in the back of her throat. It grated at him more than if she would have simply called him a liar. He stood. "It's a big day tomorrow, Helen. I'm going to go to bed." He bent for his milk glass.

"'Grandma, Dad slept on the porch floor again.'"

Isaac straightened himself from stooping for the glass. His back muscles stiffened. Helen held her phone out in front of her, reading aloud.

She scrolled her finger over her screen. "'Emily woke up crying last night. I couldn't wake Dad up. I didn't get any sleep.'"

"Helen ... "

She stood as she kept scrolling. "'I don't know what to do,'" she read. "'Dad's asleep in the backyard. I don't want the neighbors to see.'"

He vaguely remembered going out in the yard during one of the warmer nights in July. He'd lain on his back to look at the wash of stars speckled across the clear sky. When they were first dating, it was something he and Gwen would do. She knew her constellations and would point them out for him. Bleary-eyed and in a stupor, he had tried to find even one of the groupings on his own but couldn't. Even the Big Dipper had eluded him. At some point he'd fallen asleep. He looked down at the cabin's hardwood floor. "Taken out of context those sound worse than they are."

"Out of context?" She set her phone down on the arm of the chair behind her. Then she pointed at him. "I will tell you the context. You have a five-year-old son that sleepwalks and could injure himself any evening. You have a middle child absolutely riddled with anxiety and in desperate need of counseling. And then you have your eldest, made to be the mother because her father spends too much of his time passed out. That's the context. You're not able to be available to your children when they really need you."

"If anything ever threatened these kids—"

"Oh save it, Isaac." She crossed her arms. "I'm terrified to leave here on Friday. I can't live with the idea of the children being out here alone with just you. What might happen if you were dri—"

He pointed at her. "I told you already that I quit drinking." He softened the snarl in his voice. "You'll just have to trust me. I've got no booze here even if—"

"I don't trust you." She sniffed in a resolute breath. "You told me that you quit drinking," she said, nodding. "Okay. But then you also told me that you can't pick up my calls because you're so busy with work. That I believed too. Then last Thursday, I tried calling you on your phone to see if we were all set with sun block and bug spray for the kids. You didn't pick up, no surprise there, so I called your work. But, of course, I couldn't talk to you there because you are on 'administrative leave.' That's what I found out. I wouldn't be surprised if your drinking wasn't somehow connected to your being suspended."

His cheeks were warm. It was all too much and it just seemed to keep coming. He walked to the counter and thumped his glass down on it. "I'm going to bed."

"I would like some kind of agreement before either of us turn in for the night."

He turned towards her. "I already agreed to disagree."

"There's no failure in admitting that you're failing."

"Goodnight, Helen."

She reached out and held his sleeve. "I want you to have some time, Isaac. You need it. The kids need it. I can't stand idly by and watch them live in this chaos ... especially Emily. She's really too tender for this world. She needs attention that you aren't able to give. She needs to be with me."

He looked at her hand, and she released his sleeve. "Okay, then," he said, "I'll give you my answer. No."

Helen looked down at the floor. After a moment, Isaac turned and started limping toward the room where Adam had slept.

"I contacted an attorney."

Isaac stopped and slowly turned towards her. She was nodding her affirmation of what she'd said.

"I did. I've really had enough of this, and it's unfair that the decision is somehow yours alone to make. Other authorities need to be involved."

He swallowed. "Helen, you don't need ... "

She pointed her finger back toward her phone. "I showed my lawyer the texts. I've told her what I've observed, what the younger children have said to me. I've sat in the wings too long waiting for you to find the wherewithal to rise to the occasion. I only see sinking, not rising."

He stood, feeling the impact of her words crashing against him like the waves out on the dark, wind-churned lake. A gust knocked something over on the porch, and they both turned briefly to look at the dark front window.

Looking to the ceiling, Isaac steepled his hands over his nose and mouth. He sighed a warm, resigned breath into his palms. Still touching his fingertips against his lips, he looked down at Helen. She stood firm with her hands on her hips. "Can we just talk more about this tomorrow? Maybe we could do something like the kids stay with you on the weekends or—"

"She thinks I have a very good chance at temporary custody," Helen said.

He tried to imagine going to court, the kids speaking to the judge, a lawyer listing Isaac's failings into public record. "A hearing? You really want to put the kids through that?"

"I have struggled with the decision. In the end, I believe the stress they might endure is far less worrisome than the threat that living with you, in your current state, poses to them." She turned and picked her phone off of the chair's armrest. "Or you can change your mind. How all of this goes is really up to you."

"Doesn't feel like it."

"Goodnight, Isaac. You can let me know on Friday what you've decided. I don't think we should talk about this tomorrow. Tomorrow we have a special birthday to celebrate."

"I'm aware," he said to her closing bedroom door. He stood for a moment with a middle finger extended toward her room.

He stepped to the front window. The rain had died off some but the wind, if anything, had only intensified. The stirred-up landscape glowed pale blue under the full moon. He wanted to think her a bitch. He wanted to simmer in the way that she was wronging him. He wanted to believe that she was being unfair.

But he couldn't.

CHAPTER 15

Isaac lay in bed for what felt like hours after he'd finally turned in. Listening to the endless, angry wind, he knew that if he hadn't poured it down the drain, he would have had a whiskey or two or even five. It didn't feel like it really mattered. The kids were going to end up with Helen one way or another. For how long was a question over which he felt he had some control. If they could avoid the courts, maybe he could float past Helen the idea of three months. They'd be with her September, October, and November.

It could be like he'd originally imagined it. They'd get the kids involved in the conversation, get them to see that three months wasn't that long. He could explain how he'd visit them on the weekends. He could explain that Dad was hurting, and even dads need help sometimes. He could go to grief counseling, go back to physical therapy, and smooth things over with his job. If the five of them could agree on a plan, then there'd be a timeline. He could slowly count down the days.

If the courts were involved, the timeline would be up to a judge. The end date of the separation could be indeterminate. There'd likely be follow-up hearings and reports on Isaac's progress. They might require that he attend Alcoholics Anonymous or some other substance abuse support group. A judge could rule that a year or even more would be the right amount of time. Shorter than that and maybe the bouncing of the kids from their old schools to new schools and then back to their old schools would be viewed as too disruptive.

Even after deciding that he would willingly let the kids go with Helen, sleep eluded him. It was one o'clock in the morning when he checked his phone's glowing screen. He turned the light on, guessing that a glass of warm milk might be the only sleep remedy he could try. Or maybe even a few of his brother's remaining IPAs. Sitting on the edge of the bed, he spotted the orange prescription bottle on the nightstand. Whatever had rushed his brother off the island, it was urgent enough that he'd forgotten not only his psoriasis medication, but also his Ambien. Isaac popped one in his mouth and dry-swallowed it.

He waited for forty minutes but only ended up feeling like the handful of times he'd smoked weed. Loopy, he mumbled nonsense to himself and then smiled. It wasn't all that unpleasant with his mind seemingly adrift in another existence. He wasn't thinking anymore about Helen or the kids or even of having a drink. If he were going to lie awake all night, it wasn't a bad state of mind to be in.

"It's already happening," Gwen said.

He snapped his head toward her voice on the other side of the bed. Her body, from head to toe, lay completely under the covers. "Gwen?" He trembled. "How are you even—"

"It can't be stopped now. She's going to take her."

He touched the comforter and could feel the solidity of her underneath. "She's going to take all of them, but just for a short time. Just enough for me to—"

"Emily ... she's taking Emily."

He nodded. "Yes, Emily too. Your mom will be good for her, though."

For a moment, the other side of the bed was silent.

"It's hard. My words ... they're keeping me from making you understand."

"Understand what, Gwen?"

"The girls are good," she said. Her voice was fading. "You can trust them. They want to help."

Stroking the comforter, he nodded again, tears in his eyes. "Carson too. They're all good. We really have great kids, Gwen. They're great. And I'm going to be better. I can promise that." He set his hand on her shoulder. "Come out from under there. I want to see you."

"You can't trust him. He can get into your head, a hex ... poor Adam."

Isaac furrowed his brow. "Adam? What are you... ?"

She stayed with the comforter pulled over her head. "Something terrible is happening. You're not listening," she said. Her words were a lamentation.

"I'm sorry. I'll listen. Just tell me."

"I can't stay," she said in a voice that sounded as though it were coming from the far end of a long hallway.

"Don't say that ... you've barely just got here."

"I have more to tell you," she whispered, her volume fading quickly. "Emily. Remember Emily. That's when you'll know it's me. E. M. I..."

"What are you ... ?" He rolled toward the nightstand and turned on the light. He looked again. She was still there ... the shape of her still under the comforter. "Gwen?" He reached near her head and pulled the covers down.

He gasped in a painful breath. Where normally there would have been pillows, instead was the glove box and passenger side dashboard of their old car. Gwen's head lay smashed against it, her dead eyes wide open. Her face was splintered with a spider's web of blood rivulets. An open gash above her right eye bled down into her hair fanned over the cracked molded plastic of the dash. Her mouth gaped, a jack-o-lantern of bloody teeth. A jagged white of broken bone stuck up through the ripped flesh of her upper left arm.

She blinked, and her eyes rotated their focus on him. Her mouth moved as though to speak. "L.Y," she gurgled through the blood bubbling from her mouth. Then her eyes slowly closed.

"Gwen? Gwen!" His eyes snapped open into his daylit bedroom. He was tangled in sweat-soaked sheets. His heart raced like something feral trying to escape the confinement of his rib cage. Sitting up, he took deep breaths through his mouth. He glanced to his left several times, but she wasn't there. Nothing but pillows and white sheets.

He closed his eyes and the bloodiness of her was still there in his mind. He couldn't hold back what was coming. In his hospital bed, lying with his leg up in traction, he'd openly wept. It was the last time he'd really allowed himself to cry over everything that had been stolen from him. The patient sharing the room with him eventually hit the call button. Unable to calm him, the nurse gave Isaac a Xanax. She'd worried that his convulsing might tear something in his post-surgery leg. Out of the hospital, there'd been more moments of tears. Wiping with his palms into his eyes, he'd suppress them before they'd go too far. He didn't want the kids to see him breaking down.

Having seen her again so vividly, her wrecked face and body, he held a pillow over his face and sobbed. She was gone. She would always be gone, and he would forever ache for what was missing and what could have been. His kids would forever be motherless. He was alone, doing a terrible job as a single father, so much so that he had to willingly give his children up or have the courts take them away. How was this his life? He'd wanted to be so strong for the kids, and instead he'd slid into the cold comfort of whiskey and self-pity. He was no good for them. He was no good for anyone. He wasn't doing what they so desperately needed him to do.

A dream, he thought when his crying jag had finally idled down. It was just a dream. Years ago he'd gone through a period of insomnia whenever he'd go out to the field. Carson was only a baby then, and Isaac would stare into the dark ceiling of the Fish & Wildlife trailer worrying about his little boy. He'd been born slightly premature, and the doctors had a list of potential signs of long-term ailments to watch for.

Even though the doctors had said that any kind of health risk was low, Isaac couldn't shake the thought that something bad would happen while he was away. He'd finally gone to his doctor to ask about a prescription for Ambien. The doctor instead wanted him to try melatonin or an over-the-counter sleep aid. "Others prescribe it like candy, but I prefer to move slowly toward that remedy," the doctor had said. He'd warned Isaac about some of the potential side effects, like headaches, impaired vision, memory problems, and vivid dreams.

No shit, he thought. What he'd dreamed of Gwen was as real as anything he'd ever experienced in his waking hours. He picked up the prescription bottle, looked at it, and then set it down again, shaking his head. If he closed his eyes, he could still see her, exactly as he'd seen her the night of the accident just before he'd lost consciousness.

E.M.I.L.Y. What exactly had she meant? Why spell it?

He sniffed in a few ragged breaths through his nose. The crying had been good, as though he'd released something dark that had been possessing him for months. He felt cleansed. "Sometimes you just need a good cry," his mother used to say. She was right. Losing her husband while battling cancer, she knew something about grief.

Even with sunshine coming through the window, the wind still raged at the pane. Most of the lake activities he'd imagined for Emily's birthday would be out of the question. He couldn't picture casting out with bobbers so they could fish. The waves would just keep bringing their lines back to shore. Swimming wouldn't be safe. With the risk of falling branches, taking a hike was off the table too. He'd have to come up with something to keep the kids occupied.

He put his glasses on and checked the time on his phone. It was after ten o'clock. Jumping up, he started dressing. His leg barked a few complaints, but felt better than it did most mornings. He had wanted to have chocolate chip pancakes waiting for Emily when she woke up. He'd also brought a grease pen, and he'd planned for her to wake to "Happy Birthday Emily" written across the front window. Someone was talking out in the main room of the cabin. He guessed that all of the kids were up, and he'd lost any chance of surprising her. Looking at the container, he swore to himself that he'd never take Ambien again. He reached down into his luggage and pulled out the new phone he'd wrapped for Emily days before.

Opening his door, he stepped out into the living space. A banner reading "Happy Birthday" was strung from support beam to support beam. Dozens of decorative butterflies dangled from strings thumbtacked into the ceiling. Balloons were scattered across the floor and taped around the frames of the windows. Isaac blinked and then looked around the room again. "Holy cow," he said. "This looks great."

Carson and Helen were at the table hunched over the puzzle. The pieces were slowly becoming the portrait of a woman.

"Good morning," Helen said without looking up.

Carson looked at him. "Morning, Daddy. Your eyes are red."

"Probably allergies," Helen said sarcastically without missing a beat.

Isaac smiled bitterly. "Nope, just didn't get a lot of sleep last night. Had things on my mind." Screw you, you old witch, he thought.

"You seemed to be sleeping just fine when I looked in on you at eight o'clock."

Isaac walked to the counter and set Emily's gift on it. "You could have woken me up. I would have helped decorate."

"I did try to wake you up."

He sighed. Not a battle worth fighting. He figured that in her mind she already believed that he had a bottle of booze hidden in his room. Probably guessed that a hangover had kept him in bed most of the morning. "She's not up yet?"

"Not yet, but I think that's good. She had a pretty exhausting day yesterday." She sifted her hand through the puzzle pieces. "I think Ashley's up, though."

He walked around the side of the counter and took a mixing bowl from a lower cupboard. "Well, I'm going to make pancakes."

"None for me, Daddy," Carson said. "Grandma made me pooched eggs."

She laughed. "Poached, honey. Did you like them?"

"They were yummy."

She nodded. "And, certainly better for you than that heaping bowl of sugar cereal you were getting ready to make for yourself."

Isaac rolled his eyes. Yes, you're the perfect parent, Helen. Opening the refrigerator, he slid out the carton of eggs. "Hey Helen, can I use some of these blueberries?"

"Emily likes chocolate chip pancakes," Carson said.

Isaac smiled. "I know, bud. I'm going to make this first batch for Ashley."

"Don't use too many of my berries. I like to put them on my salads."

He fought the urge to tell her to just forget it. He knew blueberry pancakes would be a great peace offering for Ashley. "I'll just take a handful," he said. He occupied himself with mixing the batter and heating the skillet. A sweet bready smell permeated the kitchen space.

When the pancakes were finished, he took a plate of them to the girls' door.

"Don't wake up Emily. Let her get her rest."

He stopped with his hand on the doorknob. "Anything else, Helen?"

She didn't answer. He turned the knob slowly and then pushed the door open, closing it behind him. Instead of staring at her phone or thumbing through a magazine, Ashley was reading a hardback book. Emily slept on her back. She looked pale.

"Hey," he whispered, "you up for some blueberry pancakes?"

Ashley set the book open on her comforter. "That sounds good," she said, smiling.

The smiled melted him. He brought the plate to her and sat down on the edge of the bed. He motioned with his head toward Emily's bed. "She do okay after she finally went to sleep?"

Ashley sliced the side of her fork down through the stack of three pancakes. "I didn't hear a peep." She stabbed the fork through the mouthful she'd cut for herself and skated it through the syrup.

"Well, that's good." He watched her chewing. "Food any good?"

Still chewing, she nodded her head. "Mmm hmm."

He looked at the spine of her book. "*A Tale of Two Cities*. That was one of your mom's favorites."

"That's what Grandma said. She found it on one of the shelves next to the fireplace." She sliced the fork into the stack again. "She thought I could use a little less screen time."

Isaac rolled his eyes. "Yeah, your grandma kind of thinks she knows what's best for everyone."

Ashley shrugged. "It's actually a really good book. I forgot how much I used to like to read."

He squeezed her knee. "That would be your mom in you. God she loved books." He tilted his head and scratched his cheek. "Was never much my thing."

She finished chewing and swallowed. "These are really good, Dad. Thanks."

He squeezed her knee again. "Just wanted to do something nice for you after yesterday. Grandma says you were a big help with calming your sister down."

She glanced at Emily and then back at him. "It wasn't easy. Seemed like everything we would tell her just made her more afraid."

He raked his fingers through his hair. "Wasn't exactly an event I had on the agenda." He glanced at the other bed. "Hard to think of her as growing up. She's always just seemed so much younger than her age."

"I have an easier time picturing Carson as an adult than I do Emily."

"Yeah," he said, turning back to her. He smiled. "I did want to apologize if I've seemed like a jerk the past couple days. Something was just bothering me, and I should have just talked to you about it."

She set her fork down on the plate. "Talk about what?"

He told her about the first night and how he'd found the Ouija board out. He didn't tell her that he'd thrown it in the lake.

She was shaking her head even before he'd finished talking. "I didn't take it out, Dad. I didn't. I wouldn't do that."

"Honey ... " he started, disbelievingly.

Tears started to stream from her eyes. "I didn't, Dad. I swear to God I didn't. I saw it wasn't in the backpack, so I thought you'd taken it ... hidden it or something. I didn't—"

"Ok," he said. He shushed her. "I don't want your sister to wake up."

She wiped her fingertips over her damp cheeks. "I don't know how it got out there, but it wasn't me."

It was almost impossible to understand, but he believed her. He knew Adam wouldn't have done anything like that. He would have at least mentioned it if he had. He already ruled out Emily. Carson? Could he have come into the girls' room, found the box in the backpack, and set it up out of curiosity. Or what if he'd done it while sleepwalking? It was a possibility he really hadn't considered. If Ashley was telling the truth and hadn't somehow become sociopathic in her ability to lie, then Carson was the only other explanation. "I believe you. I do. But can you see why I might have been upset with you?"

She wiped at her remaining tears. "You should have just talked to me."

He nodded. "You're right. I should have. I really do apologize that I didn't. I guess I was just waiting for you to own up to it."

"But I didn't do it ... "

She looked on the verge of tears again. Isaac leaned forward and pulled her head into his chest for a hug. "I know you didn't. I'll figure out what happened, and I'm really sorry that I didn't just come talk to you." He kissed the top of her head. Then, he held her for a moment. His own eyes were welling with tears.

"Dad?"

"Yeah, honey."

She pulled her head back from his embrace. "You're getting syrup all over your shirt." Pulling it away from his chest, she set her plate on the bed cover next to her.

He looked down at the wet stain. "Well, that's a sticky situation."

Ashley rolled her eyes. "I think I liked it better when you weren't really talking to me. No dad jokes."

"Hey."

They laughed quietly for a moment.

"We're good then?"

She nodded.

"Good." He stood. "If you want more of those, just let me know."

She picked up the plate and fork again. "I think I'm going to be stuffed after this."

Isaac slipped his phone from his pocket and looked at the time. Eleven o'clock. "Do you think you could do me a favor and wake your sister up in ten minutes? We should really get her day started."

"I will."

Going past her bed, he examined Emily. "I hope she's not sick. Does she look pale to you?"

Ashley looked and then turned back to her pancakes. "I don't know. Maybe."

"Okay. Give me ten minutes."

In the kitchen, he poured some of the batter he'd made into a smaller measuring cup. Sprinkling in chocolate chips, he used a spoon to stir them through. As Isaac watched a stream of chip-speckled batter expand into a circle on the skillet, Emily screamed from the bedroom.

"Dad! Grandma!" Ashely shouted, her voice frantic. "Come here quick. Don't let Carson come in!"

CHAPTER 16

I saac crouched on the beach next to the jagged base of the flagpole. The majority of the pole lay on the ground pointing in the direction of Evelyn's house. He could see where a ring of rust had been eating away at the metal for years. Previous owners had handled the problem by spraying the corroded part with a rust-blocking paint that matched the color of the pole. Since the pole was hollow, and could rust from the inside too, it was a temporary solution at best. Even with no flag as added drag, the gale-force winds were too much for the oxidized metal. He was surprised they hadn't heard it come down in the night.

He stood. The wind howled in his ears. Waves hitting the shore came up some three or four feet onto the beach. The beach box was tipped on its side and emptied. Hands on his hips, looking out at the volatile lake, Isaac turned back over his shoulder and checked on Carson. He lay on his stomach with a Lego figure in each hand. He was smiling with his hair set to dancing in the wind. On top of everything else, the kid needed a haircut.

Isaac turned back toward the water. What a morning it had been. Helen had beaten him to the girls' room by a few paces. Isaac stood stunned in the doorway. Emily had sat cross-legged on her bed in a pooled stain of blood. The blood-speckled underside of the comforter was kicked down near the foot of the bed. Her little underwear and pajamas were soaked. She wailed, and would not be consoled, and claimed with certainty, when her words could be understood, that she was dying. Sitting on either side of her, Helen and Ashley kept repeating that this is what they'd talked about, that it was natural. Helen pulled the comforter back over Emily's lap.

Isaac had stood in the doorway feeling useless.

"I want Mom! I want Mom!" Emily kept screaming.

As they slowly calmed her hysteria, Isaac slipped out to the kitchen and came back with the phone. "Here," he'd said. He extended the package to Emily. "It's your birthday present, honey. I really think you're going to like it."

Still sniffling and with tears running down her cheeks, she unwrapped the gift. Her little trembling fingers worked meticulously at the scotch tape. She always tried to save the wrapping paper, a habit she'd picked up from Gwen.

"Just rip it open, honey," Isaac had said. "It's okay."

The sight of the phone brought something close to a smile on her face.

"And your sister got you a great case you can open later." At a mall kiosk he'd found the perfect one decorated in flying butterflies. "You're going to love it."

While Ashley helped Emily plug the phone into its charger, Helen went to the bathroom to draw a bath. "Just a bad dream," Isaac had heard her say when Carson asked to know what was wrong.

"This is the newest iPhone, Em," Ashley said. "A friend of mine has it, and it takes really great pictures. I can show you later."

Emily turned the phone over in her grip. "Ok," she sniffled.

Helen had come back into the room and set her hand on Isaac's shoulder. "We'll get her all cleaned up. Take Carson outside, though. He's getting really antsy," she had said.

"You're tall." From behind him, Carson raised his voice over the wind.

Isaac blinked. He didn't know how long he'd been staring at the lake, recalling the eventful morning. "What, bud—" He started to turn and then jumped with his hand over his heart. "Jesus Christ!" A man was standing ten feet from him with an American flag folded reverently in his grip. Isaac bent over with his hands on his knees. He exhaled. "Holy shit."

"I apologize if I startled you," the man said in a flat baritone voice. "We have not met officially. I'm Silas Jameson."

Isaac stood straight and extended his hand. He paused for a moment taking in Silas' amber eyes set in stark relief against his sallow face and long, gray hair. He looked to be almost flat-headed, his skull more a square than an oval. "Not your fault. I was standing here daydreaming like an idiot. I'm Isaac. Isaac Fletcher." Silas looked to be in his mid-fifties.

Instead of taking his hand, Silas offered him the flag. His meaty hands could have doubled as baseball mitts. They didn't seem to fit with the rest of his lanky body. "I found this in Ms. Cameron's yard."

Silas' fingers and palms were stained red. Isaac remembered his own hands looking the same when he'd helped his father field dress a deer.

Catching his glance, Silas turned his free palm toward his face. "I apologize for the condition of my hands. I'm in the process of pulling a hide from a carcass... a hobby of mine."

Isaac nodded. "Evelyn mentioned as much."

He took the flag from Silas' grip and set it respectfully in the beach box, as though laying it atop a casket. Given the triangular folding, he guessed that Silas must have served in the military at some point. "Thank you," he said. He stood for a moment. "So, what do you think of this wind?" He gestured toward the nearly twenty feet of flagpole lying on the ground.

Silas looked into the gust-wild branches. "I think of it as I do any other natural phenomenon."

"Fair enough."

Silas brought his gaze back down to Isaac's face. "Which is to say, it is of nature, and so has a purpose." He motioned a hand toward the trees. "A consistent, strong wind such as this serves to prune dead branches and knock over dying trees thus making way for new life."

"That's a positive way to look at things." Isaac shook his head. "All I can think about is a big branch coming down through my roof." He took in Silas for a moment. He wore black moc-toe work boots and starchy blue jeans that looked as though they'd recently come off a store shelf. More weathered looking, he also wore a sherpa-lined denim jacket buttoned to his sinewy throat. "You didn't happen to see a red or green flag over at Evelyn's, did you?" Isaac asked. He pointed a finger toward the neighbor's property.

Silas shook his head. He explained that he'd spent much of the morning picking up fallen branches. "If they were on the property, I would have seen them."

"Oh well." Isaac looked into the man's stern face. He smiled sheepishly. "Hey, look, I wanted to apologize for what you witnessed on the beach the other night." He held an invisible glass and tilted it toward his lips a few times. "Just got into a little more than I should have."

"It's none of my business."

Isaac repressed a smirk. None of his business? Then why did he tell Evelyn all the details who then told Helen? And just what the hell was he doing on the property line at three o'clock in the morning? He thought of Ashley's take on Silas. Whatever the hell a Slender Man was, it didn't sound good.

"At my age, I find myself waking in the middle of the night unable to go back to sleep," Silas said, as though he'd heard Isaac's thoughts. "I find a little walking and some fresh air helps me overcome the insomnia."

Isaac nodded. "I found once I crossed into my forties, going to bed at night has become a real crap shoot, sleep-wise."

"I suppose so."

"How tall are you?"

Both of the men turned toward Carson.

"Hey, bud," Isaac said. "That's kind of personal."

"Hardly," Silas said. He pushed his shoulders back and stood as straight as possible. "Young man, I am almost six feet five inches tall."

Carson looked Silas up and down, nodded, and then bent his attention back to his toys in the grass.

Silas looked down toward the sand. The wind twisted his long hair around his head. "I did want to ask you if everything was okay here."

"What do you—"

He pointed to the house. "When I was laboring out in the yard, I heard one of the children screaming." He set his piercing gaze on Isaac's face. "She sounded very distressed. Is she okay?"

Isaac pinched his nose between his finger and thumb, rubbing away an itch. "Yeah, I guess we're turning out to be pretty rowdy neighbors, aren't we? Sorry about that."

Silas crossed his arms. "I did very much fear that she'd been injured."

What was the best way to explain it? After a moment, Isaac decided on the truth. "I guess you could say her red-headed aunt came for her very first monthly visit." He smiled thinly. "You know, it kind of took her by surprise. Took all of us by surprise, really."

Silas stood for a moment, stone-faced, studying Isaac. "Forgive me if I'm being obtuse, but I don't always understand euphemisms. I value plain speech, so let me ask … are you telling me that your daughter is menstruating for the first time?"

Isaac nodded, feeling his cheeks flushed. "It really shook her up."

"As I imagine it would anyone." He looked toward the cabin and then back to Isaac. "We are very secluded out here, as I'm sure you know. If there is ever an emergency, you may call upon me. I served as a medic in the Navy. In addition, I am a certified nurse's assistant. Aunt Evelyn insisted upon it if I were to be her health aide."

Isaac thanked him. "That's really good to know. I should have given the idea of a medical emergency more thought."

Silas looked at him sternly. "Murphy's Law," he said.

Nodding, Isaac looked toward the cabin and then back to his guest. "Speaking of which, I should probably get in there and check on her." He looked at Carson. "Probably getting a little cold out here for him, too."

"I'm not cold, Daddy."

Silas' lips rose into a slight smile. "Children are resilient, aren't they?" He reached his hand into his pocket. "I certainly don't want to forget this. Ms. Cameron made this for Miss Emily. For her birthday." A silver chain dangled off the end of his long fingers. Its pendant was in the shape of a miniature dreamcatcher.

Isaac took the pendant and chain into his palm, and Silas released it. "This is wonderful," Isaac said. "She'll really love this. Please tell Evelyn thank you from me. Emily will thank her herself once she's up and feeling better."

Silas held up a palm. "There's no hurry for that. It's a small island. I'm sure they'll be crossing paths soon enough. Let the girl get her rest. Sleep is almost always the best remedy."

Isaac said his goodbyes and turned toward the cabin.

"Oh," Silas said. He raised his voice over the wind. "Let her know that as requested, the necklace is a dream maker."

Isaac smiled. "She'll really like that. Thanks. And thank her."

Silas nodded. "I will see you again soon, I'm sure." He turned and walked towards the trees. Then he stopped. "There was another man here ... earlier this week? I saw him boarding Mr. Caleb's boat very early yesterday morning. It was barely dawn."

Isaac lifted Carson to his feet and, with a little push of his palm between the boy's shoulder blades, got him started on his way to the cabin. "My brother," he said. "He had to leave unexpectedly."

"Pity," Silas said, "that he should have to miss the special occasion. I trust that all is well with him?"

"I think so. Did he seem okay to you ... I mean, from what you could tell?"

Silas looked at the sky as though the answer to the question were written there. He looked down again and met Isaac's gaze. "From what I remember, he seemed to be in haste. I really have nothing else to offer as to his state-of-mind."

Isaac thought again of the grad student. She had to be the reason. Oh well, he thought, no skin off my teeth. Adam wasn't really missing much of a party, anyway. "I'm sure he's fine."

"I'm sure," Silas said, and then waved his blood-stained hand before turning to return through the trees.

Isaac rubbed his leg while following Carson. Inside, everything seemed very quiet. Only Helen occupied the main living area, with her head bent attentively to the almost finished puzzle. Dressed in a white cassock with a yellow pennant stole, the woman taking shape in the puzzle had a mane of thick red hair framing her face. Her long fingers were steepled in front of her chest holding a black egg. Her hollow eyes matched the color of the egg.

"You're almost done," Isaac said.

Helen admitted that her interest had outlasted the interest of the children. "I can get a little obsessive when it comes to puzzles."

"I don't like that picture," Carson said. He kneeled at the window again racing his cars back and forth.

Tucked away in the master bedroom's closet, the clothes washer hummed into a new cycle. "Hey," Isaac said, "thanks for taking care of everything in here."

Helen pushed another piece into place. "It wasn't just me. Ashley was a big help too." She sniffed in a quick breath. "But so was the gift of the phone ... as a distraction."

"That's what I hoped when I gave it to her." He looked at the girls' closed door. "What's she doing now?"

"Ashley is showing her how to edit pictures."

Going into the kitchen, Isaac poured what remained of the pancake batter into the garbage. The dried-out pancake from the skillet followed. "Has she eaten anything yet?"

"She says she isn't hungry, just tired."

"I'll see if I can tempt her with her favorite breakfast." Hearing no objection from Helen, he stirred a fresh bowl of batter and sprinkled in chocolate chips.

Holding a plate, Isaac rapped his knuckles on the girls' door before opening it. Still looking pale, maybe more so, Emily sat in her bed scrolling through her phone. Ashley set her book down and pushed her back against the headboard.

"Anyone hungry for chocolate chip pancakes ... like maybe a certain birthday girl?"

Emily set her phone down on the comforter. "I'll have a few bites," she said. Her hair was still damp from her recent bath.

"That a girl." He sat on her bed and handed her the plate. "Do you want something to drink ... a glass of milk?"

She cut a small piece from the stack and nibbled at it. "I have water." She pointed to the nightstand.

He looked and then stared for a moment at Gwen's picture. Her smiling face seemed like something from his distant past. It was hard for him to believe that the same time the year before she was still alive. Isaac turned away from the picture and noticed for the first time that they'd opened her case and put it on Emily's phone. "Do you like the case your sister got for you?"

Chewing sluggishly, she said she loved it. With just a few bites out of one of the pancakes, she handed the plate back to him. "I'm not really hungry."

He set the plate on the nightstand. Asking her to slide over, he then lay in the bed next to her. "Let's see some of these pictures you've been taking."

Ashley closed her book around one of her fingers. "I'm going to go out and read in the living room."

"Ok, hon."

Emily leaned her head on his shoulder and held the phone so he could see it. She'd taken dozens of pictures of Ashley. Some were originals and others had been filtered through mono, silvertone, noir, and sepia.

"You've got a good eye, kid."

She'd also taken pictures of Gwen's photograph. "Mom was so pretty," she said.

"Sure was." He reached over and patted her shoulder. "I'll bet you're going to look a lot like her."

"I hope so," she said. Then she yawned.

"I should probably let you get some rest."

"No, not yet, Daddy. There's a few more I want you to see." She slid her finger, showing him different photos of the dream catcher hanging above her. "I still haven't had any dreams about anything."

Isaac sat on the bed. He fished his fingers through his front pocket. "That reminds me," he said, "Ms. Cameron wanted you to have this for your birthday." He dangled the necklace and pendant from his index finger. "She said this one's a dream *maker*. Maybe Mom will come to say Happy Birthday while you're napping."

Her eyes went wide staring at it. Turning her back to him and lifting her hair in both hands, she begged him to put it on her. His thick fingers struggled with the little clasp, but eventually got it. She turned back around with the pendant sitting against her sternum.

"That looks really good on you. You'll have to go up to Ms. Cameron's house and thank her at some point."

Emily nodded. "I will." She lay her head back against her pillow. "I want to try to sleep now."

"Good. Some more rest is probably what you need."

"Daddy?"

He stopped at the threshold.

"I'm looking forward to school," she said. "I want to see my friends again, and I promise to do better with my homework."

When he turned towards her, she was aiming the phone at him. It made a noise like a shutter click on a camera. She studied the screen and then looked at him. "You look sad in this picture, Daddy."

He forced a smile. "Sorry. Take another one."

The phone clicked again. She looked. "That one's a little better."

Leaving the room, he looked back one more time. Holding the phone in her hand, she closed her eyes.

"Happy birthday, baby girl," he whispered, shutting the door.

CHAPTER 17

"I've never seen a wind last so long like this," Isaac said. He stood at the front window looking over the agitated lake. Everything slowly darkened toward dusk.

They'd spent the afternoon in the living room. Isaac made a fire in the fireplace, which flared intermittently from the breezes that found their way down the chimney. Ashley lay curled in the overstuffed chair reading her book. Helen spent forty-five minutes with Carson on hands and knees looking for three missing puzzle pieces. Two pieces were missing from the woman's hair and one black piece for the egg. Isaac kept telling her that they were probably never in the bag from the beginning. Crawling under the table or running a toothpick between the floor planks, she'd only reply that she didn't give up so easily. Isaac breathed a relieved sigh when she finally stood, brushed off her knees, and announced, "I'm calling off the futile search."

"Me too," Carson had said, and then ran to his cars at the window sill.

Helen mentioned nothing from their conversation the night before.

Around five o'clock they checked Emily. She was still sleeping deeply. Instead of making dinner, Isaac made snacks of cheese and crackers. He hoped Emily would wake soon and be hungry for shrimp linguine, her favorite. The tiger shrimp had thawed overnight in the refrigerator and were ready for sautéing in a frying pan.

Five o'clock became six o'clock. Six had become seven.

Isaac turned from the window. He pulled his phone from his pocket and checked the time. "It's almost eight o'clock."

Helen glanced up from a book she'd found for herself on the shelves. She looked toward the window. "It's getting darker earlier and earlier. Fall is coming, that's for certain."

Taking the fire poker, Isaac stirred a few flames up from the embers in the fireplace. He added three pieces of split oak and waited until fire licked along the edges of the wood. Standing, he paced back to the darkening window. "Ashley, wake your sister up so we can at least have cake and sing 'Happy Birthday.'"

"Cake!" Carson shouted, standing. "I'll wake her up."

"No," Helen said, "you should just let her sleep. She obviously needs it."

Isaac motioned Carson toward the girls' door with a flick of his wrist. "Go ahead and get her up, bud." He turned to Helen. "If she sleeps all evening, she's going to be wide awake after midnight. Then we're going to have a really long night on our hands."

Carson opened the door. "Emily, it's time for the cake! Chop-chop!"

Helen looked up from her book. "I just think sleep is the best thing."

"Well, you're not calling the shots yet, are you?"

Helen glowered.

Ashley glanced from her book and gave Isaac a puzzled look.

"Daddy! She won't get up!"

Isaac smiled at Ashley. "Can you go help your brother? Just tell her that Dad said it's time to get up."

She nodded, closing her pages around a butterfly bookmark she'd improvised from one of the decorations. She set the book on the fireplace mantle and then walked off towards the bedroom. "Emily," she called in a sing-song voice, "time for the birthday girl to get up."

"I don't think it's good for the children," Helen started, watching Ashley disappear through the doorway, "to sense tension between us."

He crossed his arms. "Well, there wouldn't be tension if you didn't have an opposing opinion to everything I say."

"Isaac—"

"Dad!" Ashley shouted, the fear palpable in her voice. "Come here! She really won't wake up."

Isaac raced toward the girl's door with Helen following closely after him. Behind them, a squall blew open the front door sending it crashing into the wall. Helen screamed. Isaac turned. The wind storm doubled in volume as it roared past the open doorway. Something grabbed his sleeve, and he yanked his arm away.

"Dad?! Come now," Ashley shouted, grabbing his sleeve again.

He glanced once more toward the front door but then turned and rushed to Emily's bed. Carson sat in a corner of the room with his arms wrapped around his knees. He rocked back and forth, and tears streamed down his face. Helen stood at the foot of the bed pinching Emily's toes and shouting her name over and over.

Emily lay on top of the comforter with her arms at her sides, hands palm down. Her face was ashen, and her eyes were rolled into the back of her head. She breathed in rapid, shallow breaths that sounded more like panting than breathing.

Isaac sat on the bed and grabbed her by her thin shoulders.

"Dad, is she going to be okay?" Ashley whimpered behind him.

He looked at Emily, but spoke to Ashley. "Yes, she's going to be fine. Just go be with your brother." Lifting Emily's upper half from the mattress, he shook her. "Em? Come on, wake up. Em!" Her head lolled back.

"It's going to be okay Carson," Ashley said. "Don't cry."

Setting her back on the comforter, Isaac lightly slapped his fingers on her cheeks. "Em? Em?" He placed a finger to his throat and one against hers. He counted. Doing the math, he turned toward Helen's blanched face. "Her pulse is 180."

Her eyes widened. "No. No. That's too high."

"I know." Isaac shot up from the bed. His forehead beaded with sweat. "Stay here with them. I'm going to go get Silas. He has some medical backgr—"

"No, Daddy ... not that bastard!"

Isaac looked to the corner. Carson stood fiercely with his fists at his side. Looking at him in shock, Ashley remained on the floor where she had been moments before comforting him.

"They say no, Daddy. They say no."

"Who? What are you—"

"The girls. They say—"

Isaac held his palm up toward Carson. "It's okay, bud. Silas—"

"No! Don't be a goddamn gobshite!" Carson stared with tears streaking his face. He looked toward Emily and then back at his father. "Maji-manidoowaadizi. Maji-manidoo ... " His chanted words trailed off.

Isaac made eye contact with Ashley. "Ash?"

She stood and hugged her arms around Carson. "Okay, Carson. It's okay. Just let Dad—"

He pulled away from her. "Get off of me, geebag."

Isaac grabbed Helen's arm and shook her from her frozen vigil over Emily's bed.

She turned to him, slack-jawed. Her pupils were dilated. "Helen?"

She nodded almost imperceptibly.

"Watch them," he whispered. "I have to go up to Evelyn's." He furrowed his brows. "Helen?"

Seeming to snap into reality, she nodded again more firmly. "I will. Go."

He rushed from the room.

"Daddy, no!" Carson called behind him. "He'll kill you!"

"Carson, that's enough," Helen shouted.

"Quiet, Cailleach! You think she's our friend. She's not."

Isaac made strides toward the front door. It lurched on its hinges and slammed shut before he could exit. Cracks splintered through the door's window pane. A trail of water went from the doorway into the living room.

"Goddamn it," he shouted, stopping in his frantic tracks. A moment later, he glimpsed it in his peripheral vision, where his eyes had been tracing the water splotches across the floor. It wasn't possible. He turned slowly to confirm it. Swollen and warping, the Ouija game lay open on the coffee table in a pool of water shedding from it. With its point aimed toward the front door, the planchette rested in the middle of the board. Swallowing, Isaac took a step towards it.

Muscles trembling, he bent down and looked closer. The planchette wasn't the same one that he'd thrown into the lake just nights ago. Not plastic, but metal, it looked to have been at the bottom of the lake for decades. The design of branches etched into the metal was patinaed with various hues of algae green. Half a dozen stonefly nymphs crept over it, dropping to the board. They wriggled in their slow suffocation.

Behind him, the deadbolt clicked into its locked position.

"Hey," he said absently. He looked back at the front door.

Helen peeked out of the girl's room. "Isaac! What are you doing? Emily is—"

He stood dumbfounded, pointing at the board.

"Wh … what is—" She took a few cautious steps closer to the coffee table.

The planchette began to jiggle slightly, like water dripped onto a hot stove burner. Then it moved, leaving its viewing hole over the letter E. A chill slithered up Isaac's spine.

"Dad, what's going on?"

Turning, he noticed them—Ashley and Carson—standing in the doorway. He swallowed. "Ashley, I want you to take your brother into Grandma's room and close the door."

"But, Dad—"

"Ashley," he snapped.

"Okay." She nodded. Setting her hand on the back of his neck, she guided Carson toward Helen's room.

Carson looked over his shoulder. "She's here, Daddy. They're all here."

"It's okay, Carson." Ashley took him into the room and closed the door.

"Listen to her, Daddy! Listen to your wife!"

Isaac turned back toward the coffee table. The planchette hovered over the letter M before sliding to the I.

"What's—"

"Shh, Helen." He watched the metal trembling before it slid over to the L. Then the Y.

"Emily," he muttered from his escaping breath. E.M.I.L.Y.

It moved again, faster. Steadier. It spelled out 'Emily' again. And then again. And again. Each time faster until in its zigzagging frenzy it didn't seem to be spelling out anything at all.

"Gwen?" he asked.

The planchette stopped, sat for a moment, and then slid over the word Yes.

He turned back toward Helen who stood teetering. The only thing seeming to keep her upright were her hands white-knuckled over the back of one of the counter stools. "What's going on here? What is this?" she mumbled.

She saw it. It wasn't just him. It wasn't some psychotic break brought on from a mind craving liquor. "It's Gwen," he said. "It's her."

"No," she said. "No, it's not."

The piece pivoted off the Yes and then back to it.

"Look, Helen ... it's her."

He stepped toward her and pulled at her sleeve, trying to get her closer to the board.

"No," she said. She pulled away from his insistent grip. "I don't believe this. I don't believe any of this!"

The planchette started turning figure eights around the board.

Helen stumbled forward towards the game. She looked behind her.

Isaac helped her steady herself. "You okay?"

"Someone ... something ... it pushed me," she said. Her voice was reedy and trembling.

"Look," he pointed to the board. The planchette stopped over the letter M and then kept moving and stopping, pausing briefly before beginning a new word. Words became sentences: "Mom, it's me. It's Puffer."

"Puffer?" Isaac asked.

Helen's hand drifted up like a sleepy moth and covered her mouth. She stared at the board.

"Puffer? Helen what are you—"

"A nickname," she murmured. "You wouldn't even know it. She wouldn't have mentioned ..." She said that when Gwen was in kindergarten, Helen had tasked John with the chore of buying her a winter coat. He'd come home with something so thick, so stuffed with down that she could barely lower her arms. "It was a half day kindergarten. Every time I'd pick her up for lunch, I'd say, 'There's my little puffer fish. My little puffer.'" She said by the next year, they purchased a new coat for her, and the name was forgotten. "Gwen?" she asked.

The planchette moved to Yes again, paused briefly, and then skated over different letters. Either Isaac or Helen called out the words, and the sentences slowly formed. "I don't have much time," Gwen implored. "They're pulling me away."

"Gwen ... Gwen ... we love you so much," Helen said. She lowered herself to her knees as though before a shrine. "Gwen, we—"

The planchette scraped fiercely to the word No. Then letters again. Words. "You just need to listen, Mom." The planchette kept moving and stopping, moving and stopping. "Emily. She's already almost gone," it spelled out.

"Dying?" Helen whimpered.

No.

The piece moved again, its frenetic movement a cartography of communication. "Evelyn is taking Emily. She drank Evelyn's blood. She'll die in Evelyn's body. Evelyn will live in hers. Through hers."

Isaac stepped slowly away from the board. His mind burned with the race of his scorching thoughts. "No," he mumbled. "That won't happen. We're leaving. We're just going to leave this goddamn island!" He rushed for the girls' room. As he charged through the doorframe, something knocked him back into the kitchen. He caught himself on the counter. It was as though the doorway wasn't open at all, like some invisible gate, locked with spectral deadbolts, hung on phantom hinges. Shaking off his shock, he approached the threshold again.

"Stop, Isaac!" Helen shouted. "She says stop."

A smoky haze drifted through the girls' room. Emily lay on the bed with her eyes rolled up back into her head. Her complexion was nearly white, and her mouth hung open. Her rapid breaths had shallowed into something much closer to stillness. The pendant on her necklace hovered inches above her sternum, suspended by nothing. A glowing blue-green mist snaked out of her chest, through the pendant, and into the air above her. It disappeared into the wall where a second smoky trail of vapor entered, twisting down into Emily's mouth.

"Emily!" Isaac shouted, pounding on the doorframe.

"You can't stop it," Helen dictated behind him, sound-tracked by the frantic scratch of the planchette over the board. "It's already started; it's already almost finished."

The wind howled past the dark windows. The full moon's light slashed and danced in the waves. Fueled by breezes of oxygen, the fire flared and crackled.

Ashley opened the door and stood with Carson clutched at her side. "Dad," she asked, voice tremoring, "what's happening? What is happening!?"

Isaac pulled himself from Emily's door and back to the board. The piece spelled out his name. "Yes, Gwen, I'm here. I'm here."

"Dad?"

He turned toward Ashley's pallid face. "I don't know what's happening, honey ... I don't."

"It's because she's eleven," Carson said. Then: "No, it's because she turned eleven."

The game piece slid to the word Yes.

Isaac lowered himself to his knees beside Helen. "What do we do here, Gwen? I mean—"

Set off like a dervish, the piece raced around the board. Helen and Isaac looked at each other when it came to rest.

"Have to kill her?" Isaac whispered.

Helen shook her head violently. "Emily? We can't—"

"No, not Emily," Carson shouted. "Evelyn! We need to kill that old bitch."

The planchette swooped to the word Yes.

Isaac blinked. "When, Gwen? And where do—"

The piece moved, touching down slowly on letters: S.O.O.N.

Isaac pushed himself to standing. As he did, the cabin went black. Ashley and Helen screamed. Carson wept openly. The room flickered dimly with the orange light from the fire.

"Everybody," Isaac shouted, "it's a power outage. That's it." He locked eyes with Carson. "Bud, I put the flashlights back in the drawer. Get them and hand them out."

Nodding, Carson peeled himself from the wall, wiped his eyes, and marched to the drawer. He pulled it open.

Isaac turned to the Ouija board. The planchette drifted slowly toward Good Bye. "Gwen?"

"Daddy, they're gone."

"What?" He started toward Carson. "I just saw them in there."

"Not the flashlights ... the girls. They aren't talking to me anymore." He walked to her and fit a flashlight into Helen's trembling grip.

Isaac turned back toward the board. The planchette hovered a few inches above the cardboard, quivering.

"Gwen, are you still here?" It kept repeating in his head. You have to kill her. You have to kill Evelyn. He pictured Emily lying in state on her bed, the life slowly ebbing from her. "I gotta go. I have to," he mumbled. He looked towards his mother-in-law. "Helen, you'll need to watch ... Helen?" He turned to follow her terrified gaze locked on the door.

A man's silhouette stood framed in the front door's window. The doorknob turned back and forth. The deadbolt kept it from opening. On the other side of the threshold, Silas asked if everything was all right. "I heard shouting. I can restore the power for you if that's the issue. Just unlock the door."

A circle of luminescence spotlighted Silas's pale face through the glass. Carson had trained his flashlight's beam on him. "Go to hell, Silas!" he shouted.

Helen's voice started as though to scold him, but she said nothing.

Silas stood for a moment. Something like a smile whispered across his face. "That's not very polite, Master Carson." His arm reared back and his fist came shattering through the pane. Helen and Ashley's screams joined the cacophony of falling glass. He reached his bloodied hand past the jagged pieces still lodged in the window's sash. His thick fingers and thumb turned the deadbolt open.

Isaac looked around and then grabbed the skillet off the stove. "Silas, I'll cave your goddamn skull in."

The door opened slowly. Silas started to press through but then snapped his head back behind the door again. Rocketing across the room, the planchette's point stuck into the doorframe inches from his face. He pushed open the door all the way and stood framed in the entryway. He looked at the planchette and snickered. Turning from it, his amber eyes, flickering with the light from the fire, scanned the room.

Isaac checked his grip on the skillet. He took a deep breath. "Get them out of here, Helen," he exhaled.

She stood paralyzed until Carson pulled her arm. "Grandma, come on. I know the way."

Silas' eyes flashed yellow, and he locked his gaze on Isaac.

CHAPTER 18

Isaac positioned himself between Silas and the back door. The door slammed closed behind him. Carson's faded shouts of "this way, this way" came to his ear. His sweating fingers regripped the handle of the skillet. He inhaled a raspy breath.

Arms at his side, Silas advanced towards him step by step. He reached up and with one violent swing brought down the Happy Birthday banner across his path. Isaac's panted breaths burned in his lungs. "Come on, come on," he muttered in inadvertent prayer. Guessing him in range, he swung wildly towards the moon of a head. His swing stopped in midair, his wrist compressed in Silas' cold grip. Silas jerked his arm twice, and the skillet rang like a muted gong against the hardwood floor. Rearing his right hand over his left shoulder, he launched it, careening a backhand into the side of Isaac's head.

Isaac's body teetered over the back of the couch and crashed into the coffee table. He lay breathless, feeling himself on the verge of passing out. His leg felt as though someone had driven a nail right through his flesh into the heart of the bone. The pain might have been the only thing keeping him from slipping into unconsciousness. Orange and yellow light flickered around his head. His vision took in the things of the room and the shadows of the things dancing on the walls. Silas stood in the kitchen with his back to him. Drawers slid clanging open and then closed again. Isaac pushed himself backwards on his elbows towards the fireplace.

"I thought you'd give me more of a fight than your brother."

"What ..." Using the stones of the mantle, he pulled himself to standing. His leg throbbed, but held him. His hand groped down into the half-dark and then came up with a length of firewood. Silas stood with the silhouette of a meat cleaver in his hand. He glanced into the open door of the girls' room, studying Emily's prone body. Grunting, Isaac hurled the split oak across the room directly into Silas' kidneys, lurching him forward against the countertop. The cleaver dropped from his grip to the floor.

Silas stood for a moment with his hands on the counter's edge. While keeping his eyes on him, Isaac groped his hand behind him along the mantle.

Silas' head turned slowly and kept turning until his face perched directly above his shoulder blades. The rest of his body then turned slowly to join it.

Wide-eyed at the sight of a man twisting his neck 180 degrees, Isaac felt the smooth wood fumble into his palm. He closed his fingers tightly around the handle of the fire poker.

Silas started towards him again. "For belonging to such an educated man," he said, "your brother's mind, like your own, was very weak."

Isaac scowled. "You don't know shit about my brother."

Setting his hand on the armrest of the couch, Silas thrust from the elbow and sent the six-foot length of furniture sailing across the room where it crashed into the open front door.

Watching him closely, Isaac leaned for purchase into his left arm splayed across the top of the mantle. His right arm dangled behind his back, fingers twitching on the poker handle. Taking a painful breath, he blinked away the black spots floating across his vision. "Stay away from my family, you bastard." The fingers of his left hand touched upon the spine of Ashley's book on the mantle.

Silas's boots crunched over the shattered coffee table. "They'll die slowly," he said. He took a step forward. "As will you."

Isaac flipped *A Tale of Two Cities'* flapping pages into Silas' face. His hands shot up instinctively to block it. Fingers closed tightly, Isaac swung the fire poker across the space between them and into the side of Silas' head, sprawling the length of him out onto the cabin floor.

Taking ragged breaths, Isaac stood over the face-down body. Blood leaked from Silas' ear. It streaked down his face. Isaac looked through Emily's doorway. She lay as she had with the pendant hovering above her chest, a dwindling wisp of vapor rising from her sternum. The other blacker mist corkscrewed into her mouth. A cold vice clamped around Isaac's ankle.

His vision snapped to Silas' amber eyes staring at him. One palm against the floor, he was pushing himself toward standing. Wrenching his leg from Silas' grip, Isaac swung again with the fire poker. Silas caught the braided wrought iron and tore it from Isaac's grip. He swung it, just missing Isaac's kneecaps.

Stumbling a few steps back, Isaac watched Silas lurch to kneeling. He switched the fire poker into his right hand. Blood oozed from the side of his head.

"Run," a young girl's voice whispered into Isaac's ear.

Isaac limped around the side of the counter and out the back door. Passing the woodpile, he jerked the axe from the splitting block. The wind raged in the branches above him. He stopped at the tree line and looked back at the cabin. The silhouette of Silas' head and torso showed through the back window. Unmoved by the wind, a foggy, ethereal snake of vapor drifted out of the cabin's log walls towards Evelyn's property.

Isaac slid his phone out of his pocket, turned on the light, and followed its beam south into the trees. Fifty yards into the woods, he heard the screws shrieking out of the jamb as Silas smashed the back door off of its hinges. Isaac hobbled as fast as he could on a leg that felt ready to shatter with each footfall. His bruised ribs throbbed with each breath. His cheek simmered where Silas had struck him. With the wind, he had no idea how close Silas was behind him. His light flashed the trees and branches into silhouette.

He stopped when the bright orange strip flashed into his view dangling and dancing from its branch. Pressing off his light, he turned east. For a moment he stumbled forward with his arm out in the darkness in front of him. His eyes adjusted slowly to the blackness under the thick canopy. Isaac listened behind him. Anything that might have been the sound of footsteps would have been drown out by the racket of wind, branches, and leaves.

Then he was falling. The ground seemed to rise up to meet him. His spasming diaphragm constricted his attempts at breathing. Taking quick, shallow breaths he looked behind him into the swallowing dark. His hand groped the leaf litter for anything that might serve as a weapon. Scanning the area frantically, he spotted only the distorted white of the fallen birch tree that had tripped him.

Even as his breathing improved, the world remained a blur. He thrashed his hand through the leaves and fallen branches. Finally, his fingers touched upon his glasses and he rushed them on.

Recovering his wind, he crawled a few feet. He groped his hand along the ground, and his fingers touched upon the axe handle. He pulled himself to standing and limped forward, nearly dragging his inflamed leg behind him. With every step, he waited for Silas' hand to grab his neck, and the other to drive the meat cleaver down into his skull. The fiery thought of it haunted him until the stream flowed in front of him, a glowing ribbon of moonlight. He splashed his way across its cold current. "It's me!" he shouted. If they were there, he didn't want his family to run away from the sound of his crossing.

"Dad?" Ashley yelled.

"Yes!" he shouted, instantly relieved to hear her voice. He walked into the beam of light Carson had trained on him. They were huddled around Helen standing near the cyclone fence. The gate through the fence into the orphanage compound hung wide open. He stumbled towards them. "Everyone okay?" he exhaled breathily.

Ashley and Carson ran to him and wrapped their arms around him. They started talking at once about a dog that had tried to attack them.

"I think it was a coyote," Helen said, sounding as though she were mumbling it to herself as much as to them. Holding herself up with her fingers weaved into the chain links, she looked washed-out and overwhelmed.

"It came right out of the woods. It was growling," Carson said. "Grandma wouldn't go through the gate. They said we should go through the gate, but she wouldn't."

She looked at Isaac. "I didn't ... I just thought we could get trapped in there."

Carson said they were backed against the fence, and the coyote just kept getting closer. "We shouted at it and shook sticks, but it wouldn't go away. It was drooling."

Ashley said it paced back and forth as though it were trying to keep them from leaving. "Its eyes were black."

"Then Ashley made it run away. She saved us!" Carson shouted.

Isaac looked down at her. She smiled and opened her right hand. The black mace canister he'd given her for her birthday lay in her palm. He nodded. "Good thinking, kid."

She smiled, closing her fingers around the mace.

"Daddy?" Carson said, his voice full of fear.

The beam of his flashlight lit up a snowy owl perched in a tree. It held a stunned but struggling adolescent racoon in the talons of its right foot. The owl locked eyes with Isaac before lurching forward and plummeting from the large branch. Helen screamed. Silas crouched in the spot where the owl would have landed. Pinned to the ground under Silas' right hand, the racoon squirmed. Silas stood to his full height with the animal in his vise-like grip. A low growl repeated from the racoon's writhing body. A chilling breeze swept across the ground toward the orphanage compound.

Helen released a sob and collapsed backwards against the fence.

Blood still oozed from Silas' ear and covered the side of his face like a port-wine stain birthmark.

Isaac took the axe handle in both hands and stood in front of Ashley and Carson. "Everyone get behind me," he said. Ashley stayed at his side holding the mace out in front of her.

Ignoring its snapping teeth and hissed threats, Silas clamped his left hand on top of the raccoon's head. He slowly twisted the shrieking skull like a lid from a mason jar. The light went out of the little masked eyes. His own eyes closed, and Silas spoke in tongues.

The gate slammed shut. The flashlights winked out. Ashley and Helen screamed.

We just need to give up, Isaac thought. We can't beat him. He'll let us live if we just give up. Opening his fingers, he let the axe fall to the ground at his feet. "You win, Silas."

"Dad!" Ashley shouted, "what are you doing?"

Silas tossed the raccoon's limp body to the ground. "You should listen to your father," he said. His face glowed palely in the moonlight. The fingers of his bitten left hand dripped blood on the leaves.

Carson looked to the canopy, then at Silas, and back to the canopy of branches.

"Stay away from us!" Ashley screamed.

Coming behind her, Helen grabbed the mace and yanked it out of Ashley's grip. "That's enough of this. Silas wouldn't hurt us."

No, he'd kill us. He'd kill us slowly, Isaac remembered. He shook his head against the fugue clouding his mind. "Wait a minute..."

Silas took a step forward.

"Now! Now!" Carson shouted.

A sudden blast of wind through the trees rose into a crescendo of splintering and cracking. Teenage girl voices screamed in the howl of the squall. Silas snapped his gaze upward. A branch as big a round as a man plummeted out of the darkness above and crushed him against the ground under its weight.

They stood for a moment staring at Silas' pinned body. His lifeless face stared into the canopy. Isaac's head cleared.

Behind them, the gate slowly drifted open again.

Isaac looked at it ... looked at the strip of hunter's orange tied to the links. He turned to Helen. "I think you'll be safe here ... in there." He nodded toward the gate, and then bent and retrieved the axe.

"We will, Daddy," Carson said. "They said so."

Helen handed the mace canister back to Ashley. "I'm sorry," she said. "I don't know why—"

"It's okay, Grandma."

Isaac pulled his phone from his pocket. It was dead. "I have to go. I don't even know how much time I have."

"Daddy," Carson said. "I found your marker on that branch. I went due east."

"That's good, bud. You did good. Go with your grandmother and sister. I'll be back before you know it."

He watched them disappear through the gateway. It swung slowly closed again once they were all inside.

He stepped to the oak limb trapping Silas against the ground. It had to weigh two hundred pounds. The man's long, gray hair, tangled with leaves and twigs, fanned out around his pale face. Rot in hell, Isaac thought. He took deep, steadying breaths.

Silas' eyelids flickered and then snapped open. Ringed in black, the whites of his eyes were yellow with piercing, dilated black pupils. Isaac took a step back. He knew those eyes. They were the eyes that had stared down at him from the branches above the lilac bushes in his backyard before the snowy owl had retreated into the night.

Silas' arms moved, positioning his palms against the underside of the branch. The limb lurched against his effort to extract himself.

Swallowing, Isaac raised the axe above his head and brought the blade of it down. He missed the throat and instead wedged the axe into a sheath of skull. The blade scraped against bone when he pulled it out and brought it above his head again. The second swing cut clean through Silas' sinewy throat. A spray of blood exploded over the leaves and ground litter. The head itself, owl eyes and mouth open, rolled to rest within inches of the raccoon carcass. For a moment, the wind carried in it the faint chorus of cheering adolescents.

Isaac watched the body for any other movement before lifting his gaze in the direction of Evelyn's house.

"Watch over my family, girls."

CHAPTER 19

Hobbling forward, Isaac shambled along the bank of the moonlit stream. Sweat wicked from his forehead and dripped into his eyes. His soggy shoes weighed heavily on his feet. The wind raged in the canopy overhead. Roots seemingly exhumed themselves from the ground, making an obstacle course of his path. "Christ," he panted. Branches slashed at his face and clutched at his clothing. When one would get a grip, holding him in place, he'd swing the axe's blade through it. Have to get to her, have to get to her ... his only thought.

Coming close to the spot where he'd used the electrofisher, he lurched west. The breaths he took felt as though he were breathing winter air. He coughed violently against the chill in his lungs, hacking up wads of phlegm. The woods were tangled with vines and crisscrossing branches. He swung with the axe, leaving a trail of severed pieces. He could just make out a clearing of moonlight ahead of him. The branches tangled across his path almost as quickly as he was able to cut them away. Thinking of Emily as he'd last seen her, he made a final, mad rush against the web of limbs. He stumbled out into a clearing behind the looming shadow of Evelyn's house.

Mesmerized, he stared at the ground where Evelyn lay naked at the bottom of a silo of moonlight coming down through a perfect circle cut through the canopy. Even with the hurricane-like winds, the perimeter above didn't move. Not even a branch or leaf crossed into the light. Fifteen feet above him, a cloud of bats swirled round and round the shaft of bluish light, feeding on the insects drawn to it. Evelyn's body was encircled by sticks and branches with feathers tied throughout. Arms and legs spread-eagle, mouth hanging open, she rested atop a spider's web of branches as though on a giant dreamcatcher. The dark mist rising from her mouth swum through the air above him like an endless lamprey. Her palms were flat against the ground. Her wiry hair was woven with twigs.

Something jerked the axe handle from Isaac's grip. He spun around to see it being dragged into the forest by a rope of climbing ivy. Before he could even move, it had disappeared into the thick tangle of woods.

He turned back to the column of moonlight. Just above his head, a wispy, emerald worm of vapor passed through the column and down, burrowing into Evelyn's chest.

Emily.

Charging into the circle with the intent of strangling the old woman, he careened backwards onto the ground, much the way he had when he'd tried to enter Emily's room. He scrambled to his feet and pressed his palm outward, feeling the solidness of the light as though it were a silo of steel. Cold crept burning into his hand, his wrist, and up the bones of his forearm. He wrenched his hand away from the crawling chill only to fall to the ground in searing pain. "God damnit!" he shouted. Turning his palm toward his face, he studied the purple-red bruising of frostbite along his fingers. The flesh from the fat of his palm was torn off, exposing the bloody meat.

He rose to kneeling, tears spilling from his eyes, and gripped in his good hand the wrist of the wounded one. He closed his eyes against the blistering pain pulsating in his palm. "God damnit. God damnit. God damnit," he hissed through clenched teeth.

Still kneeling, he studied Evelyn's form on the ground. What he had guessed was her naked body was instead something cocooned around her torso. His eyes widened. It was human flesh. It was a blanket of skin. There was a nipple near her shoulder. Downy wisps of body hair. A few faded patches of inflamed skin were peppered across the hide.

Then he spotted it. The dark blue. The red. The yellow feathers and then the orange of the beak.

Adam's Mud Hen tattoo.

He heard Silas in his head, telling him that Adam hadn't put up much of a fight.

He turned his head to the side and threw up violently. "You bitch," he said. He spat the dripping bile from his mouth. "You goddamn bitch!"

Ignoring the pain in his hand and in his leg, he stood and circled her body. It was hopeless. He couldn't get to her protected as she was. "Jesus Christ, Adam," he repeated like a wretched mantra as he walked the perimeter. There was no way to not see his brother's skin. Isaac's hand simmered as though it had been dipped in gasoline and set aflame. Passing around the circle a second time, he spotted the bony fingers and half of the top of her age-spotted left hand lying outside the shaft of full moonlight. He kneeled to it slowly and reached out the fingers of his good hand. He could touch it. Her wrinkled flesh. The bones underneath. The thick blue veins splintering from her wrist towards each finger.

Her body stirred slightly at his touch.

Would it kill her? Would she lose enough blood in time? He imagined running back to the cabin and retrieving the meat cleaver Silas had dropped. He would sever as much of the hand as he could. It was his only choice.

Getting to his feet, he limped towards his cabin following just beneath the misty trail of Emily's drifting spirit. Reaching the back yard, he rushed stumbling through the open back doorway. The flames in the fireplace had burned down to embers. The cleaver lay on the ground in the kitchen. He picked it up and hefted it in his grip. It would easily go through the veiny skin, the flesh, the bone.

But it wouldn't kill her. He knew it.

Emily's doorway glowed with a flickering, foggy luminescence. He couldn't see through it to see her. He sat staring into it, his mind already abandoning the hopelessness of his plan. Evelyn wouldn't bleed to death. Not in time. He swung the cleaver down where it wedged into the surface of the counter.

The veiny flesh? His eyes snapped towards Adam's room. He could picture the red first aid case. His head nodded slowly at the thoughts coming together. He sprinted as much as his body would allow through the bedroom doorway and then out again through the front door to the porch. His clothes clung to his sweat-soaked body.

Minutes later, he kneeled again in the wicked clearing in the shadow of Evelyn's house. The moonlight reflected off of the molasses-colored liquid in the syringe in his hand. When they treated a river, they used three parts per million. Even in that small concentration, the stretch of water downstream would turn a shade of yellow. He stuck the needle into a thick vein on the back of Evelyn's hand and depressed the plunger. Her fingers twitched. Twenty-five ccs of undiluted lampricide surged into her bloodstream. Pulling the needle out, he tossed the syringe to the ground and stood. He looked at his arm and pulled a branch from his sleeve that clung there with twigs like fingers.

"Come on. Come on." He waited, staring at her wan face. He couldn't bear to look at the skin she'd been wrapped in. He dropped his face into his good hand. Jesus, Adam, he thought. What did they do to you? But he knew. They'd killed him. They'd killed him and—

Evelyn's body began to jerk and convulse. The bats above converged into one shadowy whorl and disappeared into the woods. The dead branches beneath her snapped under the arrhythmic spasming of her limbs and torso. Adam's skin fell from her, exposing her own withered, writhing nakedness. Foam formed at her lips and drooled down the side of her face. Her eyes popped open wide and stared wrath at him before closing again.

Something like the flat of a palm crashed into his chest and knocked him to the ground. He gasped for breath, watching the old woman's dying body. The black vapor reversed its course and turned rapidly back into her mouth like a twister above a Kansas plain.

She stopped moving. Taking gasping breaths, Isaac crawled to his knees and then to his feet. He circled the dark shrine of her resting place while slowly wrapping gauze from Adam's first aid kit around his lacerated palm. He stopped a moment and looked into the branches above him. The wind had died away. The perfect circle in the canopy had nearly closed with crisscrossed branches, allowing only flashes of moonlight.

He pulled his phone from his pocket. The screen lit up with the time: 11:37 p.m. Something about it being before midnight flooded him with relief, though he wasn't certain if it was important or not. He wasn't certain of anything.

Emily.

He limped into the darkness as fast as his rotten leg would allow. In time, the lit windows of his cabin, restored with electricity, flashed through the trees.

He found her as she had been earlier in the day, asleep in her bed. The air in the room had cleared, and she looked as though color was coming back into her cheeks. Tears in his eyes, Isaac sat on the edge of the bed, stroking her hair. He watched her small chest rise and fall. Her breaths were normal, the breaths of deep sleep. He brushed the hair aside from her face. "Em, do you think you'd want to wake up?" he asked tearfully.

She blinked her eyes open. "Daddy?" She smiled at him weakly. "Is it still my birthday?"

More tears streaked his cheeks. He nodded and then pulled her into a fierce hug. "It is, honey. It is." He kissed her hair, her cheeks.

"Why are you crying?"

"What do you remember?" he asked, sniffling. "From today."

"Taking pictures. And then just being really tired."

He nodded again, laughing joyously. "Sorry about the tears. I just can't believe my little girl is eleven years old."

She reached up and brushed her little fingers over his cheek. "That's just part of life, Dad."

He chuckled. "Dad? What happened to Daddy?"

She reminded him that she was eleven now as she groped her hand around the bed. "Where's my phone?"

He took it from the nightstand and handed to her. Looking at it around her neck, he asked her to take off the necklace. "I'd like to put some silver polish on that for you," he lied.

Reaching behind her neck and unclasping the chain, she handed it to him. "Dad?"

"Yeah, baby?" he said. He slipped the necklace into his front shirt pocket.

"I'm super hungry."

He nodded. "I'll bet. What would you say to some chocolate chip pancakes?"

She held up both thumbs.

He stood and started for the door.

"I don't like Ms. Cameron," Emily said. Her eyes were on her phone screen. "She was in my dreams. She was mean."

"I don't much like her either, kid."

She looked from her phone. "Don't tell Grandma, though. I think she's friends with her."

"I'm sure your grandma would be fine with it." His mind went to them out there in the darkness of the orphanage compound. He couldn't imagine carrying her or asking Emily to walk out there with him. He also couldn't imagine leaving her alone at the cabin.

He went to the back door with an emergency whistle he kept in his fly fishing vest. He had told both Carson and Ashley about the significance of three blasts. Without the howling wind, he guessed that the shrill sound would carry. While bringing the whistle to his lips, he spotted their flashlight beams slashing through the woods.

"We're here!" he shouted. "She's okay!"

The lights moved faster in his direction. Carson was the first to emerge into the halo of light cast from the cabin's back windows. Ashley and Helen appeared a moment later. Ashley held the flashlight. Looking haggard, Helen clung to her granddaughter's arm with both hands.

"The girls said thank you, Daddy," Carson shouted. "They told me we could come back to see Emily now."

Isaac sat down on the back steps to be eye-to-eye with his son. He hugged him and then held him out at arm's length. "I'm really proud of how you handled yourself out there. You did good." He looked at Ashley's exhausted face. "You both did."

Ashley smiled at him. "I'm going to go in and see Emily."

Isaac nodded.

Carson leaned his lips to Isaac's ear. "Silas' head was off," he whispered.

Isaac held him tight. "Don't think about that, bud. Why don't you just go in and see your sister."

Carson nodded and ran up the steps. His muffled voice shouted "Happy Birthday" from inside the cabin.

Helen stumbled and then collapsed on the step next to Isaac. He studied her in his side vision. She stared wide-eyed into the dark woods they'd just left. Her face slowly crumbled, and she lowered it into her palms and sobbed.

Isaac put his arm around her and pulled her into his shoulder. She clung to him, weeping.

"It's over," he said repeatedly, stroking her hair.

He kissed the top of her head.

CHAPTER 20

Isaac stood on the strip of beach looking over the black, glass surface of the lake. A few lights flickered in Witiko. Hopefully somebody was up. He glanced at the ridges of the cliffs. No lights. The widows had probably long since gone to bed.

Emily didn't question it when Isaac said he wanted to take them ashore for the night to stay at a hotel. "You didn't get much of a birthday, so I thought we'd get a place with a pool you could swim in tomorrow."

"Will there be Wi-Fi?" she had asked.

"Now you're asking the right questions," Ashley said.

"Just pack what you need for an overnight stay," he'd told them.

Arms hugged around her torso, Helen came down and stood at his side on the sand. "Do you think anyone will see us?"

"Somebody is up over there," he said. He pointed toward the shore. "They have a fire down by the water." Across the lake, a small, growing triangle of flames danced in the darkness not far from the pier.

"I'm going to build a helluva bonfire. Whoever it is, maybe they'll see it." He said they could wave the flashlight beams through the air too. "I'll stay up until someone comes. I don't see getting any sleep tonight." He opened his hand slowly, feeling the pull and sting of the coagulating wound.

"I'll stay up with you."

The kids were out front of the cabin. Emily begged the other two to try to catch fireflies with her. They said they weren't leaving the porch.

"Just take pictures of them," Ashley said.

"I'm going to start bringing wood down for the signal fire," Isaac told Helen. He walked up and around to the back of the cabin. Gathering an armload of wood, he started back for the beach. He glanced toward Evelyn's. Collapsing for a moment against the side of the cabin, he wept. His brother was gone. They'd killed him and skinned ...

He shook his head. He stumbled forward and then marched. He couldn't allow himself to despair. We just gotta get off this goddamned island, he thought.

He dropped the firewood onto the sand and started back for more.

"Isaac?"

He turned. Helen stood by the shore, staring at two aluminum canoes floating a few feet out in the water. Though covered in a thick stubble of algae, they appeared dry on the inside. Examining them, he could just make out enough of the letters fading in here and there through the green: Property of St. Francis' Children. He recognized them as early model Grumman's, the first company to come out with an aluminum canoe in the 1940s. A vintage one in mint condition was on display in the lobby of the Fish and Wildlife Office in East Lansing.

"They're for us, Daddy," Carson said. He came down to the beach behind him. "They'll take us to town."

Isaac looked back at his son. He nodded. "Okay, buddy."

CHAPTER 21

The canoes glided side-by-side across the water like haunted planchettes across a Ouija board. Aside from the distant lights, everything around them was a mix of blacks and blue-blacks. Clouds had rolled in and extinguished the moon. Helen sat in the back of one canoe with Emily in the middle and Carson on the front seat with his flashlight beam pointed over the water. Isaac and Ashley sat in the other with the luggage between them. Isaac slipped the necklace Evelyn had given Emily from his pocket and let it sink into the cold lake.

Emily had asked how they were moving without oars. Isaac told her it was just northbound currents on the lake. The answer satisfied her. She didn't ask again.

"I'll never understand what happened tonight," Helen whispered. "Never."

Isaac looked again at the lights of Witiko getting closer. "That makes two of us." He had no idea how he'd tell the kids about their uncle, but it would have to be something far removed from the truth. He remembered Silas' blood-covered hands, and how he'd said he'd been pulling a hide from a carcass. His brother ... the sonuvabitch was talking about his brother. He tried to understand how they'd forced Adam to write his note. How did they get him outside ... to go to Silas without a fight?

He recalled the racoon, and the way Silas had broken its neck. The gate had closed. The lights had gone out. Isaac's own mind, in the moment, had felt possessed, not his own. His first warped thought had been to give up and appeal to Silas' mercy. Helen had acted the same. Something about the racoon's death had triggered it. He didn't know how exactly, but he guessed that the dead rabbit on the cabin's lawn had something to do with Adam's sudden decision to leave. Thinking of it, of what they'd done to his brother, he sat with his hand over his mouth. He couldn't break down ... not in front of the kids.

After a moment, he fished into the front pocket of his pants and slid the car keys jangling along the bottom of the canoe.

Ashley picked them up and looked back at him with a puzzled expression.

"How do you feel about driving us into Cheboygan ... get some of those practice hours under your belt?"

She looked at the keys and then back at him. "Okay," she said, smiling.

Helen reached for Isaac's shoulder, making a bridge of her arm across the space of water between the canoes. He looked at her, and she smiled. "The children really do need you," she whispered.

He looked at her soft expression. "So, no lawyers, then?"

"I didn't say that."

Turning from her, he looked at the darkness of the looming cliffs.

Her fingers squeezed his shoulder. "We'll see, though," she said. "We'll see."

He nodded.

Isaac picked a half dozen mollusks from the rim of the canoe and set them down through the lake's surface. "Snail, snail, glister me forward," he muttered, dropping the last one into the water. It was a line from some Saginaw poet Gwen had wanted him to read. "He writes a lot about nature," she'd said. He didn't have the heart to tell her he wanted to be out in nature, not read about it, when she gifted him the book.

He vowed to himself that he'd try to read the book again ... try to see what she saw in it.

"The girls go home after this, Daddy," Carson announced. "They get to go home."

"That's good, bud."

The fire near the Witiko pier flickered and licked skyward. Sparks drifted up and then winked out in the darkness. Coming into and out of the orange light traipsed the shadows of three dogs. A person's silhouette paced around the flames.

Theresa.

He could still hear her. "They're good girls." She wasn't talking about her dogs. She was talking about the orphans. Gwen had tried to tell him as much in his dream: "The girls are good." If it wasn't for the orphans, they wouldn't have survived. Theresa knew. Gwen knew. He just hadn't really listened ... hadn't paid attention. He needed to really start paying closer attention.

"Glister us forward, girls," he whispered in what amounted to an invocation.

The Ouija board lay folded on the bottom of the other canoe in front of Emily. She held the planchette in her hand. Once she'd spotted it on the coffee table, there was no keeping her away from it. "That's from your sister," Isaac had said. "She knew you wanted one."

"Dad," Emily started in a hissed whisper. She was pointing to a greenish, luminescent spot on Carson's back. "It's a Luna moth."

It closed its wings into hands in prayer and opened them again. Isaac studied it for a moment. "Hmm, I don't think so, hon."

She looked back at him, her face a portrait of disappointment.

He smiled. "I'm pretty sure that's your mom."

Beaming, she turned her gaze back to the peaceful movements of the insect.

The canoes glided on, bringing them all closer to home.

EPILOGUE

Wearing long black coats, two women in their early seventies stood at the edge of the circle in which Evelyn had been poisoned. One wore her gray hair short and spiked. The other's white hair fell down to the middle of her back, like hanging ivy. Their faces were lit by moonlight, though there was no moon. Evelyn lay naked with her mouth and eyes open, skin wrinkled and fallen over her bones. A candle flickered on the south side of the circle, sending up a wisp of smoke. The woman with long hair bent and set a black chalice of water on the west side. "Water," she said as she rose into her stiff standing. Directly across from the candle, the other woman bent and set a handful of dirt. "Earth," she said. She rose and stood stiffly like the other.

Each extended a flat hand toward the east side of the circle and then exhaled across their palms. "And air," they recited in unison. They stood for a time looking down at the dead woman.

The long-haired woman raised her hand above her and closed the fingers into a fist. "Sister," she said, "join my poor Silas, and return to the Mother."

The candle whiffed out, and Evelyn's body collapsed into itself, turning from flesh, to black rot, to earth, and disappearing into the ground. Two groupings of turquoise rings, like miniature henges, were all that marked her resting place.

The short-haired woman lashed a kick into Adam's hide of skin. The longer-haired woman stooped and then rose, holding a syringe in her hand. She sniffed the needle and crinkled her nose in disgust. They glanced at each other and then glared out through the trees, toward the water, where a lone beam of light moved slowly across Lake Coventry.

BIO

 Jeff Vande Zande teaches fiction writing, screenwriting, and film production at Delta College in Michigan. His novels include *Into the Desperate Country* (March Street Press), *Landscape with Fragmented Figures* (Bottom Dog Press), *American Poet* (Bottom Dog Press) and *Detroit Muscle* (Whistling Shade Press). In 2012, *American Poet* won a Michigan Notable Book Award from the Library of Michigan. Montag Press released his dystopian novel, *Rules of Order*, in 2022. *The Dance of Rotten Sticks* is his first horror novel.

Made in the USA
Monee, IL
21 September 2024

65565286R00163